C000055007

Little
Girl
Gone

Margaret Fenton

Aakenbaaken & Kent

Little Girl Gone
2nd Edition

ISBN: 978-1-958022-08-5

Chapter One

I dread September every year. The summer heat lingers, oppressive and unwelcome. The kids in Birmingham have been back in school for two weeks, long enough for the excitement of new teachers, clothes, and school supplies to wear off. Classes and homework have become things to be endured. The lush green hills surrounding the city begin to fade to an unappealing dull brown, and it seems the crisp cool nights and the red and gold foliage of fall will never arrive.

Other typical late summer colors emerge, too. Like the black and blue of bruises on a child's legs, peeking out from under a pair of shorts at recess. There's the chalky complexion of the child who never gets enough to eat in the cafeteria, or the rusty skin of the one who never gets a bath. Reports of abuse and neglect made by teachers skyrocket in September, swamping the Jefferson County Department of Human Services, Child Welfare Division, where I work.

To no one's surprise the murder rate also spikes. The woman found in the ravine was the area's forty-fifth homicide of the year. I'd like to say the news of the poor woman's death was more than mere background noise read by the perky morning anchor while I half-dried my hair in my usual scramble to get to work. I'd like to say I paid attention. Paused for reflection, a moment of silence, a prayer, anything. But I didn't. It was Tuesday, the first of September, and another school year was well underway. It was the busiest time of the year for me, and I was struggling every day just to keep my head above the flood of new investigations and everything that went with them.

I parked in the lot behind our downtown office at five to seven. Russell, my cubicle-mate, trudged in ten minutes later. As usual, his highlighted blond hair was still wet from the shower, his newspaper was tucked under his arm, and he clutched a cup of to-go coffee.

Russell and I are not morning people. Both of us usually start out in a bad mood, but lately his had stretched into a day-long thing. His boyfriend of nearly a year, Heinrich, moved back to Germany recently to be with his family. They were trying to decide whether to maintain a long-distance relationship and Russell was miserable. I was on the verge of placing a call to Munich and begging Heinrich to get on a plane back to Alabama.

I updated my To Do list for the day as Russell settled himself at his desk. Every day he sipped his coffee, perused the paper, and read me little bits of news before he checked his voice and e-mail messages

"You hear about the body they found?" he asked, skimming the front page.

"There was something about it on TV. She was found in a drainage ditch or something?"

"Uh-huh. Behind that fancy new golf resort they're building in Homewood."

"Russet Ridge? Strange place for a body." The half-completed complex would feature a world-class golf course, five-star restaurants, and a hotel with a shopping area and a spa. It was going up in one of Birmingham's more affluent suburbs where murders weren't supposed to happen.

"Yeah, it doesn't sound like the usual stuff."

The "usual stuff" was drugs and domestic violence. They were two of the most common causes of death in Jefferson County. And two of the most prevalent reasons why caseworkers like me and Russell took children into the State's custody.

Russell continued reading. "It says here she was shot in the head at close range. Found by some kids out playing over the weekend. Poor things. If she was in the water in this heat for more than a day, even it was shallow--"

The bagel with cream cheese I'd wolfed down for breakfast suddenly lurched in my stomach. "Russell, please."

"What?"

"I don't really want to hear the details."

"I didn't know you were squeamish."

"Can I at least finish my first cup of coffee before we discuss decomposing bodies?"

"Sorry. Anyway, your boy Kirk Mahoney wrote this story."

At the mention of Kirk's name, an uninvited image of his spiky black hair and blue eyes flashed into my mind. I felt a strange tightening in my chest and a tingling sensation just in front of my left ear where he'd kissed me last. I rubbed the spot, then tucked a strand of blonde shoulder length hair behind my ear. "He's not my boy."

Kirk was anything but my boy. More like my nemesis. One who had dogged me relentlessly after the tragic death of one of my young clients this summer. He'd turned out to be quite an ally, though, when it came to putting the pieces of that case together. I hadn't seen him in over a month. "Besides, I have a boy,

6

remember? Grant."

"Oh, right."

"What's that supposed to mean?"

"Nothing."

Grant was my boyfriend. As much as he could be. We hadn't seen much of each other lately due to my thirteen hour days and his computer firm being awarded a contract to outfit an entire new medical clinic. Grant owned a company called High Tech, and they were installing all of the facility's new PCs and other equipment. We'd squeezed in a handful of dates in August before the days got so crowded. Our relationship now consisted of a lot of sleepy late-night phone conversations.

I focused again on the list of tasks in front of me. I prioritized it into things I had to get done today, things for tomorrow, and stuff I'd get to when I could. Russell logged on to his computer, and I picked up the phone to arrange some IM's with clients. IM's were intervention meetings, during which the caseworker and the clients worked toward addressing the problems that had led to the department's involvement. Strict guidelines dictated when they had to be done, and I was falling behind in scheduling them.

I was on my third phone call when Jessica, our unit secretary, appeared in the doorway of the cubicle. In her hand was a thin brown folder.

"Claire."

"Oh, no. Come on. You're kidding, right?"

"Sorry. You're next on the assignment rotation." She said it with a smarmy smile. Jessica was the type of person who enjoyed giving people bad news. "Mac says tag, you're it."

Mac McAlister was my boss, the Unit Supervisor. He and I have kind of a love-hate relationship. Okay, maybe not that strong. More of a like-dislike relationship. His somewhat tepid support of me after my client's death in June still rankled. I had no doubt that if that case had gotten any uglier, he would have thrown me under the bus.

"Damn," I muttered, and held out my hand for the file.

"He'll be by in a minute to give you the rundown."

"Thanks so much."

"No problem," she called as she walked back to her desk.

I could feel stress tightening my shoulders. Mac entered the cubicle and leaned his own beefy shoulder on the filing cabinet. His ring of white hair needed a trim, and his out-of-style tie hung inches too short. He fingered the cigar in his pocket, no doubt longing for the good old days when he could light up at his desk. I picked up the folder Jessica had brought me and read the highlights while he talked.

"One of the Homewood police officers found her sleeping under a cardboard box behind the Piggly Wiggly on Highway 31. They thought for a second they had another body on their hands. The reporting officer, Mary Nobles, thinks she's about thirteen. The girl won't give her name or address."

"Runaway?"

"That'd be my guess. Or a throwaway. That's all I know for now. Go over to Homewood and pick her up, get her something to eat and see what you can do with her."

"Wonderful. I suppose HPD can't be bothered to bring her here?"

"I didn't feel like arguing about it. They said they were busy."

"Like I'm not?"

"Touch base with me after you get her some breakfast."

"Okay."

I kissed my plans for the day goodbye and gathered my purse and briefcase. I drove my aging white Honda Civic to Third Avenue North and made my way to the Red Mountain Expressway. The morning commute traffic was at its peak, but I was headed south out of the city so it didn't slow me down. I took the expressway and within ten minutes pulled up to the square, beige-bricked police department headquarters.

I checked in with the officer at the desk, and as I was signing in I heard a familiar voice.

"Well, hey there, Miss Conover."

I looked up from the sheet to see an officer enter from the back of the station. He was in uniform, his gun dangling from his right hip.

"Oh, hi, Officer Ford."

"Chip, please."

"Chip," I repeated with a nod. Chip and I had worked together on a couple of pickup orders, taking kids into custody. He loved his job as a cop, worshiped his badge, and probably slept with a loaded gun under his pillow. He was a big ball of us-against-the-scum-the-earth, Dirty-Harry-movie fueled testosterone. I couldn't stand him.

Chip ran a hand over his dark blond high-and-tight. "You here for the girl?"

"Yeah."

"She's in the break room. I'll take you back."

I clipped a temporary pass to the pink and white lanyard around my neck that held my DHS ID and entered the back of the station with Chip leading the way. "She's not real talkative," he said.

"So I hear."

"Mary's one of our best officers and she hasn't been able to get jack out of her. I told the girl that if somebody had messed with her, all she had to do was tell me and I'd take care of him. Put him under the goddamn jail, you know what I mean?"

I winced in frustration. Chip had just made my job a hell of a lot harder. If this girl was a victim of sexual abuse, the last thing in the world I wanted him to talk about was what could happen to the perpetrator. First, prosecution in most cases was unlikely, and second, most kids didn't want the abuser to go jail, especially if it was a loved one. For many kids the thought of putting daddy or uncle in prison was too much to bear, no matter what he'd done. I needed to figure out what had happened first, make sure she was safe, and let justice sort itself out later.

A small room off the narrow hallway held two tables and a couple of vending machines. An old color TV was perched on top of a humming refrigerator. A fluffy morning talk show played with the volume muted.

A uniformed black policewoman sat in silence at one of the tables, writing on a thick clipboard, next to a teenage girl. The girl had an open can of Diet Coke in front of her. Standing in the doorway of the break room, I got my first look at my new charge.

9

Chapter Two

The girl was a skinny thing. But naturally so, not the kind of thin that's the result of malnutrition or an eating disorder. She was tall for her age, too. Her hair was one long length, straight, and jet black. Out of a bottle. She hadn't been on the street long because the dye job was new. Her doe-brown eyes were heavily outlined in kohl eyeliner. Heavy makeup attempted to cover the freckles on her nose. She had cheap silver jewelry on her pale wrists and fingers, and at least three earrings in her left ear. Her short fingernails were painted black. She wore black pants and a clinging black T-shirt with something resembling a ghostly skull in gray on the front. A Goth, for sure. Or possibly an Emo. A red book bag hung by its strap on the back of her chair.

I took all this in within a millisecond as Chip sauntered into the room ahead of me. "Hey, girl," he said, "your social worker's here."

Officer Mary Nobles saw me standing in the doorway and rose, signing a page on her clipboard as she joined me in the hall. Her athletic frame towered over me. She handed me the clipboard and I signed the pickup order. She gave me my copy and said, "Good luck."

"Still not giving her name, huh?"

"Nope. I found her about four-thirty this morning when I was out on patrol. She was sleeping under a cardboard box behind the grocery store. The backpack's the only thing she had on her. We searched it. No drugs or weapons. Just an IPod, a plain black sweatshirt, some makeup and a hairbrush."

"No phone?"

"Nope."

"And no ID, obviously."

"She's a little young for a driver's license, I think, but no school ID or anything. We notified all the local precincts, and the County, but nobody's reported anyone missing that matches her description. Like I said, good luck."

I stood in the doorway again and eavesdropped on what Chip was saying to the girl.

"Remember," he said, "if anyone's touched you the way they shouldn't, you just let me know. I'll make sure they never do it again."

My client rolled her eyes. So did I.

"Thanks, Chip," I said. "I can take it from here."

11

"Oh, okay." He met me near the door. "I guess I'd better get back to work."

"Yeah."

"Did you hear about our homicide? I got to work the crime scene."

Out of the corner of my eye, I could have sworn I saw the girl flinch.

Chip bragged on. "You should have seen the stiff. She'd been lying in that ditch for about two days. Not a lot of water, but enough to do some damage. All bloated--"

"Chip--"

"Plus, it's still hot out, so the smell--"

"Chip! Please."

"What?"

"I don't want to hear the details." Was it my imagination or was my new client's breathing more rapid and shallow than it had been a minute ago?

"Really? I didn't think you had a weak stomach."

"Yeah, well, I do, so spare me, okay? You'd better get back to work."

"Sure, okay. Take it easy. Bye, kid," he called to the girl before leaving. I released an audible sigh of relief and sat where Officer Nobles had been, across from the girl.

"Hi," I said. "I'm Claire Conover. I'm a social worker with DHS."

"Hi," she said in a faint voice.

"Did the police tell you anything about what's going to happen next?"

She shook her head.

"Okay, first of all, are you hungry?" Maslow didn't invent his hierarchy for nothing. Physical needs first.

A pause, then a nod.

"What do you say we get out of here and hit McDonald's for breakfast? My treat. Then I'll fill you in."

"Okay."

She slung the stained red backpack over her shoulder, and I signed out at the desk. There was a McDonald's on Green Springs Highway on the way back to the office. I opted to go in rather than drive-thru.

I told her to order as much as she liked, and she ordered two Egg McMuffins, a hash brown, and another Diet Coke. I wasn't hungry but ordered a sausage biscuit anyway, and a coffee. I didn't want to just sit there and watch her eat. Besides, girls this age tended to talk more openly when some other activity was going on.

I carried the tray to a table. While she munched her potato, I picked at my biscuit, and after we'd eaten for a few minutes I said, "What's your name?"

She took another Mcbite of McMuffin and ignored me.

"Look, unfortunately this isn't a question I can just skip over. I have to call you something. So what'll it be? Jane? As in Jane Doe?"

She scowled. "Call me Sandy."

"Okay, Sandy."

"But that's not my real name."

"I didn't think it was. Can you tell me where you live?"

She shook her head.

"How old are you? Surely you can tell me that."

She thought for a second. "Fifteen."

Girls who lie about their age always age themselves up. I guessed the truth was more like thirteen, as Mary Nobles had suspected. Or maybe even twelve.

"What's your mom's name?" I asked, knowing full well what the answer would be. Sure enough, she shook her head.

"If you don't want to go home to your parents, what about another relative? A grandmother? Or an aunt or uncle?"

She shook her head again.

"A friend's house? Maybe I could call one of your friend's parents?"

Again, a no.

"Okay, Sandy. Here's the deal." I leaned forward, getting her full attention. "I don't know what's happened to you or why you were sleeping behind the grocery store. And you don't want to tell me, right?"

She nodded.

"You've run away from home, I suppose. Maybe something happened, or someone hurt you. Maybe you got in an argument with your mom, or dad, or stepdad, or sister or brother."

No reaction.

"This isn't the first time I've seen a girl who's run off. One time I had a fifteen-year-old who was much in the same situation you are. She was homeless, and when I met her she wouldn't tell me anything. I wound up having to put her in foster care. With strangers. People she didn't know at all. She'd been there about two days when she cooled off and got homesick for her family.

13

Turns out she'd gotten into a fight with her mom because she wouldn't let the girl go to a party. She wanted to go home. But it was too late. Once the judge signs that order putting you in my custody, there's no going back. You can't just go home. You can't go home until the judge says you can, and that could take months. It was three months before that girl could go home and be with her mom and dad and brother and sister. Three months before she could go back to her school, and her friends. Just because of a stupid fight that got completely out of hand. Do you understand what I'm saying?"

"I understand."

"Are you sure you don't want to tell me what's going on? Or give me someone I can call?"

"Nope."

"You understand you might not be able to go home for a while?

"A long while?"

"Yep."

"Okay," she said.

I sat back in the hard plastic chair and studied her as she ate. What was with this kid? I'd given her my scariest story: *You're-going-to-live-with-total-strangers-and-you-can't-go-home*, and she hadn't shown a drop of emotion. Not a tear, not a fear, nothing. She ate quietly, took a sip of her drink. She had a distant expression on her face. Detached. Shut down. She'd been traumatized, for sure.

She finished her second breakfast sandwich and wadded the wrapper up.

"Get enough to eat?" I asked.

"Yes, thank you." Someone had taught her some manners along the way.

"All right. Let's go to my office. I need to find you a place to live."

I peppered her with questions on the way to DHS. What grade are you in? What's your favorite subject in school? What music do you listen to? What movies have you seen lately? Like sports? Anything to learn a little more about her. All of my questions were answered with the typical stony silence or a shake of the head. After a few minutes, I gave up.

I brought her up to my cubicle. Russell was out, so I cleared a few things off of his desk and parked her there.

"Do you want to call someone? You can use that phone."

"No."

"I'm afraid I don't have much for you to do."

"That's okay."

"Are you tired?"

"A little." No wonder. She'd been up since four-thirty. And sleeping on concrete, which wasn't exactly comfy.

"We have some beds downstairs. Do you want to go lie down?"

"Okay."

She grabbed her backpack again and we took the stairs one flight down. I made my way through the lobby to the north side of the first floor, where the Overnight Unit was headquartered. Two caseworkers screened and handled emergency investigations from five in the evening until eight in the morning and on weekends. Sometimes they had to bring kids into care in the middle of the night, so next to their office was a large room they jokingly called Hotel DHS. In addition to two baby cribs, there were four cheap metal cots with flimsy canvas-covered mattresses on top. A stained pillow crowned each one.

I searched around in a large cabinet outside the room until I unearthed a twenty-year-old set of pink and blue floral sheets. At least they were soft. I made the bed for her and found an old pink blanket with a giant hole in one corner.

"There you go."

"Thanks."

"No problem. Do you remember where to find me if you need anything?"

"Yes."

"There's a bathroom in the lobby, by the way."

"Okay."

"If you can't find me, just ask someone."

"Okay."

I peeked in the door for a moment, covertly watching as she sat on the cot, rummaged in the red backpack, and extracted the mp3 player. She placed the earbuds in her small ears and lay down, eyes closed. I could hear a tinny version The Cure's *Lovesong* through her headset. Who the hell are you and what happened to you, I thought. And, where am I going to put you? Then I realized exactly where she would do well. If it was my lucky day.

15

Chapter Three

I took the stairs two at a time. Back in my cubicle, I checked my email and printed today's 621. The 621 Form was the list of foster placements, updated every day and distributed to all the social workers. Three pages long, filled with three columns of small print. I scanned it, all the time muttering a small prayer of "please, please, please" until I found the name I was looking for. <u>Sandler, Nettie/T.J.</u> said the first column. The next column was the number of foster children currently in the home. She had four, which meant she wasn't maxed out. The limit was six. The next column said <u>Open</u>.

"Yes!" I said to myself and pumped a fist in the air. I buzzed Mac and told him about breakfast.

"She didn't tell you anything? No name, nothing?"

"Nothing. I told her the scariest version of what was going to happen to her, about going to foster care and everything, but she didn't crack."

"Where are you placing her?"

"Nettie Sandler's got an opening, according to today's 621. I'm about to call her."

"Yeah, I think that'd be good. Keep me posted."

I called Legal first and spoke to the secretary. Got Jane Doe's case, aka Sandy, on the docket for the following afternoon's shelter care hearings. Then I called Nettie.

Nettie Sandler was a wonder. A black woman from Greene County in rural west Alabama, she married at age thirteen and had ten children by the time she was twenty-six. All of her children were now successfully grown, and they had blessed her with twenty-five grandchildren and countless great-grandchildren who were scattered around the country. Several years ago Nettie and her husband T.J., a retired railroad engineer, had come to the conclusion that their empty house was too quiet and had signed up to be foster parents. I sent my toughest cases to them, including teens that had a criminal record a mile long. I had never seen Nettie fail to reach them. Something about her kindness and her ability to make them feel at home did the trick. That, and her cooking. Nettie could cook better than anyone I knew.

She answered the phone after the first ring. "Hey, Nettie, it's Claire Conover."

"Hi, sweetheart!" Nettie called everyone sweetheart. "You got one for me?"

"I do. She won't tell us her name or her age or anything, but she's going by the name of Sandy. She's about thirteen or fourteen. The police found her asleep under a cardboard box behind the Piggly Wiggly about four-thirty this morning."

"Lord Almighty. Poor baby. Where's her mamma?"

"Don't know yet. My guess is she's a runaway. The police notified all the local law enforcement agencies when they found her, but no one's claimed her so far."

I knew there was no way Nettie was going to refuse her now that she knew the story. But I asked anyway. "Can you take her?"

"Of course, bring her on over. I'll get a bed ready. Bless her heart. Bring her whenever. I'm here all day."

"Thanks, Nettie."

I went downstairs and eased my head through the door of the room where Sandy was resting. Her music still played softly, but I could tell by her slow, deep breathing that she was asleep.

I went back upstairs and did as much paperwork as I could for her file, which was difficult considering I didn't know her real name. No way to run a history on her to see if she'd been in our custody before. No way to sign her up for Medicaid. No way to request her school records. In the end, I did little else but type up my court report for the next day and finish the paperwork to place her in foster care. I made all the required copies and stopped by Mac's glass-fronted office at the perimeter of our unit to get his signature on a fifty-dollar voucher to get her some clothes and personal supplies.

It was twelve-thirty by the time I finished everything, plus some items on my list from earlier. I had a one o'clock intervention meeting scheduled in a conference room. I went downstairs to check on Sandy, who was awake and staring at the ceiling, earphones still in place.

"You okay?" I asked.

She removed the music. "What?"

"You okay?"

"Yeah."

"You hungry? I've got about a half hour before my meeting if you want to run out with me and get something."

"No, I'm okay, thank you."

"All right. I'll be in the conference room upstairs if you need me. Just ask the front desk to call me. After my meeting, I'm taking you to your foster home. Your foster mom's name is Nettie Sandler. I think you'll like her."

18

"Okay."

"Do you have any questions for me?"

"No."

Back in my cubicle, I prepped for the IM. Thankfully it was a short one without too much drama. An hour later, I chucked the paperwork on my desk to deal with when I had time and grabbed the digital camera out of my desk drawer.

Sandy was sitting up on the cot, scrolling through the songs on her IPod. "You ready to go?" I asked.

"Yeah. What's that for?"

"I have to take your picture."

"Why?

"For our records. Stand up for me."

"Wait." She retrieved a plastic hairbrush from the bag and brushed her long black hair, then ran a finger under her eyes to touch up her makeup. "Look okay?" she asked.

"Gorgeous. Smile pretty."

She scowled, and I snapped. Much more realistic.

I took one more for good measure, then returned the camera to my desk. I'd print the pictures later. After getting my things, I met Sandy in the lobby.

Riding in the car would give me one last opportunity to talk to her. Once we'd fastened our seat belts and I'd cranked up the A/C in my car to combat the humid heat outside, I said, "So, have you given any more thought to what we talked about earlier? About anyone you want to stay with?"

"No."

"Don't you think your mother is worried out of her mind?"

"No."

"What about your dad? He must be frantic."

"I never see him. He's in prison in Mississippi."

"How long's he been there?"

"Off and on since I was about two."

"Where?"

She shrugged.

"What's he there for?"

Another shrug.

Well, hallelujah. A nugget of information. "What's his name?"

She ignored that one. I couldn't think of anything else to ask, so I said, "We're going to go to Family Court tomorrow for your hearing. I'm bringing Nettie a voucher so she can take you and get

19

you some clothes and things."

"Clothes for court?"

"Yep, and for school." We'd have to discover her real name first, but I was confident someone would claim her soon.

"School! I'm not going back to school." She tossed her head.

It was the most emotion I'd seen out of her all morning, but I wasn't about to get into that fight now. I let it go.

"For now let's worry about getting you settled, okay? I'll give you my number if you need anything, or if you think of someone you want me to call."

She nodded, and we rode in silence going west down Bessemer Superhighway to the suburb of Midfield. Nettie and T.J.'s long driveway was directly off the busy four-lane road, but the house was far enough back on the hill to mute the traffic noise. The original part of the house had been hand-built in the early 1940s by T.J.'s coal-miner grandfather. It had started as four rooms, and grew as each successive child had arrived. It was now a sprawling brick-and-wood ranch with a maze of six bedrooms tacked on wherever there was space. It was large and comfortable and homier than any house designed by an architect.

I knocked on the carport door and heard Nettle shout, "Come in!" The door led us into Nettie's huge, cluttered kitchen, painted a butter-yellow and smelling of fresh bread, tangy barbeque sauce and spices. Floral-curtained windows overlooked the garden in the back, and old appliances hummed quietly.

Nettie was setting the rectangular rustic table for seven. Her gray and black hair was pulled into a bun. Her cocoa-colored face was dotted with dark freckles, while dimples framed a bright white smile showing only a few laugh lines. Nobody meeting her for the first time was ever able to guess her age of seventy-five.

She greeted me with her usual "Hi, sweetheart," wrapped her plump arms around me in a hug, and introduced herself to Sandy. I sat at the kitchen table and checked my messages with my cell phone while Nettie gave Sandy a tour of the house and showed her where she would sleep.

Nettie joined me, alone, in the kitchen after the tour. "She's gettin' settled. I got her in the room with my ten-year old girl, Kedisha. I think they'll get on just fine. The rest of them will be home in just a while. It gets as crazy as Bedlam around here at three-thirty."

I cleared the phone and smiled. "I bet." I told Nettie about the hearing and gave her the voucher for the clothes. She said she'd

20

take Sandy to do some shopping in the morning.

"That should cheer her up some," Nettie said. "I ain't never seen no teenager that didn't love new clothes. Nobody's called for her?"

"No, not yet. I'm starting to get a little worried." I could think of only two reasons why her mother hadn't contacted the police. First, she didn't want her, which made her a throwaway and meant she'd spend the rest of her adolescence in foster care. Second, she wasn't from Birmingham and had made her way here somehow. Probably by hitchhiking, which was dangerous and might explain the underlying trauma. I wondered if the police had started to contact other counties in the area, and made a mental note to call Mary Nobles tonight when her shift began.

"Sandy?" I called out toward her room. "Can you come here a sec?"

She joined us at the table, next to Nettie and across from me. Nettie instinctively reached up and began stroking her back in a light, comforting rub.

"I have to go back to work. Here's my card. It has my cell phone number on it, so you can reach me twenty-four-seven, okay? If you want to tell me anything, don't hesitate to call."

"Okay."

"You sure you don't have any questions before I go?"

"No."

"All right. Then I'll see you and Nettie at the courthouse tomorrow afternoon."

"Right."

Nettie gave me another hug goodbye, and I spent the afternoon doing home visits. Both were unannounced, and both went better than I expected, a welcome surprise. I finished the last one at four-thirty and came to the happy realization that I'd gotten all the starred items on my To Do list done and might get off work at a reasonable hour. I grabbed my phone and speed-dialed Grant Summerville's number.

It took him a few minutes to answer and when he did, he was grunting. "Oh, uh, hello?"

"What are you doing?"

"Crawling... around... uh... in... the... ceiling."

"Why?"

"Running... um... cable."

Grant was a scarecrow of a man. Six-foot-five and floppy, from his curly brown hair to his long arms and legs. And clumsy

21

didn't even begin to describe him. I hoped he wouldn't fall through the plaster.

"Let me call you back in... a minute," he said.

"Sure."

Five minutes later my phone sang its tune. "Sorry about that," he said. "What's up?"

"I'm actually going to get off work at five, like normal people. I was hoping we could have dinner at my place."

"Damn. I have to get the rest of this section wired tonight to keep on schedule. I already told the guys we'd be here late. I'm sorry. Can I take a rain check?"

"Sure." I sounded hurt, and he heard it.

"I really am sorry. This weekend, I promise. I promise we'll see a movie and go to dinner or something, okay?"

"Okay."

His voice dropped to a sexy near-whisper. "Claire, I do miss you."

That made me smile. "I miss you, too."

"I'll call you tonight."

Going home to an empty house didn't appeal to me today. I scrolled through my phone list and called my father.

"Hi," I said. "Got plans for dinner?"

"No, not especially."

"I thought I'd pick up something from the Diner." The Bluff Park Diner was our local cafeteria-style restaurant, just down the street from my father's house.

"Sounds good, just get me my usual."

Thirty-five minutes later I arrived at Dad's. DR C CONOVER was stuck on the mailbox in white letters. The C stood for Christopher, the DR for his Ph.D. in Psychology. I eased my Honda into the space behind my father's hybrid. The bumper of the hybrid was covered in stickers advocating human rights, environmental conservation and political views.

I took the Styrofoam boxes containing one daily special and one vegetable plate into the kitchen and set them on the harvest gold kitchen counter. "Dad?" I called.

"In here."

He was in the dining room. Newspaper was spread over the table, and Dad was painting an ocean-blue and earth-green peace sign on a poster sized piece of white cardboard attached to a one-by-two. Another sign drying nearby read NO MORE WAR. "What's all this?" I asked.

22

"Just getting ready for the rally tomorrow."

"Rally?"

"Parents for Peace. We're holding a rally tomorrow at Kelly Ingram Park." Dad's long gray-blond ponytail was hanging over his shoulder and threatening to dip into the green paint. I tucked it in the back of his T-shirt. "Thanks."

"You're welcome. I thought that organization was for parents of servicemen. And women."

"Nope. For any concerned parent. And I'm a parent. I know, because the evidence is right here." He leaned over and kissed me on the cheek. His blue eyes, the same shade as my own, twinkled at me above the bright white scar on his face.

Dad had gotten the scar from a beating when he was a Freedom Rider in the nineteen sixties. My parents were both very active in the Civil Rights movement before I was born. They supported any human rights cause, whether it was eradicating poverty, equality for women, or world peace. My mother, who died of breast cancer when I was thirteen, took me and my younger brother to soccer games in between planning meetings for the National Organization for Women. Their passion for advocacy and helping others had been handed down to me, the social worker. And to my brother, a nurse in Orlando.

"I brought dinner. It's on the counter."

"Let me finish this placard and we'll eat. Do you want a drink?"

"No, I don't think so. Although--" I was interrupted by the ring of my cell phone. I checked the caller ID to find Nettie's number.

"Hello?"

"Oh, Claire." Nettie, and her voice was breaking.

"What's wrong? Is it Sandy?"

"Yes. Lord bless her, she's gone."

Chapter Four

"Gone?"

"She must've gone out the window," Nettie said. "Oh, Lord, please keep that baby safe."

"How long ago?"

"I can't rightly say. The other kids got home right after you left, and I introduced Sandy and fed them all a snack. After she ate she said she wanted to take a shower. After her shower she went in her room. About five-thirty I went in to tell her to wash up for supper and she was gone."

I glanced in the kitchen to see the clock on Dad's microwave. Five-forty-one. It might not be too late to find her. "Hang tight, Nettie. I'm on my way."

I hung up and whispered a sharp, "Shit."

Dad, finishing the last of the peace sign's circle, asked, "Problem?"

"The girl I took into custody today just pulled a Houdini out the window. I gotta go."

Dad followed me into the kitchen and watched as I scarfed down ten bites of beef tips and rice. "That's all you're going to eat?"

"I'll come get the rest of it later." I wiped gravy from my lips and planted a kiss on his cheek. "Bye."

I made a quick detour to my office downtown, signed in with Joel, the nighttime security guard, and dashed to my desk to print two sharp copies of Sandy's picture. Her blue-black hair contrasted drastically with her pale face and the tea-colored wall behind her. I slipped the photos into my purse and raced to Nettie's.

She let me in the carport door, sniffling and dabbing her eyes with an old fashioned lace-trimmed handkerchief. "I'm so sorry. I should've watched her more careful."

"It's not your fault." I checked the time again. It was six-twenty. I had about forty-five minutes of faint daylight remaining. "I'm going to go look for her."

Back in my car, I hung a left out of Nettie's driveway and headed toward downtown Birmingham. I followed the route we'd come earlier when I dropped her off, and remembered we'd passed several shops a mile or so down the road. I drove slowly, angering the drivers behind me as I scanned the roadside for a little girl.

At the next major intersection, strip malls and chain restaurants clustered all four corners. I pulled into the parking lot of a fast-food fried chicken place and went inside. The overweight teenager behind the counter asked brightly if she could help me.

I showed her Sandy's picture. "Have you seen this girl? She would have come in sometime in the last couple of hours."

She shook her head. "Sorry, haven't seen her."

I left the rich aromas in the restaurant and sat in my car, surveying the shops around me. A lot were closed for the evening. The Dollar General was still open, and loitering in the parking lot were three African Americans. Two men and a woman, talking animatedly. The woman was clearly flirting. I parked the Honda a few spaces away and started toward them, Sandy's picture in hand.

The guys, in their mid-twenties, shot me a nervous look. Both were both dressed similarly in baggy jeans and long jerseys. One had long, braided hair. I belatedly wondered if I was walking into something I shouldn't, and was thinking I should just turn around and leave when the bald guy said, "We gotta dip," to the girl. Both men got into an older Chevy and, stereo thumping, squealed out of the parking lot. The woman and I watched them go.

"Hi," I said. Now that I was closer, I was surprised to see she was more of a girl than a lady. Her clothes were tight, and included a white tank-top low-cut over breasts that were big for her age. The makeup covering her dark skin had been applied with a heavy hand and her curls were elaborately styled in an up-do. It was hard to place her age, but I guessed somewhere between thirteen and sixteen. Way too young to be flirting with twenty-something men. It made me wonder what she trying to get from them, and vice versa. Sex? Drugs? Both?

She scowled, and raked me up and down with a look. "Whaddya want?"

"I wanted to know if you've seen this girl?" I held out Sandy's picture. She took it. One of her long nails had a glittering butterfly on it.

"Why? She yo' daughter?"

"No." I didn't elaborate.

"What you want with her then?" She handed the photo back.

"Have you seen her? It would've been within the last couple of hours."

"I ain't been here that long."

"Have you seen her? Please, it's very important."

"Why?"

"She's missing. She could be in danger."

The girl narrowed her long-lashed eyes and studied me. She

26

had a pretty face, large dark eyes, and slightly gapped teeth just a little too big for her face. She'd grow into them.

"You ain't no cop."

"No, I'm not."

"I know. You ain't got the attitude. And you said you wasn't her mamma."

"No."

"Oh," she said. "You her social worker, huh?"

Wow. "How'd you know?" I asked with a smile.

She shrugged. "You just look like a social worker."

"Thanks, I think. You know many of us, do you?"

"Not really. I ain't seen that girl."

A string of Dollar General customers were leaving the store. I fished in my purse for a card and handed it to her. "Will you call me if you happen to see her?"

"Yeah."

"What's your name?"

"Why?" Suspicious, this one.

"No reason. I just like to know who I'm talking to. I'm Claire."

"Duh. I know. I can read." She waved the card at me.

"And you are?"

"LaReesa."

"LaReesa what?"

"Jones." It was a common enough last name, but it made me wonder if she was telling the truth.

"How old are you?"

"Twenty."

"Yeah, right."

"Sixteen."

"Not quite, I think."

"Okay, I'm thirteen. Damn."

"That's more like it. You live around here?"

"Why?"

"Just curious. It's the social worker in me."

"You gonna put me in foster care?"

"Why, do you need a place to stay?"

"No, I live with my mamma."

"Where?"

"In an apartment, around the corner."

"Does your mom know where you are?"

"She's at work. Shouldn't you be lookin' for that girl?"

27

"I'm going in just a second. What's your mom's name?"

"Damn, you nosy, ain't you?" She turned her back on me. BABY GIRL was printed in white letters on the butt of her azalea-pink pants. I'd pushed it enough.

"Sorry. Anyway, please call me if you see that girl, okay?"

"Whatever."

I got back in my car and spotted a Texaco gas station on the opposite corner. I drove across the busy street and parked in front of the door. A young man, his hair in dreadlocks, stood behind the bullet proof glass enclosed counter.

He smiled at me. "Hey, can I help you?" His eyes were bloodshot and half closed.

"I'm looking for this girl," I answered through the round speaker, flashing Sandy's picture again. "She would have come in sometime in the last couple of hours."

He studied it. "Oh, yeah. I seen her. She used the phone. I remember."

"She came in the store? Did she say anything to you?"

"Nah, man, not really. She was sorta cute, you know? But she just wanted to use the phone. She made a call and then waited outside on the curb until she left."

"Left? How?"

"About thirty minutes after she showed up, some big-ass SUV came and got her."

"I don't suppose you saw the driver or got the license number?"

"Nah, man, I was busy."

Busy smoking dope, I guessed. "What color was the SUV?"

"Um, dark. Blue."

"What make?"

He shrugged. "I didn't look that close, man."

"Do you remember what time this was? When she got picked up?"

"Like, maybe like a half-hour ago."

I sighed. "Thanks."

I sat in my car for a minute, then walked back in the store. Marijuana Man was sitting on a stool now, watching a sitcom on a small color TV. He raised his eyebrows when he saw me.

"Have you made any calls on that phone, since she came in?"

"Naw. How come?"

"Can I see the phone?"

He passed it to me through the little slot at the bottom of the window. It was a black phone, cordless, with a small green screen above the numbers. I searched the buttons.

At the bottom right of the keypad I found what I was looking for. A small button, labeled "REDIAL". I searched through my purse until I found a pen and an old Taco Bell receipt. I pushed "TALK" and then the redial button. A number scrolled onto the screen. I wrote it down as it appeared. It started with 205, which meant it was local, and then 910. I knew the land-line phone numbers around Birmingham pretty well, and that prefix wasn't one I recognized. That made me think it was a cell phone. I put the phone to my ear and listened.

Whoever it was didn't answer the phone. I got a standard electronic message, not the voice of the phone's owner, or their name. The message informed me that I'd reached the 910 number and invited me to please leave a message. What the hell, I thought.

"Hi, this is Claire Conover and I'm trying to reach Sandy. Please have her call me." I left my number.

I hung up. I had no expectations that my message would be returned by anyone, but at least I had a phone number.

I returned the phone to the man behind the counter and wished I knew a way to determine whose number the phone had just dialed. I guess the phone company would have records. Maybe the police could get them. I'd ask Mary Nobles.

I returned to Nettie's. Nettie, T.J., and a racially diverse group of children ranging in age from four to ten were seated at the table in the kitchen, chattering happily between bites of brisket, corn, and potatoes. Both Nettie and T.J. urged me to fill a plate, and I was tempted, but in the end I thanked them and Nettie walked me to my car.

"No luck?" she asked.

"No." I told her about what I'd discovered at the gas station. "So someone came and got her. An adult, or at least someone old enough to drive. And at least I've got their phone number, if nothing else."

"Lord, I hope she's safe."

"Me, too."

Nettie agreed to call me immediately on the off chance that Sandy returned to her house. I sat in my car in her driveway and dialed 411 to get the non-emergency number for the Homewood Police Department. I asked for Mary Nobles and was transferred to her.

"I was just about to go on patrol. What's up?"

I relayed the story of Sandy's disappearance. She took my report over the phone and said she'd get the word out to the other city police departments in the area, as well as the Jefferson County Sheriff's Office. I gave her the number I thought Sandy had dialed. She said she'd get it traced.

"By the way," I asked, "have you checked with the surrounding counties to see if anyone's reported her missing? Maybe she's from Blount, or St. Clair, or Tuscaloosa."

"Not yet. They usually contact us when a parent makes a report knowing the kids will often head for the city. I was going to check with them tomorrow if we hadn't heard anything."

"Okay, I'll keep you posted if I hear from Sandy."

"Same here."

I paged Mac and updated him on Sandy's departure. I told him everything I'd learned at the gas station and about the phone call. He took it in his usual, official manner. Runaways weren't all that uncommon in our unit. Still, he wasn't thrilled about it.

Dad was out, his house dark and his car gone. No doubt he was at a Tae Kwon Do class, or water aerobics at the Rec Center, or any one of a hundred other activities and organizations that had kept him busy since my mother died seventeen years ago. My brother, Christopher Junior, was just ten when she died. I was thirteen; an angry, grieving, confused, emotional mess of a teenager. Dad handled the chaos well, knowing when I needed a parent and when I needed my space, and what could have descended into a relationship full of rebellion and rancor blossomed into one of closeness.

I unlocked the door and headed for the fridge, intent on finishing my dinner. But Dad had beaten me to it. All that was left was a few grains of rice and a bite of green beans. My part-time vegetarian father had given in to temptation again.

I rummaged around in his refrigerator for a while, and not discovering anything worth eating, drove the last mile home. I'd bought a small nineteen-fifties house in the area seven months ago, and had transformed it into one that reflected my tastes. After parking in the carport on the side of the little black-and-white cottage, I made my way down the dark hilly driveway to the mailbox. Flyers, bills, nothing of interest. I unlocked my front door with the same sense of accomplishment that I felt every time I came home.

I switched on a few lamps and changed into shorts and a T-shirt. Foraging around in my own fridge didn't reveal anything to get excited about, so in the end I toasted my last bagel and scraped on the last lump of cream cheese.

The third, smallest bedroom in the house was my office, where I booted the computer. I logged on remotely to the server at work and added an addendum to my report for Sandy's case. *On September 1, between approximately three-thirty and five-thirty p.m.,* I typed, *the Dependent left her foster placement and is currently on runaway status.*

That was not, not, not going to make Judge Myer happy. I dreaded the shelter care hearing tomorrow and the dread was all mixed in with worry about whether Sandy was safe. And who had picked her up in the blue SUV? Her parents? A friend? What in the world was Sandy up to?

And why was I this concerned? It's not like I hadn't had a runaway teenager in my caseload before. I'd had many, actually. But they tended to be older, and more streetwise. Usually when they ran, they ran to their drug dealer or their gang members. My runners were usually experienced in taking care of themselves. Something Sandy, I believed, wasn't.

I printed a few copies of the addendum and filed them in my briefcase. Trying to put Sandy's whereabouts out of my mind, I worked on case narratives for the home visits I'd done. When I was halfway through typing the second, my instant messenger on my phone ding-donged like a doorbell and a window popped up.

Hightech00 asked "wyd?"

That was Grant, and wyd was geek-speak for "what are you doing?"

"working," I typed back.

"me 2. Did u enjoy your evening off?"

"never got it. 1 of my girls ran away."

"u find her?"

"No."

"sorry."

"me 2. I'm worried."

Grant and I chatted online for a few more minutes. He updated me on his project and what was going on at the store. After a while I began to yawn and typed, "going 2 bed, talk 2 u tomorrow."

He responded with "*smack*", a kiss. I remembered the feel of his lips and the smell of his skin and wished it were the real thing. Then he typed, "gnst." Good night, sleep tight. With Sandy missing, fat chance.

I managed to spend a few hours in dreamland, and went in early again Wednesday morning. Wednesdays were even tougher than Mondays. At least on Monday I'm refreshed and rested after two days off. Wednesdays are just a reminder that there are two more days until the weekend.

My mood was as sour as ever as I surveyed my calendar for the day. One IM this morning and paperwork. Russell arrived in his usual state and unrolled the newspaper.

"Hey, check it out. They printed a composite sketch of the dead woman from yesterday. The police are asking anyone who recognizes her to call." He passed me the first section.

The sketch was computer-generated, in color, and took up most of the first page. The woman had auburn hair and brown eyes, a heart-shaped face with fair skin. The hair curled loosely around her face, to her shoulders. She'd been pretty before dying in that ditch. A pretty, real person. The thought made me sad.

The small article, credited to Kirk Mahoney, stated that the victim was approximately thirty-five years old. No tattoos or scars except for a mole on the left side of her neck.

I handed the paper back to Russell. "Surely someone will know her."

"Probably."

He read me other news from the paper before checking his messages. I spent a busy couple of hours doing paperwork and returning calls, then at ten-thirty left for my IM, which was to be held at my client's house on the east side of town.

I was only a couple of blocks away from the office when my cell phone chimed. The caller ID said DHS.

"Hello?"

It was Mac. He skipped the pleasantries and said, "Homewood Police Department just called. They want to you go immediately to Forest Glen Townhomes, off Valley Avenue." He read me the address and how to get there.

"They say why?"

"Nope. It was Chip Ford who called."

My heart leapt. Sandy, it had to be. She'd been found again. Or she'd gone home. Maybe this townhouse was where she lived, and she and her mother had patched things up.

"Cool, thanks, Mac."

"Maybe they found your little girl."

"I hope so." Please, God, I hoped so.

Chapter Five

I cancelled my intervention meeting with my clients, then drove as fast as I legally could over Red Mountain to Homewood. I turned off Valley Avenue onto the road that led to Forest Glen Townhomes, ascending the mountain from the south. I kept an eye on the road while looking for the sign to the complex.

Forest Glen's entrance was on the right, leading to a row of eight conjoined two-story dwellings. Each unit was painted a different pastel color, giving the place a pleasant, feminine feel. Nice.

Mac's directions said to meet the police in unit number six, and I didn't need to be a detective to tell me which one it was. Three police cars and a van were parked in front of the light yellow house.

My feeling of dread returned. Why would it take three cops to return one small girl home? A herd of patrol cars could only mean big trouble.

I found a space several doors down from number six and made my way to the white-painted front door. It was wide open. A steep set of tan-carpeted steps rose directly in front of me. I could see a living room to my left, decorated in a traditional style with lots of beige and dark red accents. All the stuff looked relatively new. Faint voices came from that direction, somewhere toward the back of the house, and an additional buzz of conversation floated down from upstairs.

I found a newly renovated kitchen at the back of the house. Light tan walls and stainless steel appliances. The house was remarkably clean and free of clutter. Two officers were looking through the cabinets. I asked for Chip, and they directed me upstairs.

I made my way back through the living room. Not only was it immaculate, it was devoid of any objects that might tell me anything about who lived here. No photos, collectables, nothing. Just one generic abstract painting over the fireplace.

"Hello?" I called, and started up the steps.

I was halfway up when a familiar voice behind me said, "Well, hel-lo gorgeous."

I stopped cold and turned. Sure enough, at the bottom of stairs stood Kirk Mahoney, his topaz-blue eyes narrowing as he smiled.

"Fancy meeting you here," he said.

"How did you know it was me?"

"I'd recognize you from any angle. Especially that one."

I shot him an annoyed look.

"And your car's parked outside, an old white Honda Civic with a DHS parking decal, desperately in need of a trip to the car wash. What's up?"

"I don't know."

"What do you mean you don't know?"

"The police called and asked me to meet them here. What are you doing here?"

"Following my story."

"Your story? You mean the red-headed woman in the ravine?"

"So you do read my articles." He climbed the stairs until he was on the step below me, matching my height. He leaned close until we were almost nose to nose. A tingly feeling started in my legs.

"It's good to see you again," he said.

"Kirk..."

"Yes?"

"Seriously, what are you doing here?"

"I heard on the scanner that this could be where she lived. My Jane Doe in the ditch. So she had kids, huh? You taking custody?"

"I--" I was interrupted by the sound of a man clearing his throat at the top of the stairs. "Oh, hello."

"Can I help you two?"

"Chip Ford called for me. I'm Claire Conover, from DHS."

"Oh, yes." He shouted for Chip over his shoulder, then looked at Kirk. "And you are?"

"Kirk Mahoney, from the <u>News</u>."

"We aren't ready to make a statement yet."

"Can you tell me if this is where the dead woman lived?"

"Really, we're not--"

"What about her name?"

"Let's step outside." He brushed past me and practically escorted Kirk out of the front door just as Chip appeared at the head of the stairs.

"Hi, Claire."

"What's going on?"

"Come on up."

I met him on the landing. The townhouse had three bedrooms on this level, and I could see a neat bathroom as well. I gave Chip a quizzical look.

Then I noticed he was holding something in his hand. A photograph. Not a regular snapshot, but a wallet-sized head shot. A

34

school picture. He held it out to me.

It was Sandy. No doubt about it. Her hair was a pretty, dark red set off by the dark green tunic-style top she was wearing, and her wide smile revealed a crooked eye tooth. She looked a little younger in the picture, which made me think it was last year's yearbook picture. "That's her. That's Sandy, isn't it?"

"I thought so."

"She lived here? It was her mother who was killed in the ditch by the golf course?"

"It looks like it. The mother's name was Jean Chambless, and her daughter is Samantha."

"Poor kid."

"We need to talk her. Now."

Uh-oh. "Mary Nobles didn't tell you?" I asked.

"Tell me what?"

"She ran away."

"You're freakin' kidding."

"I'm not. I took her to her foster parents about three yesterday. She went out the window sometime between three-thirty and five-thirty."

"Goddamn it. The detective is going to want to hear this. Let's go outside."

Chip followed me down the stairs and outside. We waited on a tiny patch of grass while the man who had greeted me talked with Kirk near one of the police cars. Kirk, the lavender sleeves of his dress shirt rolled as usual to just below the elbows, scribbled rapidly in a pocket notebook while Chip and I watched. The two men finished their conversation, shook hands, and Kirk closed the notepad. He glanced my way and winked, then mouthed "see you," before roaring away in his sporty silver Infiniti.

I watched as the car crested a hill and disappeared from sight. I was still staring down the road as the detective joined us. "Jonathan Stringfellow," he said, and held out his hand.

I shook it. "Claire Conover."

"You and that reporter fella know each other?"

"Yeah, we do."

He waited.

"It's a long story." I brought my mind back to the present and focused on the detective. He was older than me, but only by a few years. Early forties, maybe. Brown hair and tan skin. Slightly chubby. A strong southern accent and deeply receding hairline were his only remarkable features. A silver wedding band squeezed his left ring finger.

"Did Chip show you the picture?" He pronounced it pit-chure.

"Yes, and I'm sure it's the girl I took into custody yesterday."

"We'll need to speak to her."

I squirmed. "That's going to be problem." I related all that happened the day before, including what I'd discovered at the gas station.

Chip said, "Why the hell wasn't the foster parent watching her? Jesus Christ, I can't believe she'd let a kid go off like that."

Pissed, I jumped to Nettie's defense. "My foster parents aren't wardens, Officer Ford. They can't be expected to know what the children are doing every second. If I'd known--"

Detective Stringfellow held up a hand. "It doesn't matter. I'm sure anyone who could've prevented this would have. You said she used the phone at the gas station. You didn't happen to write down the number she called?"

"I did, actually. I gave it to Mary Nobles. She's working on it. Hang on." I trotted over to my car and dug through my purse until I came up with the Taco Bell receipt where I'd written the number. I handed the small scrap of paper to Stringfellow, who copied the number into a notebook and then pocketed the slip.

"Detective, can I look around a while? See San--Samantha's room? Maybe I can get some idea of where she might have gone."

"I was just gonna suggest that. We've just about finished going through everything. Haven't found much of importance. No list of any family, address book, phone numbers, baby pictures, nothing. Nothing in the girl's room except clothes and what looks to be some old notebooks from school. It's. . ." He searched for words and finished with, "weird."

The detective walked me back into the house, and at the top of the stairs showed me Samantha's room. The walls were painted a soft celery green. The bed was covered with a striped comforter, bright lines of fuchsia, turquoise, and the same green that decorated the walls. The furniture was simple and white, and from the lack of scratches and wear, I guessed it was fairly new, too, like the stuff downstairs.

Samantha's single bed was against the far wall. I sat on it and picked up one of the many stuffed animals lying there. This one was a small teddy bear, white, cute and very soft. I hugged it to my chest and surveyed the room.

A cork bulletin board hung on the wall behind me. I saved it for later. Two full laundry baskets and a pile of clothes sat at the foot of the bed, some clothing trailing from there to the closet in front of me. A desk was to my left, underneath the window. A few notebooks lay on top of it next to a bottle of lavender nail polish. To my right, a waist-high, three-shelf bookcase, held more stuffed animals, a jewelry box, and a few books. *Harry Potter. The Lion, the Witch, and the Wardrobe. The Hobbit.* Samantha liked fantasy.

I rose from the bed, opened the jewelry box, and found a mass of cheap silver and gold earrings, necklaces and bracelets. I closed it and went to the desk.

The drawers held old school papers, marked with grades that were mostly average, the occasional "D" or "Needs Improvement" scrawled across the top. Her teachers were fond of using red pens. A few sketches were mixed in with the schoolwork, amateur drawings of palm trees and beaches and dogs and cats and flowers.

I finished searching the desk and opened the closet. Several pictures were taped to the back of the door. Somebody named Zac Efron smiled brightly at me. A collage of several photos surrounded a teen-magazine article about him. They were joined by photos of Liam Hemsworth, in scenes from *The Hunger Games* movies.

A sheet of lined notebook paper hung under the actors' pictures. SAMANTHA was written in big rainbow-colored bubble letters along with "Best friends forever, Marci" and several little hearts.

Shoes spilled from a wicker basket on the floor of the closet. Clothes hung haphazardly from plastic hangers, and sweaters lined the top shelf. I poked around in the corners of the closet, but didn't find anything hidden.

Good Lord, how had this apparently normal teenager wound up sleeping under a box behind a grocery store, her murdered mother all over the news?

It seemed the only other clues to Samantha's life were on the cork board hanging behind me. I went back to the bed and studied it.

It was a standard, office-issue bulletin board, about three feet wide and a two high. Three four-by-six photos were grouped together in the upper left corner. It looked like a fourth was missing. I studied the other three.

In the first, Samantha and three friends mugged for the camera on a picnic table. Samantha leaned against the knees of a young man seated on the tabletop, who playfully held two rabbit-ear fingers over her head. The others were a husky boy and a beautiful Latina girl, their arms wrapped around each other. The next photo was of Samantha and the same dark-haired girl, smiling in a pose in front of the boy whose legs she'd been leaning on in the first photo. He was taller than both of them by a few inches, making him about six feet tall.

The next picture showed a larger bunch of kids, six altogether. The shot was spontaneous, taken while none of them looked directly at the camera. Four girls and two boys slouched in front of a set of blue lockers. Sure enough, the tall boy was in the photo again.

His hair was the golden brown of bread crust, his skin tan. The hair was curly and long, with an outward flip that must have required some work. In this picture he wore a black and red hoodie, his hands shoved into the front pockets as he talked to Samantha.

So Samantha had a boyfriend. Or at least a crush.

I looked over the rest of the stuff pinned to the board. A calendar with a picture of a covered bridge, but had no notations on it. A postcard from New York City had been pinned toward the bottom. The back was blank. A bookmark with cats on it was stuck next to it. Finally, a pin-back button asked, "If I got smart with you, how would you know?"

I was reaching over to unpin the clearest of the photographs of Samantha and her friends, the one of the four of them on the picnic table, when Chip Ford's voice called out, "Hey, Detective, I think we found something!"

Chapter Six

I left the photo on the bulletin board and went to find Chip. He was in the master bedroom. I had time to notice the four-poster neatly made with a burgundy printed comforter before concentrating on what Chip was holding.

He stood in front of a dresser, an open box in his hand. Something in French was printed on the top. A single-bottle wine box, the kind of wooden thing you get when you buy the expensive stuff. Not that I was an expert on fancy wine. Mine tended to come with a screw-top from the Piggly Wiggly.

Detective Stringfellow entered the room. "Whatcha got?" he drawled.

Chip put the box on the raised bed so we could all see. "It's got some papers in it."

The detective sorted through the small stack. The first item was a birth certificate for Jean Marie Riley from thirty-five years ago. Five years older than me.   Another birth certificate, this one on blue paper, for Samantha Jean Riley. She had been born on March 15, in Mississippi. She would be fourteen next year. I wondered when the Riley family had become Chamblesses. Likely Jean had gotten married, either to Samantha's father or someone else, and changed their names.

Stringfellow continued to dig through the papers. He pulled out two obituaries, neither one with a picture, both for people named Riley. Jean's grandparents, or parents, I guessed. Several snapshots were at the bottom of the box, one of a middle-aged couple with 1985 written on the back, the other a black-and-white portrait of a woman from the 1930s. An undated photo showed a guy with long hair standing next to a classic shiny Ford Mustang. *Kenny Thigpen* was scrawled in loopy handwriting in pencil on the back. From the young man's mullet-styled hair and acid-washed jeans, I'd wager it was taken in the late eighties. Next were two baby pictures of Samantha. And another one of Samantha, taken at a fair when she was about ten, in front of a Ferris wheel.

That was it. Well, at least I had a name. Several, in fact. Samantha Jean Riley. Or Samantha Jean Chambless. Or Samantha Riley Chambless. I'd run all of them through the system when I got back to the office, with the help of Michele, our records clerk.

The detective was glancing through all the items again as he replaced them in the box. I watched, then said, "I wonder. . . "

"What?"

"If the guy with the long hair is Samantha's father. She said he's in prison in Mississippi."

Stringfellow looked at Chip. "Go call the folks over at MDOC," he said, meaning the Mississippi Department of Corrections, "and see if a Kenny or Kenneth Thigpen is a guest of the State."

"Gotcha."

"Detective? Did you see the photos of Samantha and her friends on the cork board in her room?" He nodded. "Could I take one of the pictures? I'd like to go over to the school and see what I can find out. Maybe she ran to one of her friends' homes."

"I'm getting ready to send an officer over to the middle school now if you'd like to tag along."

I checked my watch. "I can't. I have to be at Family Court in under an hour for Samantha's Shelter Care hearing. By the way, did one of your officers take one of her pictures off the board?"

"No. I noticed one was missing."

"Samantha must have it."

"Go ahead and take one if you need it, but I want it back. And I want us to keep in close touch, okay? Let me know what you find out."

"I will."

I rushed to Samantha's room and took the picture of her and her three friends down from its place. My time-check had sent me into something of a scramble. I hadn't realized it was so close to one o'clock.

The detective and I exchanged cards and I said goodbye. I headed for West End and parked in the lot in front of the stately Jefferson County Family Court. The architectural beauty of its somber red-brick façade was somewhat diminished by the razor-wire that surrounded the G. Ross Bell Youth Detention Center next door.

I climbed the marble stairway in the atrium to the courtrooms on the second floor. The wooden benches used by the public were jam-packed. That meant a huge docket today, and with dismay I realized I could be here all afternoon. No rhyme or reason dictated the order of the cases Judge Myer heard. If you were lucky, you were on top of the stack.

On a whim, I hurried to the judge's courtroom. It was five after one. Social workers, attorneys, and court appointed advocates were starting to amble in. The atmosphere was casual and professionals who had business with the Court were pretty much allowed in and out of the courtroom as they liked, unless a trial was going on. I greeted two lawyers and a colleague, and was relieved to see George, the usual bailiff, sitting in the small box to the right of the judge's bench.

George was in his late sixties, maybe early seventies. The few strands of thin gray hair he had left were combed from ear to ear over his round head. He'd been bailiff for all the judges elected for years, long before I'd started at DHS five years ago. In social worker life-span, I was a long-timer and therefore a familiar face to just about everyone here. George saw me and winked. He loved a good blonde joke, and was a shameless flirt.

I made my way to his box. "Hey, handsome."

"Well, here I was just hoping that a pretty girl would come my way. What's cookin', beautiful?"

"Have I ever told you that you're my favorite bailiff in the whole wide world?"

"Uh-huh. I bet."

"I need to get out of here ASAP."

"What's in for me?"

"My undying gratitude? My first-born child?"

"Don't want no more kids. Can't get rid of the ones I got."

"Please?" I batted my eyelashes in an exaggerated manner.

"Just because I love you. Which case you here on?"

"It's a Jane Doe, but I found out her name this morning. She's the daughter of the woman that was murdered a couple of days ago out in Homewood."

"Damn, poor kid." He searched through the stack of yellow folders on his desk until he found my case, and placed it on top of the stack. "You owe me another one."

"I owe you a million. By the way, what do you call an intelligent blonde?"

"I don't know."

"A Golden Retriever." He laughed.

I joined the growing ranks of my colleagues in the gallery, and we chatted as we waited for Judge Clayton Myer to take the bench. I spotted Brian Shoffner, the DHS attorney, and gave him a quick update on the latest about Samantha's case. He consulted with Monica Langford, Samantha's court-appointed lawyer, and filled her in on what had happened.

At one-twenty, George the Bailiff stood up and announced, "All rise!"

We did as ordered. Judge Myer took the bench, his boyish

41

features made more severe by his authoritative black robes. He heard one case for a private attorney, then reached for the stack of yellow folders on his desk. The courtroom was silent as he read, to himself, all the documents in the first folder, including the Petition for Custody, the police report, and my court report. Then he frowned. "Miss Conover?"

I joined Brian and Monica in front of the bench. "Yes, Your Honor."

"Anything new on this case? She still on runaway?"

"Yes, sir. The Homewood Police Department contacted me this morning. It seems my Jane Doe's real name is Samantha Chambless, and her mother is the woman found murdered on Monday."

"The one out by the new golf course?"

"Yes, sir. The police are very eager to talk with Samantha and are trying to locate her as well."

He sighed. "Poor kid. Mr. Shoffner?"

"We request that she be placed in the State's custody until a more suitable placement is available."

"Ms. Langford? Do you have anything you want to add?" I couldn't imagine what, since she hadn't even met her client yet.

"No, Your Honor."

We waited we he wrote a few sentences on an order. "Okay. Samantha Chambless is hereby placed in the custody of the State of Alabama until this court deems otherwise. Surely she must have a relative out there who wants her. Claire, if one surfaces, get with Brian and request an immediate hearing."

"Yes, sir."

Judge tore the form with the order on it into its separate sheets, keeping the white one for the court, handing a copy to Brian and Monica, and giving me the last.

"And Claire," he said as I took the order.

"Yes, sir?"

"Find her."

Chapter Seven

I practically sprinted out of the courtroom door, my watch taunting me with how fast time was passing. It was already ten after two. If I was going to make it to Samantha's school before everyone left, I'd have to hustle.

I got to E.W. Dodge Middle School just as a long line of yellow buses were queuing in front of the doors. The building was relatively new, fewer than ten years old, a modern temple of learning in dark red brick and glass. Inside, I was sure, were the most up-to-date textbooks, computers, and materials. A far cry from the materials the students in the older inner-city schools had available.

I jogged to the main office and asked to see the principal. The lady manning the desk hemmed and hawed until I showed her my DHS ID. That got her attention.

She showed me to a room behind the long counter where a man sat behind an enormous polished wooden desk. He was younger than I'd expected. And more attractive. Instead of the fat, bald, bad-breathed men who had reigned my middle school, Mr. Eddy had thick, wavy brown hair and a nice tan, accented by a white golf shirt with a little blue devil on the pocket.

We shook hands and he offered me a seat. A studio portrait of him, along with a pretty wife and two adorable young girls, sat on a lateral filing cabinet behind his desk. Trophies shone next to it. I suspected Mr. Eddy had a coaching background.

"How can I help you?" he asked.

"I'm here about Samantha Chambless."

"I thought so. The police were here earlier wondering if she'd been to school."

"Has she?"

"Not since Friday. I saw her as she lined up to get on the bus. I wished her a good weekend, and she waved to me. That was the last time I saw her."

"What did she look like?"

"What do you mean?"

"I've seen a picture of her with red hair, but when I met her Tuesday, it was jet black."

"It was red, as usual, on Friday."

I thought about that for a second until he continued. "The police asked me for a list of her friends."

I fished a notebook and pen from my briefcase, then grabbed

the photo I'd taken from Samantha's pin-up board out of my purse. "I'd like the same list, and I was wondering if you could identify these kids." I handed over the picture.

"Yes, the police had a picture, too. The boy she's leaning against is Braden Hawthorn. The girl is Marci Silva, and Marci's boyfriend is Kyle Weller."

"Is Braden Samantha's boyfriend?"

He shrugged. "Trying to keep up with all that stuff gives me a headache."

I laughed.

"I suppose she and Braden have been spending more time together, but what that means I have no idea."

"What else can you tell me about Samantha?"

He reached to the right side of his desk and opened a blue folder. "She moved to Homewood last year, entered the seventh grade here last January. She was promoted to eighth this year. Her grades last semester were average, mostly C's but a couple of B's. She seemed to acclimate without too many problems. Her teachers have reported no discipline problems, this year or last."

"No sudden changes in her behavior, or grades?"

"Not that I'm aware of. I'll check tomorrow with the teachers just to be sure, and let you know if they report anything."

"Where'd she go to school before here?"

He checked the folder again. "Tunica, Mississippi."

Tunica was a gambling town, filled with riverside casinos that drew a lot of trade from nearby Memphis and other southern cities. I wondered if her mother had worked in a casino.

"Can I have the addresses for Braden, Marci, and Kyle? I'd really like to go by their homes today and talk to them."

I knew he wasn't supposed to give them to me, but I was hoping he would anyway. It would save me a lot of time. He hesitated a second before typing on the small laptop on his desk. In moments, a printer behind him spat out pages that he passed to me.

"I have to get outside for bus duty," he said.

I followed Mr. Eddy to the hall, where I could hear the echoing cries of "E! W! DODGE!" and "GO! BIG! BLUE!" as the cheerleaders practiced in the gym across the passage.

"Was Samantha a cheerleader?" I asked.

"No, she wasn't. She wasn't really involved in any extra-curricular activities, to my knowledge."

"Was she popular, would you say?"

He shrugged. "Not extremely. I wouldn't say she was the

most outgoing girl in school, although I did see her with friends most of the time. Usually Marci and several boys. I'd describe her as an average eighth grader. I know that's not much help."

"It's okay. Thank you for your time, Mr. Eddy," I said. "And for your information." We shook hands again, and I handed him a business card in case anything came up.

A loud tone blared, making me jump. He laughed. "Uh-oh, look out. The stampede has begun."

Classroom doors flew open with a series of bangs, followed by the shrieking and shouting of hundreds of middle school kids as they escaped for the day. Mr. Eddy beat the crowd outside to the buses as I waited for it to thin so I could leave.

Royal blue metal locker doors slammed all around me, and over the din I heard a clear "Hey, Miss Claire!"

I turned to see Kate, my friend Michele's thirteen-year-old daughter, coming down the hall. Her book bag hung heavily from her shoulder. "Hey, Kate. How are you?"

"Fine, thanks." She was nearly taller than me, and never seemed to be troubled by all the things that had plagued me during my eighth grade year: frizzy hair, pimples, oversized teeth, and baby fat. Her long brown hair fell perfectly straight: her tan skin, smooth.

"What are you doing here?" she asked.

"Working. I just had a meeting with Mr. Eddy."

"Lucky you," she said, and blushed. I imagined she wasn't the only one with a crush.

She continued. "I bet you're here about Samantha Chambless. I heard her mom was murdered. Everybody's talking about it. I hope she's doing okay."

Me, too, I thought. The police's visit to the school must have set the grapevine on fire.

Suddenly I realized that if I wanted to know what was going on in the eighth grade, I should ask an eighth grader. "Can I give you a ride home, Kate?"

She hesitated, biting her lip.

"Unless you want to ride the bus with your friends," I added.

"No, not really. I just need to let my mom know."

I pulled out my cell phone and dialed DHS's number, then punched in Michele's extension. After shouting my request to Michele over the din and getting clearance, Kate and I made our way to my Honda. I lined up behind the buses and a few carpool cars, and we waited to exit the parking lot.

Kate put on her seatbelt and I asked, "So, do you know Samantha Chambless?"

Her deep blue eyes turned to me. "I know who she is. We spoke a few times last year, but not a lot. We weren't, like, friends or anything."

"Was she a nice girl?"

She shrugged.

"What about Braden Hawthorn? Was he her boyfriend?"

"I guess."

She was shutting down on me, and I couldn't figure out why. "What does 'I guess' mean?"

"Yeah, they hung out together. I've seen them a lot in the halls, holding hands."

"Have they been dating a long time?"

She squirmed in her seat and shrugged again.

"What is it, Kate? Does something about Samantha bother you?"

She took a deep breath. "I--we, like, almost everybody--called her Sammy the Slut behind her back."

"I see. How come?"

"'Cause she was one."

"In what way?"

She was quiet as I put the car in gear and pulled out of the school's lot. I made a left and headed for Edgewood, the neighborhood where Michele, Kate, and sixteen-year-old Ian lived.

"I'm not going to tell your mom anything we talk about." I threw that out there, hoping to get her to talk.

"I feel bad now for calling her names. After what happened to her mom. Where's she going to live?"

"I'm not sure yet. Probably, eventually, with a relative. Why was she a slut?"

"Last semester," Kate said as she stared out of the window, "there was this rumor going around that she let Tucker Bell touch her. . ."

"Touch her?"

"Down there. And up her shirt. And then I heard she gave him a. . . I mean, she. . . " She was really flustered now.

"She what?"

"She kissed his. . ."

"Oh." Kate was a good kid. Smart, and big-hearted. I was glad she was still somewhat innocent, and felt uncomfortable using words like "blow job" in front of adults. I knew plenty of kids who

46

wouldn't have thought twice about it.

"I see."

"Then, I heard she went all the way with Braden Hawthorn. That's why he's so in love with her. He follows her around like a puppy dog. It's disgusting. Yuck." She made a gagging sound.

I had a suspicion that Kate's reaction had a deeper meaning. The emotion that had surfaced as she mentioned Braden made me think she liked him herself.

"Braden's a cute boy."

"Ick."

Uh-huh. Sure. "What about Marci Silva? Do you know her?"

"I know her better than I know Samantha. We went to elementary school together. She and Kyle have been going together since last year. I haven't heard that's she's done anything with him, you know, like Samantha."

If the rumors were true, Samantha was at best sexually active. At worst, promiscuous. Sometimes early seductiveness or sexual activity could indicate a history of sexual abuse. Since the research estimated that two out of ten girls would be victims, it wouldn't surprise me. And the odds went up significantly if her mother had been married more than once.

I changed the subject, much to Kate's relief, and we chatted about books she'd read lately until I made a left onto Broadway and pulled behind Ian's compact car at Michele's house. Kate asked, "Do you want to come in?"

"No, that's okay, thanks. I need to get back to work."

"Okay. I guess I'll see you."

"See you."

It was still too early to go by Samantha's friends' homes. I wanted to wait until later, to catch their parents at home. So I went back to the office and, once in my cubicle, greeted Russell and picked up the phone.

Detective Stringfellow picked up after the second ring. "What'd you find out?"

I summarized what Principal Eddy had told me, and my conversation with Kate. The detective was not a dumb guy. He asked, "Think she was sexually abused?"

"I don't know. I'm going to talk to her friends tonight, see what they can tell me. Hey, I forgot to ask you earlier, who identified her mother? From the picture in the paper?"

"A friend of Jean's named Leslie Brasher. They used to be neighbors at Forest Glen until Leslie bought a house in Leeds a month ago." Leeds was a suburb east of Birmingham. I guess the city's founding fathers had been fond of merry old England, since so many of our local towns seemed to be named after English places.

"Have you talked to Jean's coworkers yet? Where did she work?"

"We don't have any information on that yet."

"What do you mean?"

"No one has come forward from any place of business at this time. Jean's friend Leslie didn't know if she even had a job or what she did. Leslie said Jean was very secretive about where she got her money. She never talked about work, but she left the house every day, though not always at the same time. She just told Leslie she was taken care of."

"That's weird." Any form of real estate in Homewood didn't come cheap. Where would Jean get money for a mortgage, and all that new furniture, if she didn't have a job? Alimony, maybe. Maybe she'd found herself a sugar daddy, then divorced him. It made me more curious about the mysterious Mr. Chambless.

Stringfellow interrupted my musings. "And there's more. Kenny Thigpen? The guy in the picture?"

"Yeah?"

"I think you might be right about his being Samantha's father. And, he got out of the South Mississippi Correctional Institution in Leakesville six days ago."

48

I digested Detective Stringfellow's news about Kenny Thigpen. "What was he in for?"

"He's been in and out of jail for various things since 1989. Mostly drugs and probation violations, but this particular trip to the hoosegow was for armed robbery."

"Wonderful. I wonder--"

"If he's driving a dark blue SUV around Birmingham?"

"Exactly."

"Me, too. I've got a call in to his parole officer, asking him to check on Thigpen's whereabouts and have him call me, but I haven't heard back yet. Oh, and we got the results of Jean's autopsy, too."

"And?"

"The coroner placed her time of death between six in the evening and midnight Saturday. She was killed with a thirty-eight caliber bullet. One shot to the forehead. I think she knew her killer. He was pretty close to her when he fired. It didn't look like she was running away, and she didn't have any defensive wounds. No scratches, or anything like that."

"Did they find the gun?"

"Nope, no weapon recovered. Be interesting to see if Mr. Thigpen has managed to get his hands on a thirty-eight. Mary Nobles traced that phone number, too, the one you got at the gas station."

"And?"

"It's a cell phone, and it belongs to guy named Patrick Merrick. Mr. Merrick said he had no knowledge of anyone named Samantha Chambless and said he hasn't received phone calls from anyone by that name. Are you sure you got the right number?"

"I just hit redial on the gas station's phone. The man at the station said he hadn't made any calls on it after Samantha did, but to be honest, he wasn't really sober."

"What do you mean?"

"He was pretty stoned. Maybe he just didn't remember."

"Damn, it was a good lead, too."

"I'll check in with you tomorrow, after I talk with Samantha's friends," I said.

"Okay, and I'll call if I hear anything about Kenny's whereabouts."

We disconnected. I decided to be lazy and took the elevator to the fourth floor. The office of the director of Jefferson County DHS, Dr. Teresa Pope, was on this floor. I'd crossed her one too many times this past summer and was actively avoiding her as much as I could. My destination was the Records Department.

Well, "Department" might be an overstatement. It was really just Kate's mom, Michele, who manned the desk, and Dolly, who managed the physical files in the basement. Michele was busy typing on her computer as I approached her desk. It was in the customer service area when the building was Barwick's department store many years ago. She slid the window open and said, "Hey, thanks for taking Kate home. It was a real treat for her not to have to ride the bus."

"My pleasure. She was a great help. Did she tell you what's going on?" I leaned against the counter.

"I heard about her classmate's mother. Is that your baby?"

"Yep."

"You always get the doozies."

"That's what I keep telling Mac."

"Where's she going to live?"

"She's on runaway right now."

"You're kidding."

"Nope, bolted from the foster home yesterday."

"Bet that made Mac happy."

"To say nothing of Judge Myer, and the police."

"I'm glad I'm not you."

I laughed. "Thanks. That case is why I'm here. I need a records check on the girl and her mom. I know the girl was born in Mississippi, so you're not going to find a birth certificate, but I need to see if she has a Medicaid history or has ever been in our custody before. She was born Samantha Jean Riley, but now she's Chambless. So I need to check Samantha Jean Chambless, too. And Samantha Riley Chambless."

Michele was writing the names on a sticky note. "What else?"

I had a sudden thought. "Check Samantha Thigpen, too, please. That's her father's name, we think. And I need to check on mom's history as well. Any abuse or neglect reports against her. Or if she's ever received public assistance. Her name is Jean Marie Riley, or maybe Jean Marie Thigpen. Or Jean Riley Thigpen, or Jean Thigpen Chambless."

Michele had moved to her second sticky note. "Good Lord, this will take a while."

"Sorry."

50

"Tomorrow okay?"

"I suppose."

"I'll do what I can today before I leave."

"Thanks."

Michele and I made lunch plans for Friday, and I took the stairs back down to my desk. Russell had left. I did paperwork and made phone calls until the clock on my phone said five-twenty.

Braden Hawthorn lived southwest of downtown, in an area of Homewood that bordered my neighborhood, Bluff Park. His subdivision was a newer one comprised of large homes that peered down the side of Shades Mountain and into Oxmoor Valley below. My father's house was at the crest of the mountain, not but a mile or so away. Both he and Braden's parents had shelled out big bucks for the sweeping view of the valley, only Dad had done it in the nineteen-sixties. I realized with a start that Dad--and the Hawthorns--could probably see the new golf course and resort being built below. The area where Jean's body had been found.

All the houses looked like cousins. Different floor plans, but all built of red brick, wood siding, and dormer windows. All had spacious two-car garages on the lower level, making them three stories tall. I parked in the street near the mailbox and made my way over the small lawn to the black front door.

The sheet that Mr. Eddy had given me identified Braden's parents as Deborah and Don Hawthorn. Don opened the door. Braden had gotten his hair from his dad. Dirty blond and curly. His father's features were sharper, his skin paler. He was dressed comfortably in shorts and a touristy T-shirt from Las Vegas, covering a small tire around his middle.

"Don Hawthorn?"

"Yes?"

"I'm Claire Conover. From Jefferson County DHS."

"I assume this is about Samantha Chambless?"

"That's correct."

"The police were here earlier. I can't believe it, about her mother. They said Samantha ran away. She still hasn't been found, huh?"

"I'm afraid not."

"Come in."

I stepped into to a wide expanse of high-ceilinged great room, dominated by a large dark green sectional sofa. A coffee table sat in front of it, and on it lay part of a newspaper, two plastic cups, and an empty bowl. A large flat-screen TV played a game show. Mr.

51

Hawthorn grabbed the remote and shut it off.

"Deborah?" He cleared some of the newspaper off the couch so I could sit. "We have a visitor!"

Deborah entered from what I assumed was the kitchen, drying her hands on a dishtowel. Here was where Braden got the rest of his good looks, including his skin, eyes, and lips. They were eating Italian for dinner: I could smell marinara sauce.

"Yes?"

Don said, "Miss Conover is here from DHS, and she wants to talk about Samantha and Braden."

"He's upstairs doing his homework. Do you need him?"

"I'd like to speak to the two of you alone first, if I may."

We all sat on the sectional sofa. Deborah asked, "How can we help you?"

"Samantha's in the State's custody. My custody. I really need to find her. I'd like to ask Braden if he's heard from her. I understand Braden and Samantha have been seeing quite a lot of each other."

A solemn look passed between the Hawthorns.

"Did either of you know Samantha?"

Deborah cleared her throat. "Not much." She shot another glance at her husband, and continued. "We didn't exactly get off to a good start with her."

A clomping sound came from the stairs near the front door, and a slight blond girl skipped into the great room, dressed in blue shorts and a pink shirt with Tinkerbell on it. From her features, she was clearly Braden's sister. I placed her age at about ten. "Mom, can I have a popsicle?"

"Take it upstairs. Your dad and I have company."

We waited while she went into the kitchen. She rummaged around in the freezer, taking her time, nosy about my presence but trying not to be obvious. I wondered if big brother had sent her down to see what was going on.

"Excuse me." Don went into the kitchen. I could hear the low rumble of his voice, then the pink shirt vanished up the stairs. He rejoined us on the couch. "Sorry. That's our daughter, Brianna."

"You were saying, about Samantha and not getting off to a good start?"

Deborah was choosing her words carefully. "The first--and only--time we met Samantha, it was a Thursday night about a month ago. Don and I went out to dinner after work, just the two of us. Braden was to stay home and baby-sit Brianna. We have very strict rules when the kids are home alone. No visitors. Period. We got home a little earlier than expected, and Samantha was here. Upstairs, in his room. Braden says nothing happened, and they were both dressed. Well, mostly dressed, but still--"

Don interjected, "He's only just gotten off restriction."

That would certainly jibe with what Kate told me earlier in the car about Braden and Samantha having a sexual relationship. I also wondered how Samantha had managed to get to her boyfriend's house. She was far too young to drive. Had her mom dropped her off? If so, neither had called first to get permission from Mr. or Mrs. Hawthorn. It made me wonder just how supervised Samantha had been.

Deborah said, "As you might imagine, we were both very upset. He's only fourteen. And he was supposed to be watching his sister. Then, when I asked Samantha to leave, she had the nerve to get smart with me. She said she didn't see what the big deal was, that they weren't fooling around or anything. I just told her call her mother or whoever had brought her here and get out. I mean, can you imagine? Here was this kid I don't even know, mouthing off to me when she's just been caught with my son. . ."

She was really getting agitated. Don put a calming hand on her knee and said, "We haven't seen her since. What do you need from us?"

"Mostly I need help monitoring Braden's communications. I have reason to believe Samantha could be in serious trouble. She may try to reach out to him."

"We can check his cell phone and his email, and let you know. Do you need to talk to Braden tonight?"

"I'd like to if it's okay with you."

Don shouted, "Braden! Come down here a minute!"

No response. Don excused himself again and after a moment the two of them came downstairs, Braden's lean frame dressed in athletic shorts and a white T-shirt, no shoes or socks. The white headset from an IPod was draped around his neck. I noted again what an attractive kid he was, more so in person. He remained standing.

"Sorry, couldn't hear you calling me with my music on." I wondered if that was the truth or passive-aggressive teenage rebellion. Fourteen was a tough age, and it seemed like the Hawthorns were in for it.

I introduced myself to Braden. "I understand the police have spoken with you already? And you're aware Samantha's mother has been killed?"

Braden nodded, and his mother winced. So much for protecting her baby from the horrors of life.

"Samantha may be in very serious danger. Has she tried to call you? Or contact you in any way?"

"Nope."

"Braden," his mother said.

"No, ma'am," he corrected himself.

"Did she ever mention any trouble? Any worries about her mother? Did she seem different lately?"

"No, not really."

"Not really?"

"No."

"I need for you to call me if you hear from her." I handed him one of my cards. "Any time of the day or night, okay? It's very urgent."

"I will. Where's she going to live? I mean, when she comes back?"

"Hopefully we can find a relative who is willing to take her."

"Someone here in Birmingham?"

"We'll see. Do you have any idea where she might have gone?"

"No, ma'am. Can I go finish my homework?"

"Go ahead," his father said.

After Braden went back upstairs, I passed out more business cards and shook hands with the Hawthorns. "Thanks for your help. I just hope she's okay and that we can find her."

Deborah made a wry face. "Forgive me for saying so, but part of me wishes she'd just stay gone. Or that we'd never met her in the first place."

54

Mr. Hawthorn showed me out, and I spent a minute leaning against my car, studying the house. The developer had clear-cut the whole area when the neighborhood went up, so all the trees were still practically saplings. No old-growth near the house, which meant that if Samantha was sneaking in, she wasn't doing it through Braden's window. No way to get up there. But both his parents worked, so she could be coming here after school. I'd pay a visit the next afternoon and see if she was here.

I hit Oxmoor Road and drove down the valley to my next destination. Marci Silva's parents lived in a subdivision just off busy Lakeshore Drive, near Samford University, in an area of older homes that were just as affluent as those in Braden's neighborhood, or maybe even more so. A huge white house complete with columns and a large three-car garage. The Silva's lot was bigger than the Hawthorn's, and the old-growth trees the Hawthorns were lacking could be found in abundance.

I rang the small rectangular bell by the door. It was opened by a professionally dressed middle-aged woman, her long dark hair pulled into a knot on top of her head.

"Mrs. Silva? Are you Marci's mother?"

"I am Doctor Silva." Her answer was tainted with the hint of a foreign accent. Spanish, maybe.

"Sorry. Dr. Silva. I'm Claire Conover, from DHS."

"DHS?"

"The child welfare department?"

"Ah. You are here also about Samantha? Please come in."

"Thank you." The small foyer was crowded with a mahogany sideboard, with intricately carved doors. It looked old. And expensive. Dr. Silva led me into the living room, where more heavy dark furniture gave the room a formal feel. She turned on two lamps and gestured toward the couch. I sat. The cushion barely gave under my weight.

"I'm so sorry to have to disturb you. I'm looking for any information you might know about Samantha Chambless. I suppose the police have been here already?"

She nodded. Her gaze flicked to the front windows, covered in heavy rust-colored drapes and sheers, as if she could still see the cop car parked outside. "They were here a couple of hours ago. They said that Samantha's mother had been murdered. And that Samantha had run away."

"I'm afraid so. Do you know Samantha well?"

"Not very well. She and my daughter have been friends for a few months. I have to say I was not pleased with their friendship."

"Why?"

"I tried to tell Marciana that Samantha was not a good friend. But she is thirteen." She shrugged. "She will not listen."

"What were your objections to Samantha, exactly?"

"She was not of our class. I don't know how else to explain it."

"I see. Any particular behaviors that worried you?"

"Samantha was just. . .common."

I wondered what that meant. Clearly the Silvas were much wealthier than Jean and Samantha. Was that what she meant? She didn't elaborate. I pushed for an answer. "I'm sorry, but I need to ask what you mean. Some of Samantha's friend's parents have indicated that they didn't feel like she was supervised very well. Would you agree with them?"

"I would. Her mother was a single parent, and I'm sure that was difficult, but there didn't seem to be many rules where Samantha was concerned. I didn't know Jean well, I only met her twice. But like I said, they were common." She didn't go on, and I still wasn't sure exactly what she meant. I didn't know what to ask next.

I took a few seconds to glance around the room. "You have a lovely home, by the way."

She smiled. "Thank you."

"May I ask where you're from?"

"Brazil. My husband and I are Brazilian, but Marciana was born here."

"And you're a doctor? Of?"

"Political Science. I teach Latin American Studies. My husband is a doctor as well. He is a professor of Economics. He has a class tonight."

I smiled. "That's interesting." I didn't know what Jean Chambless had done for a living in her mysterious, short life, but I was pretty sure it wasn't anything as prestigious as academia. I continued, "And Marci has a boyfriend, correct?"

Her face lit up. "Yes. Kyle. A very nice boy. His father is an executive. In construction. And Kyle, he plays the American football. Very talented. He will go far."

So no problems with the boyfriend. I wondered what her reaction would have been if Kyle's daddy was, say, a steelworker.

"Is Marci home?"

"Yes, she is in the family room. Do you need to speak with her?"

"If it's all right with you."

She left the room and returned moments later with the girl I'd seen in the photos in Samantha's room. She wore a thin blue baby-doll tee, and her thick, dark hair was pulled into a cloth band. Her long tan legs contrasted with short white shorts. She was taller than I'd imagined. And stunningly beautiful for her age.

She took a seat in the chair next to her mother's. "Hey."

No trace of a foreign accent, I noticed. "Hey. I'm Claire Conover. Did your mom tell you why I'm here?"

"Yeah, the cops were here earlier asking about Sam."

"Have you heard from her? Talked to her?"

"Nope, not since Saturday. She called Saturday morning. We were supposed to meet at the mall, but she called to say she couldn't make it, that she didn't have a way up there. That was the last time I talked to her." Marci fidgeted with her ponytail, tightening it and running her fingers through her hair.

"Do you have any idea where she might have run to?"

"Nope."

"Was she in any kind of trouble? Did she talk to you about anything she was worried about?"

"No, never."

"Ever mention anything about her mom or any threats to her?"

"Nope." She took the ponytail down again. Put it up again.

"Ever mention her dad?"

"She just told me he was in prison. I wish I could help, really. I'm really worried about her."

"Me, too." I found my business cards in my purse and handed one each to Dr. Silva and her daughter. "Will you call me if you hear from her, please? And the police, of course."

"Of course," Dr. Silva answered. "Right away."

As I stood to leave, the sound of a key clicking in the front door got our attention. A hulking gray-suited man in a neat blue tie walked in. He had salt-and-pepper hair and a moustache. "Cecile?" He spotted me and gave a small bow. "Oh, my apologies."

Mrs. Dr. Silva suddenly seemed flustered. She didn't introduce me. "Thank you for coming. I shall explain everything to Fernando." Her speech was rushed.

"Sure. Thanks for your time." She showed me out. Quickly. I had the impression Mr. Dr. Silva was not going to be pleased with

57

any of this mess.

It was getting late, close to seven-thirty, and I was tired and hungry. I decided to forgo the visit to the Weller's until tomorrow and drove back to Bluff Park. My father's lights were on when I swung into his driveway.

He was in the den, watching a British crime drama on TV. I sank into one of the two overstuffed recliners and accepted his offer of a glass of tea. He brought it to me and asked, "Find your kid?"

"She's still on the run. Had her court hearing today and Judge Myer was not at all happy with the situation."

"She'll turn up. They usually do, right?"

"Right. How was the rally? Did you bring peace to the world?"

"It was good. We had a good turnout. Good speakers, and I think the letter writing campaign to Congress will go well. You should write one."

"I know. Where was the rally again?"

"Kelly Ingram Park."

"Any trouble?"

"No, only a couple of counter-protesters who came out to wave the flag."

Kelly Ingram Park, formerly known as West Park, was in the shadow of the skyscrapers downtown, a few blocks from my office and across the street from the Sixteenth Street Baptist Church. A moving place, from the statue of the attacking police dogs to Reverend Fred Shuttlesworth's upside-down quote of "Segregation is a sin," which I'd been told he'd written in his own blood while hanging by his feet after a brutal beating. I hadn't been down to the Civil Rights District in a while.

Dad said, "I was talking with a cop today. He said there's been a lot of drugs in and out of that neighborhood lately, and people sleeping in the park. Especially teenagers. It's a shame that we even have homeless people in this country, and we really should--"

"What'd you say?"

"I said we really should work on increasing funding for--'

"No, about the teenagers."

"Oh. Apparently lately it's become a hangout for teenagers, homeless and otherwise."

"Huh." I knew of several places where homeless teen clients of mine gravitated. Mostly the girls. The Rest Stop Inn in North Birmingham. Summer's Truck Stop off Interstate 65. Places where a young girl could go and do a trick for money or booze or drugs. I prayed Samantha hadn't fallen into all that yet. She had no street knowledge.

I stayed to share a pan of frozen spinach lasagna with Dad before driving the five minutes to my house. I was looking forward to getting out of my clothes and into a hot bath, then into my comfy pj's with a good book. My headlights illuminated the front of the house as I turned into the driveway, and I caught a glimpse of a man in cargo shorts sitting on my front stoop, his elbows on his knees.

Christ, here we go again.

Chapter Ten

He had a six-pack of beer. He opened a green bottle with a small hook on a pocketknife and held it out to me. "Hi, honey, welcome home."

I didn't take the beer. "Kirk--"

"I know, I know, you're damn glad to see me."

"What are you doing here?"

"Drinking. Join me."

I took the sweating Heineken and eased down next to him on the stoop. He was on his third. My porch light was off, most of my elderly neighbors were asleep, and the only light shone from the streetlamp two houses down. Crickets sang in the grass around us. The beer was still cold and tasted good.

"You're home late," Kirk finally said. "Been working?"

"Yep."

"All this time?"

"I had dinner with my father."

"Oh. Not Minivan Man?" That was his nickname for Grant, since the only time he'd seen him was when Grant had been in his van with the computer store's logo on it.

I didn't feel like discussing my love life, or much else, with Kirk. And I sure as hell wasn't about to let him in the house. The last time I did that we wound up pressed against the stove with our lips locked in a hot kiss. While Grant and I hadn't really discussed the state of our budding relationship, it was kind of understood that we wouldn't date other people. I wasn't sure dating was what Kirk wanted anyway. I had a feeling I knew what Kirk wanted, and dwelled on that thought for a moment.

"Claire?"

"No, not him."

"You're awful quiet tonight."

"What are you doing here?"

"Maybe I just wanted to see you."

"Kirk, I'm exhausted, it's late, and I'm not in the mood for your shit. What do you want?"

"Wow. Okay. Excuse me, I'll get right to the point. I got a tip that Jean Chambless's daughter is missing."

"No comment." My whole body ached with tiredness.

"C'mon."

"Kirk, you know I can't say anything to anyone about my cases. Especially you. We've had this conversation at least five times. I almost got fired three months ago because of you and what you printed in the paper."

"I know, and that was a mistake. I give you my word I won't use your name."

"No."

"Fine. I was hoping we could work on this case together, help each other out. But forget it." He rose off the step and grabbed the remainder of the six pack, leaving in a huff. I'd been ugly to him, and I felt guilty.

"Kirk."

He turned.

"I'm sorry. I'm very tired. I'm sorry I snapped at you. If you want to work together, we can. But I meant what I said about not being able to tell you anything. It'll have to be a pretty one-sided relationship."

"It already is." There was a tenderness in his voice.

"It's the best I can do, for now."

He rejoined me on the stoop. I could feel the warmth of him against my shoulder. "So where do we start?" I asked.

"You tell me."

I thought. "Detective Stringfellow said Jean Chambless has-- had--some mysterious source of income. She apparently had money, owned the townhouse and all, but no one seems to know where the money came from. No co-workers came forward to identify her, just a former neighbor. And Stringfellow didn't find any stuff at her house to give him a clue to her past. No pictures, documents, nothing."

"That's weird."

"Definitely. I'd like to go talk to the ex-neighbor, if you want to come with me. I'll need to find her address. And phone number. Her name's Leslie Brasher, and she lives someplace in Leeds."

"I can do that. When do you want to go?"

Tomorrow was Thursday. I had a staff meeting in the morning, then lunch with Royanne, my best friend. I wanted to go search around Nettie's neighborhood again, and then get to Kyle Weller's house at some point in the evening. "If we could set something up right after lunch, that'd be great. I'll make up something to tell my boss about where I'm going, if he asks."

"I'll call you in the morning, after I find a phone number."

"Use my cell."

"Of course. It's kind of fun, sneaking around with you again like this."

62

"Not so much."

He leaned over and kissed my right cheek. "See you tomorrow."

After he left I unlocked the door to my cool, empty house. Grant had left a sweet good-night message on my machine, and I grappled with another twinge of guilt, knowing I would never tell him about my attraction to Kirk. I skipped the bath, fell into bed and into sleep and naughty dreams.

The staff meeting in the morning dragged on for an hour and a half. I rushed out of the office as soon as I could get away, and by ten-fifteen was searching the area around Nettie's neighborhood in Midfield. I didn't have a whole lot of hope that I'd find Samantha, but it was the last place she'd been seen. I had a limited amount of time before I had to pick Royanne up at the bank headquarters downtown where she worked.

I cruised through the strip mall where I'd been yesterday, checked again with the high-as-a-kite gas station attendant who said he hadn't seen Samantha since she left. As I was creeping through the parking lot of a McDonald's, I spotted a familiar pair of bright pink pants, sashaying toward the highway.

Hitting the button to roll down the window, I called "Hey!" LaReesa Jones, startled, turned to me.

"Jesus!" she said.

"Sorry. What are you doing here?"

"What the hell, you followin' me?"

"LaReesa, it's ten-thirty on a Thursday morning. Shouldn't you be in school?"

"Didn't go today."

"Yes, I see that. May I ask why?"

"It's a holiday."

"I happen to be intimately familiar with the school system's calendar, and today is not a holiday."

"Teacher work day."

"Nope."

"I couldn't go today. My mom is sick. I had to give her medicine and stuff."

"Well, if she's that ill, shouldn't you be home with her?" I popped the locks on my doors. "Get in."

"Why?"

"Because I'm going to take you home and talk to your mom."

"I told you, she's sick."

"Get in, LaReesa."

"What if I don't?"

"Then I put in a call to the police, then the school, and we start an investigation. Officially."

She shot me a look that was meant to set me on fire, and slammed the door after she sat down. "This is *bullshit*."

"Seat belt, please." She strapped in and I asked, "Where am I going?"

No answer.

"My office, then?"

She swore again, and pointed. "Around the corner and up the hill."

I drove as she directed, and before we'd gone a mile I pulled up to a brown brick, L-shaped apartment complex. Black bars covered all the windows and doors, including little cages for the air-conditioners. A large dumpster crowded the parking area, which was virtually empty save for a beat-up pickup and a rusty old Dodge up on blocks. Staircases flanked each end of the building.

I shut the car off. "Which one?"

"Top of the stairs, on the right."

"C'mon."

I locked the doors and followed a still-angry LaReesa up the concrete stairs. The handrail was loose. At the top I waited while she dug a key out of her tight-fitting pants. She was wearing the same shirt she wore the day before, I noted, now dotted with a small food stain.

I followed her into the dim apartment. The blinds were shut tight. A broken tan recliner, its footrest sticking halfway out, was the only seating in the living room. Next to it sat an octagonal end table, with several library books, an empty Pop-tart wrapper, and a glass on top. I picked up one of the books.

I recognized the cover. Trixie Belden. An older edition of The Mysterious Code. I looked at LaReesa. "Who's reading this?"

"Me."

It was below her grade level. "Do you like it?" I'd enjoyed the series when I was a kid.

"Yeah. It's about these kids, and they have a club called the Bob-Whites."

"I know. I used to read them."

A cheap particle board entertainment center held an older black television and nothing else, the remote control sitting on top. A dining set made of glass and black metal filled a corner, and the table was covered in papers, mail, and other junk. A set of cabinets separated the dining area from a kitchen that consisted of little more than an old refrigerator, a two-burner stove, and a sink.

"Where's your room?"

"We ain't got but the one." She pointed.

I peeked in the bedroom off of the living room. Long and narrow, it held a full sized mattress on the floor and an old dresser, painted black. A homemade rack for hanging clothes, made of two-by-fours and an old shower curtain rod, sat against the far wall.

"Where do you sleep?"

"Here." She pointed to the recliner.

I strode into the kitchen and turned the cold faucet at the sink. Nothing. Tried the hot one. Nothing.

I felt the refrigerator. It was cold, a good sign. I wrenched it open and the door squeaked.

"Hey!" LaReesa cried.

Four or five little brown cockroaches scattered from underneath when the door opened. The fridge held mustard, a jar of strawberry jam, one Tupperware container, and two Cokes. A search of the cabinets revealed more roaches, a half-empty box of Lucky Charms and two cans of cream of mushroom soup.

My memory went back to one of the first cases I'd ever worked as a child welfare agent. The parents were mentally challenged, with two charming kids under six. The house was barely more than a two room clapboard shack that should have been condemned. After the investigation, I'd stood in Mac's office taking deep breaths, trying to hold back the tears and failing.

"But they aren't hungry?" Mac asked.

"No, but--"

"And they have shelter?"

"You could call it that."

"Then what is it?"

"It's just--I mean--they're just so *poor*."

He met my gaze, his dark eyes hardened, a man who'd seen it all. "You can't fix everything, Claire."

How many times had those words echoed in my head in so many homes like LaReesa's?

I jerked my mind back to the present. "Is this all you have to eat?"

"My mamma's going shopping."

"Yeah? When?"

"When she gets paid. She works two jobs, you know."

Today was the third of September. Her mom should have been

paid two days ago. She wasn't due for another paycheck for at least four days at the earliest, and likely not until the fourteenth. There was no way this meager amount of food would last that long. Not for two people.

"Where's your mom now?"

"At work."

"Where?"

She named a dry cleaners not far away. "I don't always stay here, you know. Most of the time I'm at my grandma's." Her arms were folded across her chest now, and she radiated anger. And defiance. "I ain't needin' nobody to take care of me. I don't need no social worker."

"Where's your grandma's house?"

"On Eighth Avenue."

"All the way over there?"

"It ain't that far."

It was at least a mile, probably closer to two, and she'd have to cross the busy Bessemer Road.

"Come on." I headed for the door.

"Where?"

"I want to talk to your grandmother."

"Why?"

"Come on."

I waited while she relocked the door, and we drove by her instructions to a small shotgun house on the busy avenue. I parked on a side street. LaReesa led me through the rusted gate at the sidewalk and to the front door. The house looked careworn, the lawn overgrown, the front porch littered with a broken baby swing, a rusted charcoal grill, and two old-fashioned outdoor metal chairs with peeling paint. She knocked.

"Who   is   it?"   called   a   feeble   voice.

"It's Reese, Grandma."

I heard the click-thud of several locks being turned. Then the door opened and everything went south.

Chapter Eleven

The elderly woman who opened the door saw me first, and her expression turned quizzical. Then she caught sight of LaReesa, hiding behind me, and the wrinkled frown went to fury.

"What the hell you doin' out of school?" she shouted.

LaReesa shrugged and looked at the ground.

"Are you LaReesa's grandmother? I'm Claire Conover, with DHS."

"DHS! Oh, my Lord. What's she done?" Her hand went to her chest as she opened the door wide. LaReesa skulked in behind me. Grandma's appearance was deceiving. She was a little stooped lady, draped in a purple and blue floral housecoat with thin grey hair tight in small rollers, but she had the roar of a monster. "You been skippin' school? I'm gonna tear the hide off you--"

"Look, Mrs.?"

"Jones," she said, eyes narrowed and glaring at LaReesa beside me. "Estelle Jones."

"Mrs. Jones, I'm not here to get LaReesa in trouble. And this isn't even an official investigation, as far as DHS is concerned. I happened to run into LaReesa today and wondered why she wasn't in school."

"That's a damn good question!" She moved toward LaReesa, wild-eyed, her open hand half raised.

Before she could slap the shit out of her, I quickly side-stepped to shield LaReesa from the blow. "Whoa. Let's just calm down." I took out my phone so I could call the police if I needed to.

She retreated, still glaring. "You go and get DHS called on us!"

"I didn't do nothin', Grandma."

"Why don't we sit down and talk about this?" I said.

Mrs. Jones gestured to one of the three mismatched sofas crowded into the room. I glanced around. The house was small, and I could see straight through to the dining room, kitchen, and closed door back door beyond. The walls were the color of orange sherbet, and the whole house had a pervasive smell of cooking oil and dried sweet flowers from the numerous jars of potpourri that were open around the room.

Mrs. Jones sat on a light blue Victorian sofa, and I sat on the overstuffed brown one opposite her. LaReesa curled onto the green one, her legs beneath her.

"Like I said, this isn't an official investigation, but it may turn into one unless we can come to some sort of agreement, okay?" Both of them nodded. Mrs. Jones was finally calming down. A toddler about two years old and wearing nothing but a diaper walked with unsteady steps from the kitchen, his little index finger in his mouth. LaReesa jumped up, scooped him into her arms and took him through a door off the dining room. She joined us again, saying, "I put him in his crib, Grandma." LaReesa looked at me. "That's my auntie's baby."

"Oh. He lives here?"

"Uh-huh. Him and my two other cousins."

"How old are they?"

Mrs. Jones answered. "That was DeCameron. He's twenty months, DeCora is six, and DeCaria is ten. The girls are in school, where you should be," she finished with another glare at LaReesa.

That was a lot of kids to feed, especially if you included LaReesa in the mix. "And you have custody of them?"

"Not LaReesa. Just those three. Their mamma's locked up for possession."

"I'm sorry."

She shrugged. "I can only do what I can."

"Are you married?"

"My husband died sixteen years ago."

"I see. I'm sorry, again." I continued. "You know, when LaReesa gets in trouble, there are other ways of dealing with it than slapping her." Grandma looked at me like I was nuts. I had no hope she'd actually stop hitting LaReesa. After all, she'd been raising kids long before I was born, and old habits were hard to break.

I focused on LaReesa. "And you have to, *have to*, go to school. Got it? I'm going to come up there and check on you regularly, and if there's one more unexcused absence, I won't have a choice about doing an investigation, understand?"

"Whatever."

"You go to Midfield Middle?"

Mrs. Jones answered, "Yes, she's in the eighth grade."

"Why weren't you in school today?"

"I didn't feel like going."

"How are your grades?"

"They're okay, I guess."

"You get along with the other kids? Have lots of friends?"

"Yeah."

"What about your teachers?"

68

"They're okay."

Something else was going on, but I couldn't say what. She was keeping something back.

I nodded and stood. I had a lot of other questions. Like how could Mrs. Jones afford to keep these three children and LaReesa? What was her source of income? Did she receive any help from anyone? Welfare, or child support? I held the questions for now. She was angry, and I didn't want to push it with her. This relationship would take a little time to develop. I thanked her for taking the time to talk to me, and told her I'd stop by within the next few days to check on things. I received a surly nod in return.

LaReesa walked me outside. At my car door, I said, "So I'll see you tomorrow at school."

She looked at the ground and kicked a weed growing in a crack in the sidewalk with the toe of one of her old Sketchers.

"Bye," I said.

She didn't say anything. Kick, kick.

"LaReesa, what is it?"

"You know when you asked me about why I didn't go to school today?"

"Yeah?"

"It was cause I didn't have nothin' to wear."

"What do you mean?"

"We wears uniforms at school. I only got the one white shirt, and I washed it too late last night. We ain't got no dryer that works, and when I woke up it was still wet."

"Have you told your mom you need some school clothes? Or your grandma?"

"They know. Mamma ain't got no money right now cause she got to pay the fees to get the water cut back on. And Grandma said she couldn't buy me none, either. She ain't got the money." She wouldn't look at me.

"What if I got you some clothes? Would you promise me you'll go to school?"

"New clothes?"

I grinned. "I'll see what I can do. What size are you?"

She flashed me her gap-toothed smile. "A fifteen. Can I pick them out?"

"We'll see, okay? No promises, and you've got to be in school. Deal?"

"Deal." We shook on it.

As I drove away, late to meet my best friend for lunch, I

caught sight of LaReesa in my rearview mirror, still smiling.

Royanne forgave me, after some pleading, when I picked her up twenty-five minutes late. We arrived at Los Compadres Mexican Restaurant at the peak of the lunch crush and had to wait another fifteen for a table. We got seated, and Pablo brought us drinks and a hot basket of chips with salsa. I nibbled on the corner of a chip, thinking.

"Hello?" Royanne said, waving at me. "You okay?"

"Yep. I need school clothes for a thirteen-year-old girl."

"Uniforms?"

I nodded. "I have a list of resources back at the office, but I've already hit most of them up for other clients. And this particular girl isn't in our custody, so I can't get a voucher from Mac."

"I could call Reverend Jim."

Royanne belonged to one of the many mega-churches in the area, a Methodist one, and Jim was her pastor. "Would you? That'd be great. I'd love a cash donation, but if he has any uniforms that would be helpful. She said she's a fifteen, size-wise."

"No problem."

I had an idea. Royanne's kids, three of my favorite little people on earth, were two-and-a-half, four, and seven. "And, if you have any of your kids' clothes you want to give away, I also have a twenty-month-old boy and a six-year-old girl who could use clothes. There's a ten-year-old girl, too."

"You know, it's probably time for me to go through their closets. Most of Olivia's stuff might be too girly for the little boy, but I'll see what I can find. She might have some T-shirts that would work. And I'll ask at her daycare."

"Thanks."

Pablo brought our lunches, and just as he set the steaming plate down in front of me, my cell phone chimed. "Sorry," I said to Royanne. I flipped it open and said hello.

"Where are you?" Kirk asked.

"Lunch. You?"

"Office. I tracked down Leslie Brasher. She's at work. She can meet us about one-thirty, okay?"

I glanced at my watch. That gave me an hour, roughly. "Where?"

"She an assistant manager at the Home Depot in Trussville. Off Gadsden Highway. What are you eating?"

70

"Mexican. I'll meet you there."

"Have a Margarita or two. They'll weaken your defenses."

"Kirk--" I could have slapped myself as soon as I said the name. Royanne's eyebrows shot toward the ceiling and she choked on her refried beans. Shit.

"See you." I closed my phone.

"Kirk?" she asked. "Who's Kirk?"

I struggled to come up with a lie and failed. "Nobody. Don't worry about it."

"Kirk. Wait a minute. Kirk Mahoney? That wasn't the reporter from this summer, was it?"

"We're sort of working a case together."

"Really?" Her tone was sarcastic.

"It's no big deal. But it is top secret. If anyone knew I was even talking to him--"

"What kind of case would have you two working together?"

"Have you been reading his articles in the paper lately? He's been following the story about the dead woman found out by the new golf resort in Homewood."

"What's that have to do with you? Oh. . ." It dawned on her. "She had kids?"

"Kid. Singular. A daughter. Now she's mine. And that's all I can say. Kirk is helping me locate someone who might know them. A relative, or someone to take custody."

"Oh. Does Grant know you're talking to Kirk?"

"Roy, it's not like we're dating. It's work."

"Uh-huh."

"It is."

"I hope you don't screw up this thing with Grant."

"I won't."

"Because I'll kill you."

We quickly finished our meals and I dropped Royanne off at the towering Birmingham Financial Bank downtown, then took I-59 to Trussville, one of the larger suburbs on the east side of downtown. The Home Depot was easy to find. The orange and tan structure perched on a hill just off the main highway through the city. I parked and spotted Kirk in front of the sliding doors. The heat was radiating off the blacktop parking lot, and I immediately felt myself flush.

"You drink that Margarita?"

"Kirk--"

"If I had a dollar for every time you said my name in that

exasperated way--"

"You'd be a rich man. Let's just go do this, okay?"

"Okay."

The automatic doors slid open and we entered the cool concrete-floored warehouse. Kirk asked for Leslie Brasher at the customer service desk and soon we were joined by a husky woman who I swear had to be over six feet tall. She'd spent a good deal of her life outdoors. Her skin had a thick, wrinkled look of tanned hide. Mostly gray hair hung all the way down her back in a braid, and a plain navy T-shirt was largely hidden by an orange apron and a belt to support her back. I chuckled to myself to see Kirk practically stand on his toes, trying to match her height.

"Can I help you?"

Kirk introduced himself and asked if we could talk outside. We followed her to the side of the store near the garden department, which was filled with late-summer editions of colorful flowers.

"What do y'all want to know?" Leslie asked.

Kirk said, "You were the one who recognized Jean Chambless from her picture in the paper?"

"That's right. Poor Jean. I can hardly believe she's dead."

"I'm so sorry. Were you close friends?"

"Why?"

I jumped in. "I'm Claire Conover, from DHS. I've got custody of Samantha. I'm trying to find someone---a relative or a family friend---who would be willing to take her in."

"Oh. You know, I didn't think about that. I guess she's going to need a place to live. How's she doing?"

"Actually, she's sort of run away on me. Do you know anyone she might have gone to?"

"No, I don't. Sam. Poor girl. She was really giving her mother fits for the last six months or so."

"In what way?"

"Just teenage rebellion stuff. She's thirteen, you know. It happens."

"Can you be a little more specific?" Kirk asked.

"Sam had a boyfriend. Jean thought she was too young, so they would get into it over that."

"Jean didn't like him?" I asked.

"Braden's a nice enough boy, but Jean thought they were moving a little fast for their age, sexually, if you know what I mean? And the computer. The computer was a big issue. Sam spent a lot of time online, sometimes sneaking on in the middle of the night.

That's all I know. Jean and I were more neighbors than friends. We'd have the occasional cup of coffee together if we both happened to be sitting outside on a nice morning. She would talk about the struggles of being a mom, but that's about it. She wasn't an easy woman to get to know."

Kirk asked, "Do you know where she worked?"

"No idea. There were lots of things about her that just seemed off. I told the police all this when I called about her picture in the paper."

"Off? Like what, for example?" I asked.

"Well, the work thing. Jean never talked about it, never mentioned it. She'd leave the house at all different hours of the day and night, so for a while I thought maybe she did shift work. At a restaurant, or a factory. One day I just flat-out asked her where she worked, and all she said was she didn't want to talk about it and changed the subject, fast. Very strange."

"Did she seem financially stable?"

"Oh, yeah. Nice new car, all new furniture. That's another thing, come to think of it. All the stuff in that townhouse was delivered new. The furniture, the appliances, the beds, all of it. It wasn't like a moving van ever showed up, just truck after truck from all these local stores. Weird, huh?"

"Weird," I agreed.

"And she never seemed to hurt for money. Never mentioned any debt or anything."

"Did you keep in touch with her after you moved?"

"Not at all."

I looked at Kirk. I was out of questions. He offered a hand to Leslie, who shook it, and then mine. Kirk and I both handed her our cards in case she thought of anything else, and thanked her for her time.

"Can I ask a favor?" Leslie asked me.

"Sure."

"When Sam turns up, will you let me know? I know it may sound silly, but I just want to know she's safe."

"Be glad to."

We said goodbye again and Kirk walked me to my car. "What do you think?" he asked.

"Jean shows all the signs of--"

"A woman on the run."

"Exactly."

"But from what?"

73

"Good question."

"So what's next?"

"I went to see the principal at Samantha's middle school. They moved here from Tunica, Mississippi. Maybe that's our next angle."

"Road trip! Cool! Shall I book one hotel room or two?"

"Kirk--"

"There's that tone again. Can't we be friends?"

"No."

"Why?"

"Because."

"You hate me that much?"

"I don't hate you. I have a boyfriend, and the flirting makes me uncomfortable." Especially after what happened in my kitchen a couple of months ago, but I didn't say that.

"Okay. Got it. No more flirting. Understood." He pulled a serious face.

I laughed. "Good luck with that."

He smiled. "I like it when you laugh."

"Kirk--"

"That's not flirting, that's complimenting."

I returned to the subject. "So what about the Tunica thing? I don't know where to start."

"No problem. I'll get on it. I'll call you when I know something."

I unlocked my door, and Kirk gallantly opened it for me. I waved out of the window as I drove toward the busy highway. Once on the interstate headed toward DHS, I replayed our conversation with Leslie over again in my head. Something she said was bugging me, but I couldn't think what.

The computer. That was it. Leslie said Samantha spent hours on the computer. In my tour of Jean's townhouse, the one thing I didn't see was a computer.

Chapter Twelve

Just to be sure, I dialed the Homewood Police Department. I asked for Detective Stringfellow and was told he was out. Would I like to have him paged? Yes, please.

I was back at my desk before he called back. "What's up?" he asked.

I told him about talking with Leslie Brasher, and the squabbling that went on between Samantha and her mother about the computer. "But I didn't see a computer at the townhouse. Did you take one?"

"Nope. No computer that I remember. Maybe her mamma got tired of all the fussin' and got rid of it."

"Maybe. Did you find any bills or anything at Jean's? If there was a bill for--"

He finished my thought. "Internet services. Gotcha. Good call. We did take some bill stubs outta the drawer in the kitchen. Let me go give them a look-through and I'll call you back. You'll be at your desk?"

I glanced at the digital clock on my desk phone. "For a while." I had to run up to records and talk to Michele, then do a sneak-by Braden Hawthorn's house this afternoon, and go talk to the Wellers. Time to find out if Marci Silva's boyfriend, Kyle, knew anything about Samantha's whereabouts.

It was twenty minutes before Stringfellow called back. "Sure enough. One bill stub from Charter Communications, dated August twentieth, and there's a handwritten notation that it was paid on the twenty-second." I could hear him rifling through some pages. "Says here they got digital cable and internet services. Something called the Biggest Value Package..." He read for a second. "Looks like they got all the movie channels. Huh."

I said what he was thinking. "So Jean wasn't hurting for money." Movie channels and high-speed internet access were luxuries. They were the first to go when pennies needed pinching. I knew that from past personal experience.

"Apparently not. And she had a computer with internet access, or at least she did about eight days before she was killed."

"So where's the computer?"

"Good question. What do you do with a computer you no longer want?"

"Sell it. Or give it away." I had a thought. "I've got a contact at the News. I wonder if Jean Chambless placed an ad to sell a computer recently. I'll ask him to check. A long shot, but I can ask."

"Might be good to talk with Samantha's friends, too. See if any of them know what happened to it."

"True. I'm following up with a couple of them this afternoon. I'll start asking about it."

I went to see Michele, stopping by one of the vending machines on my way to buy a Diet Coke. It was getting close to four, and I needed a caffeine boost. Michele was winding down for the day, finishing up a few reports. I accepted her offer to step into her glass-enclosed area and have a seat. I slouched down to rest my head on the back of the chair and closed my eyes, rolling the cold soda can across my forehead.

"Stop that. You're too young for hot flashes."

I laughed.

She asked, "Long day?"

"They all are. Did you have a chance to check on Samantha and Jean Riley or Thigpen or Chambless or whatever the hell their names are?"

"I did. And it was a bust. Sorry."

"Somehow I knew you were going to say that."

"I called over to the courthouse. No marriage records under any of those names. I called Legal, and Samantha's never been in our custody. No Medicaid record for her, either. Speaking of which. . ." She reached in a plastic stacking tray and handed me a stack of forms about a quarter of an inch high. Records for my other clients. Great, more filing for me.

I went back to the topic at hand. "Well, at least we know Samantha hasn't been in our custody. Maybe I'll call Family Court and see if she has a juvenile record." I peeled myself off the chair and thanked her again.

"No problem. We still on for lunch tomorrow?"

"Yep. See you then."

Back at my desk, I checked my messages and returned some phone calls. I called Family Court's records department, and was told Samantha had never been arrested. I was almost sorry since I was so desperate for any information about this mysterious girl. Anything would help.

I started to call Kirk, then decided to do it from the car on my way to Braden Hawthorn's house.

He answered on the first ring. "Hello, gor. . .I mean, hello."

I stifled a giggle. "Hi. How's it going?"

"Fine, thanks. And you?"

I summarized what I learned from Stringfellow about the computer. "Can you see if Jean Chambless had anything for sale in the classifieds?"

"Sure. I'll call you back." Ten minutes later he had bad news. "Nothing. Sorry."

"That's okay. I knew it was a long shot. And now we have a missing computer on top of everything."

"Makes me wonder just what was on it."

"Yep."

"So when are we going?"

"Going?"

"To Tunica."

"Kirk--"

He laughed. "Seriously. We need to get over there."

Somehow I thought Kirk could do just fine by himself. "So how about I call a hotel and get us some rooms?"

"I've got things to do tomorrow."

"Okay, so we'll go Saturday."

"Kirk. . ."

"What?"

I couldn't think of a really good reason not to go. "Okay. A day trip. I don't want to stay over."

"Understood." We hung up.

First was a quick trip to Braden's. I sat in the car and watched the house for a second, trying to decide whether it would be worth it to go to the door. In the end, I shut the car off and walked up.

Braden answered the door, again in shorts and a blue E.W. Dodge T-shirt, IPod ear buds in his ears. "Hey," he mumbled.

"Hey."

"What are you doing here?"

"Just checking on you. You heard from Samantha?"

"Nope. Nothing."

We stood in silence for several seconds. Finally, he opened the door wider. "Come in?"

I stepped into the cool house. "Where's your sister?"

"She's upstairs, playing."

"Oh."

I started to wander. Peeked into the kitchen, which was purple and gray and clean except for a couple of dishes in the sink. Through there to the dining room, and back to the living room.

Braden followed me, and asked, "What are you doing?"

"Just looking."

"For Sam? She's not here."

"Then you won't mind if I look around upstairs?"

He looked uncomfortable, and I could see the hesitation in his eyes.

"Well?"

"Fine."

He followed me up the stairs. We turned right to Brianna's room. She was on her bed, surrounded by several stuffed animals, brushing the hair of a Barbie. We said hello, then I looked into the next bedroom, which was Braden's. No evidence of Sam, no photos, just a few posters of high-end sports cars on the gray walls. When I opened the closet, he exclaimed, "Hey!" The closet was a mess, a jumble of clothes and sports equipment and other junk. But no Samantha.

I looked through the playroom, then went downstairs to the garage and storage room. Braden followed me back to the master suite on the main level, which was beautiful. Still no Sam. We went back to the living room, where I asked him to join me on the couch.

He was furious. Fuming. I wasn't sure why. Because I invaded his space? Because I didn't trust him? "I'm sorry you're mad. I just wanted to be sure she wasn't here."

"Whatever."

"Why are you so upset?"

"I told you I haven't heard from her, and you didn't believe me. And then you go fucking around through all our stuff."

"Look, Braden, Samantha cares about you. She may try to come here. I can't emphasize enough how much I, and the police, need to talk to her. You really don't know where she is?"

The anger on his face softened, and for the first time I saw real concern. And fear.

"I don't know where she is. Or where she could be. Me and Marci--that's her best friend--we keep calling her cell trying to figure out where she might have gone, but we haven't been able to find her."

"Okay. I believe you. Look, if you hear from her, please call the police. Or me. She could be in some serious mess."

"I will."

I didn't believe him. "Did Samantha tell you anything that was going on? Something she was worried about? Afraid of?"

"No."

"Did she ever talk about being sexually abused?"

"No! Never. Why? Was she?"

"I don't know. Were you having sex with her?"

He shrugged, shook his head, then nodded. "But we were careful. We used a. . .you know." Lord, the kid couldn't even say the word "condom." I hoped he was telling the truth. I changed the subject.

"Did you guys chat online sometimes? Instant message each other?"

"Yeah."

"She got in trouble sometimes for using the computer too much, I hear."

"Yeah. Sometimes she'd surf around late at night. Go to chat rooms and Facebook and stuff. Used to piss her mom off."

His expression was laden with worry. My heart went out to him. "What kind of computer did they have?" I asked.

"What do you mean?"

"When the police went through the house after the murder, they couldn't find a computer."

"That's weird. They had a laptop. A kick-ass new Dell Ispiron. Sam loved it."

"Do you know what might have happened to it?"

"No. Sam texted me last Thursday night on her cell. Said she was trying to find a ride to the mall Saturday. Then I saw her at school on Friday. That was the last time I talked to her."

"They had a lot of new things. Furniture, the computer, TV. Did Samantha ever talk about why? Or where the money came from?"

"Nope."

"Do you know what her mom did for a living?"

"No. We never talked about that kind of stuff."

It was looking more and more like a dead end. I stood. "Well, thanks, Braden. I appreciate your help. I just wish I knew where she was. If you had to guess, where would she run? Did she ever mention any place she wanted to go?"

"Disney World. And New York."

"Why New York?"

"Sam wants to be a model. She could, too. She's real pretty."

Braden walked me to the door. I reflected on our talk on my way to Kyle Weller's house. I didn't have a whole lot of hope that Kyle or his parents would be able to fill in any blanks. Any more than Braden did. He seemed genuinely puzzled as to where Samantha had gone.

Kyle's house was on a road called Kensington. I threaded through the neighborhood, impressed with the size of all the houses. It seemed the Wellers would qualify as the most successful of Samantha's friends, and least financially. What must it have been like to be the poorest girl in this crowd? I found the address I was looking for, a huge stucco house painted a light cream. I rang the bell.

I knew the man who opened the front door.

Chapter Thirteen

I knew him, all right. But from where? He was tall and blond and round. His suit jacket was absent, so were his tie and belt, and his dress shirt was open at the collar. With that body, he could have been a bouncer. But according to Cecile Silva, Marci's mother, he was an executive in construction.

"Can I help you?" He had a rich, deep voice.

"I'm Claire Conover, with the Child Welfare Department."

"Frank Weller." We shook hands. His grip was strong and hurt my fingers. "You're here about Samantha? Come in."

The inside of the house was gorgeous, too, with lots of arches and tall ceilings. The furnishings were all modern textures in neutral colors. He led me to a large living area where we sat on comfortable white sofas in front of the fireplace. A large flat-screen television hung above.

"The police were here earlier. I told them I don't know where Sam is. I've only met her once."

"Has Kyle said anything about where she might be? Where she might have gone?"

"Nothing. He's..."

"He's what?"

"My son has always been a little difficult. Rebellious. Especially now that he's a teenager. He doesn't tell us much."

I wondered who "us" was. The missus Weller, I assumed. If she was home, she wasn't making her presence known. I didn't hear anyone else in the house.

"I see. So he has behavior problems?"

"Oh, no. Nothing that I would consider out of the normal range. He just can be a little difficult sometimes. So I'm afraid getting any information out of him will be hard."

"You know he's dating Marci Silva?"

"Oh, yes, that's been going on for several months now. We're very fond of Marci, and her family. But Samantha, we didn't know her very well."

"I see."

"The police asked us to monitor Kyle's email and phone calls and text messages, and we will. But I doubt he'll be able to provide much information."

"Has he talked at all about Samantha or what happened to her mother?"

"Very little, so far."

"Could I meet him?"

"I'm afraid he's at football practice until six. I have to go pick him up in just a minute."

"Oh. He plays for the middle school?"

"Yes, he's played football for years. He's a defensive tackle. He's quite good."

"I see. Do you have any other children?"

"No, just Kyle." He stood. "I wish I could be more help."

I had the sudden feeling I was being shown the door. Why the rush to get me out? Kyle couldn't wait for five minutes? I stayed seated. Mr. Weller started to look uncomfortable.

"Mr. Weller, I'm so sorry to have to disturb you like this, and I really appreciate your help. Is your wife at home?"

"No, I'm sorry. I'm not sure where she is."

"Oh. You know, I can't help thinking that you look really familiar."

"I run a large company. I'm in the news quite a bit. Look, Miss Conover, like I said, I'm sorry we can't be more help." He gestured toward the door.

I gave up. "Thanks for your time." He shook my hand again before I left. I got in my Civic. He was backing out of the driveway by the time I fastened my seat belt and cranked on the A/C. He was sure in a hurry to get somewhere. I thought about following, to see if he really was going to E.W. Dodge, but abandoned that idea. I was getting paranoid. I was hungry, and I wanted to go home.

My house was cool and quiet, as usual. I changed and was thinking about dinner when my cell phone sang its ring.

"Hey," Grant said.

"Hiya."

"You doing anything for dinner?"

"I was just contemplating that. You finished at the medical clinic?"

"Yep, I'm home. Want to go get something?"

That sounded great. "Sure. Where?"

"Italian?"

"Works for me."

I changed again, refreshed my makeup, and by the time I was finished, Grant was in my living room. "Ready?" I asked.

"You look great." He kissed me.

"Thanks. You do too." He did, in dark jeans and one of his usual polos. This one was gray. Brown hair curled low on his forehead, a day's growth of stubble looked sexy on his face.

We drove back to Homewood, to Gianmarco's, one of our favorite restaurants. I never had to look at the menu: the veal was delicious and the only thing I ever got. We ordered wine and chatted for a while before the food arrived. We were just about finished with the meal when he asked, "So what do you want to do Saturday? Wanna see a movie? Or maybe some music? I think there's a good band playing over at Sloss Furnaces."

Saturday. Shit. "Oh, um. . ."

"What?"

"I think I'm going out of town."

"Really? Where?"

"I have to go to Mississippi. To Tunica. It's for work."

"Oh."

"I have this kid, see, and she's run off. She used to live in Tunica, and I have to go over there and see if I can figure out where she might have gone. Maybe she has relatives or friends she might have run to, see, and I just need to go over there and get some information. So I won't be in town, see?" I was babbling like an idiot.

"It's okay. Some other time."

He sounded so disappointed. Then he asked, "You going by yourself?"

"Yeah. Well, maybe."

"Maybe?"

"I might be going with a. . .well, a co-worker of sorts."

"I see."

I shoved a forkful of polenta in my mouth. Why not tell him? Why not tell him I was going away with Kirk. Wait. Not going away with Kirk. Going to Tunica. On business. Tell him, I thought. I should tell him. I shoveled in more polenta.

"Male or female?"

I choked, coughed, swallowed, and whacked myself on the chest for a minute. After a sip of wine, I asked, "What?"

"Who are you going over there with? This sorta-co-worker? And are they male or female?"

"Oh, well, it's not really a co-worker. You want some more wine?"

"No. Not a co-worker?"

"I can't really talk about it."

He was getting pissed. I could tell. I'd come to learn over the last month that Grant never really leapt into anger. It came upon him slowly, gradually, and thankfully, rarely.

83

"What do you mean you can't talk about it?"

His voice was louder, and the people at the next table turned and glanced at us.

"Can we talk about this in the car? Please?"

He pushed his platter away. So did I. The ever-watchful waiter came and cleared the plates, and Grant requested the check. We sat in silence a few moments until the waiter brought it, ran his card, and he signed it. The food was sitting heavy in my stomach. What the hell had just happened?

In the dark van, I fastened my seat belt and so did Grant. He didn't start the engine.

"So are you going to tell me?" he asked.

"What?"

"Good God! Who you are going to Tunica with, for God's sake!"

"I could get in real trouble if anyone finds out."

"Who the hell am I going to tell?"

"It's a reporter. A guy. Kirk Mahoney."

"Wait a minute. The same Kirk Mahoney that wrote all that crap this summer about you and your case?"

"That's the one."

"And now you're going to Mississippi with him?"

I thought about telling him the whole story. But I couldn't. It would violate the confidentiality of the case, and I didn't want to do that. I thought about what to say. "Look, Kirk's been writing articles for the paper on a murder. That murder is related to my case. That's all I can say. I'm just desperate to find someone who might have some information on my girl, that's all. Kirk has been really helpful."

"Then why all the secrecy? Why did you get all whacked-out when you were telling me about it?"

"I could get in a lot of trouble if Mac finds out I'm talking to him."

"Like I'd tell your boss. I don't even know your boss."

"I know."

"So why, then?"

I didn't look at Grant. "I don't know."

I couldn't see his green eyes in the dark, but I could feel them studying me. Then he cranked the engine, roughly.

"Yes, you do."

I stared out the window the whole way home and we didn't speak. He walked me to my door. I knew the answer before I asked the question, but asked it anyway. "Come in?"

"No, thanks."

"Oh. Thanks for dinner."

He reached over and played with the ends of my blonde hair lying on my shoulder. His strong hand was warm. I could feel it through my thin shirt. "Look, Claire, if you want to date other people--"

"I don't!"

"We never really talked about it. I mean, if this guy--"

"I don't, Grant. I really don't. I don't even want to go to Tunica with him, but I have to, for my case."

"Okay." He gave me a half-smile. "I'll call you tomorrow."

"Okay." He walked down the concrete path, towards his van. "Grant!"

He turned around. I didn't know what to say. I'm sorry seemed appropriate, but sounded like I was guilty. Don't worry? No. I had a million questions I wanted to ask, but didn't. In the end, I just waved. I watched his van pull away, then turned and rested my forehead on the door. I felt like I'd lost something. Something really valuable, and it was all my fault.

Friday morning it was pouring rain, the outer bands of some tropical storm that had hit Mobile. I'd slept only four hours, tossing and turning most of the night before finally drifting off around three. All night I was dying to call Grant, to ask him to come over, or let me go over there. I wanted to talk to him. Hug him. Hold him. Things between us were not good, and I was miserable.

I dragged myself to the shower and dressed. I was late for work, and I didn't care. As I was gathering keys, purse and briefcase, my cell phone rang. The caller ID showed the office. It was my friend Beth, one of the two receptionists who manned the front desk. "What's up?"

"Where are you?"

"Headed in. Why?"

"Someone's here to see you. He says his name's Kenny Thigpen, and he's here about Samantha Chambless."

"No kidding?"

"Yep. Oh, and call Tom."

"Call Tom" was code for "have security standing by." Code to say the person at the office to see me was angry, crazy, or dangerous. Why "call Tom" was the code was a mystery. In the five plus years I'd been at DHS, we'd never had a security guard named Tom. The current one was Earl, and he was about a hundred and seven years old and spent most of his time asleep in a vinyl-covered chair by the front door.

"Really?"

"Uh-huh."

"I'm on my way in."

I raced as fast as the traffic and rain would let me, parked in the lot behind the building and went in the back door. I took a convoluted route past the Overnight Unit's offices, down a hallway and came out behind Beth and Nancy's desk at the front. Beth was on the phone. Nancy reached over and gave me a playful punch on the shoulder hello. I asked her, "Who's my guy?" while I nodded toward the somewhat crowded waiting room.

She pointed. "The Nervous Nelly. See him? The one with the shaky leg."

I looked at the rows of plastic chairs, facing a wall of public-service posters. He was in the fourth row, arms crossed, his blue-jeaned knee twitching rapidly up and down.

Then I saw why Beth had said, "Call Tom." He was bald, his head shaved down to a shiny scalp. His only hair was on his face, in the form of a pointy dark blond goatee that reached almost to his chest. He was thin, like in the picture I'd seen at Jean Chambless's apartment. He wore a black Harley-Davidson T-shirt, and a chain was draped from his back pocket to a belt loop on the front of his jeans.

But it was the tattoos that were disconcerting. A spider web stretched out along one side of his neck, almost reaching to his right cheek. Down his arm I could make out a Confederate Flag, some sort of bird, a barbed wire, and one that looked like an X with a upside down V on top of it. My stomach sank as a realized that one was a white-supremacist tattoo. Some of them were plain black ink and looked like he'd done them himself, probably in prison.

"Call Tom, indeed," I whispered to Nancy. "I'm going to go find us a room on a very crowded floor. Would you let Earl know to walk by every few minutes?"

"You got it."

I dropped my stuff off at my desk, then found an empty conference room on the third floor. I taped a quick "Reserved" note on it and went down to fetch my visitor.

"Kenny Thigpen?" He stood up quickly. He was nervous, and the emotion looked totally out of character. He wiped his hand on his jeans before he shook mine. "I'm Claire Conover."

"I wanted to talk to you about my daughter."

"Yeah, I'm glad you're here, and I'm sorry you had to wait. Let's go upstairs."

I led him to the glass-fronted room. The third floor held the cubicles of the foster care and adoption social workers, and plenty of people were around. I indicated a chair for Mr. Thigpen and sat across from him where I could see out of the room.

"You're Samantha's father?"

He nodded. "Not that I've really been around much."

"How did you find out that DHS has custody of her?"

"I just got outta jail. I've been tryin' to call Jean for days. Tried up in Tunica first, finally found someone who told me she was here and gave me her number. Never could get no answer at her house. Then the phone got cut off, and I got worried. Then my probation officer called, said the police here in Birmingham had called and Jean was murdered. They wanted to know where I was last weekend. I called the cops here, and they put me through to some dude named Stringfellow. I got a meeting with him today, too. He gave me your name. When can I see my daughter?"

I wished I had an answer for him. "I do have custody of Samantha. However, we have a little problem." I took a deep breath. "I took her to her foster mom's house two days ago, and she left. Ran away. The truth is, I don't know where she is. The police are looking for her, and I am, too."

I stopped there, waiting to see how he was going to take it. Was I going to get yelled at? Threatened? Or would this be a relatively calm reaction? He placed his fingertips together under his chin. "I see," he said.

So far, so good. "Mr. Thigpen, I can't tell you how sorry I am that this happened. I promise we're doing everything we can to find her. Anything you might be able to tell me would be very helpful."

I saw Ancient Earl walk casually by, his hand on his nightstick. He glanced in, and I gave him a subtle nod. He kept walking.

"Tell me about you and Jean, and your relationship with Samantha."

He sat back in the hard chair. "Like I said, I ain't been around much. I been in prison in Mississippi off and on for lots of years."

"For?"

"Drugs, mostly. Then I got busted robbin' a store, tryin' to

87

get money for drugs."

"So what about you and Jean? How did you meet her?"

"We was in high school together, in Biloxi, Mississippi. Long time ago. We never dated in high school, never hung out together. Then one night a few years later, me and some buddies were at Casino Magic. She was dealing blackjack, and we started going out. We got married about six months later, and Sam came along a few months after that."

"Why'd you divorce?"

"Yeah, well, I got this drug problem, see? Started with alcohol. I drank a lot when I was datin' Jean, then started on the hard stuff after we got married. Coke, pot, pills, whatever. I hate that I screwed up our marriage, and I can't say I blame her for leavin' me. I got pulled over, high, and went to jail. She forgave me the once, but the second time I got busted that was it. Like I said, can't blame her. She didn't want Sam around all that stuff. I didn't neither."

"When was the last time you saw Samantha?"

"It was a few years ago. Jean worked at Casino Magic till the big storm, you know?"

"Hurricane Katrina?"

"Yeah, the place got destroyed and they didn't open back up after. So Jean got another job and she and Sam moved to Tunica. Jean brought Sam over to tell me bye before they left. I went back to jail right after that. I was a mess, but I'm in treatment now. Sam wrote me a couple of letters when I was in the joint. They was real sweet. I'd really like to see her when she gets found. I'm so sorry she's lost her mamma like that."

I saw his jaw tighten as he swallowed. He put a hand up and covered his eyes for a second. That got to me. I struggled to control myself and said, "I'm sorry, too. The little time I got to spend with Samantha, she seemed like a very sweet girl."

He looked up. "Jean was a great mamma. Whatever else, she took good care of Sam."

"Did Jean ever do drugs?"

"Oh, no, never. She never would. She drank some, but that was it as far as I know."

"Do you know where she worked in Tunica?"

"One of the casinos. I ain't sure which one."

"What about other family? Does Sam ever visit her grandparents?"

"They're all dead, my parents and Jean's. Jean ain't even got nobody to bury her, I don't reckon. I gotta go over and ask that Stringfellow guy about it today, I guess." He teared up again and wiped his eyes.

"You said the police asked where you were on Saturday?"

"I was at home. By myself. Watching football on the couch. I ain't got nobody that can swear to it, though. That's what I told the cops."

"Mr. Thigpen, I want to get your contact information, so I can call you when Samantha shows up." He gave me an apartment address in Gulfport, Mississippi, along with a phone number. He didn't have a cell phone. "I guess I don't have to tell you that in order to have custody or visits with Samantha when she's found, you'll have to pass drug tests."

"I know."

"What's your employment situation?"

"I restore and repair cars. Me and a friend got a place down on the Coast."

"I'll let you know as soon as I find out where Sam is. Here's my card so we can keep in touch." He took it, and shyly reached out a hand to mine. I shook it.

"Thanks."

"One more thing. You drove up here?"

"Yeah."

"You've got a place to stay?"

"I drove overnight and I'm headin' home as soon as I talk to that policeman."

"What do you drive?"

"Why?"

"When Samantha disappeared, she was picked up by someone in a blue SUV."

He laughed, tentatively. He looked uneasy all of the sudden. "I wish I could afford something like that. I got a seventy-one Mustang. A coupe. One I restored myself."

"Thanks for coming in." I walked him downstairs and saw him to the door. We said goodbye, and I pretended like I was going toward the elevator. As he headed across the street, I turned around and went back to the glass door.

His car was across the street and down about half a block. I saw him dig in his pocket and pull out a key. Then, damned if he didn't unlock an older blue SUV, get in and drive it toward the expressway.

Chapter Fourteen

The SUV was an Explorer. The paint job was navy, with a black luggage rack on top. A big-ass, blue SUV. Damn.

If Kenny Thigpen had owned a cell phone, I would have marched straight up to my office and called him. I would have demanded to know why he didn't tell he was cruising around Birmingham in a blue SUV. Even after I said his missing daughter was picked up in one.

But if he knew where his daughter was, why come here? Why come down to DHS and make his presence known? Especially if he'd just murdered his ex-wife. Why not just grab Samantha and take off to Mississippi, or wherever? It made me wonder if he had anything to do with Samantha's disappearance. But why didn't he tell me what he was driving? It didn't make any sense.

I went back to my cubicle and called Stringfellow. Told him about my visit with Kenny and that he could be heading Stringfellow's way in a blue SUV. I asked him to have Kenny call me. I updated him on my visits with Samantha's friends, too.

I got my cell out of my purse and called Kirk to let him know about my conversation with Kenny Thigpen. I told Kirk that Jean had worked in one of the casinos in Tunica, so we were on the right track.

After we hung up, I left my cell phone on my desk. Hoped it would ring. It was up to Kenny to contact me, since I had no real way of getting in touch with him until he went home.

And I hoped Grant would call, too. It was almost ten-thirty. He'd be busy installing computers at the medical clinic now. I picked up the phone, put it back down. I wouldn't know what to say if I did call him. I started some paperwork, tried to lose myself in the forms and not think about him. It didn't work. After an hour, I shoved the silent phone in my pocket and went to find Michele.

She was in her office, typing rapidly on her keyboard. "Hey," she said. "Sorry. Let me just wrap this up and we can go. Where do you want to eat?"

We talked about where to go for a while, then she asked, "You okay?"

"Yeah, I guess."

"You seem a little bothered."

"I'm okay. Hey, while I've got you here, can you run a name for me?"

"Sure."

"Frank Weller?"

"Ah, yep. We have a record on him from last year. I remember that one."

"We do? You do?"

"Wait till you see it."

So Kyle's father had a DHS record. Well, well. No wonder he'd looked familiar. I'd been hoping my fuzzy memory was wrong.

Michele entered a few keys into her system, then wrote a number on a sticky note. "You want to run down and get the chart before we go?"

"Would you mind?"

"No, go ahead, we've got time."

I made my way to the basement, where sweet Dolly fetched the thick russet file for me. I leaned against the wall outside the file room and opened the chart.

The first thing I saw was a picture, and at the sight of it my stomach clenched, then dropped. God Almighty.

The photo was of Kyle's face, but it bore little resemblance to the one I had from Samantha and Jean's townhouse. Both his eyes were swollen and blackened, and an inch-long red cut ran along the top of his cheekbone, from just underneath the corner of his eye toward his ear. It gaped open and needed stitching. Someone had wiped most of the blood off his face, but a smear or two still remained. Another small, round bruise was on his forehead.

Two more pictures were paper-clipped under the first one. The next was of the front of Kyle's neck, where a wide red patch flamed across it underneath his jaw. I noted the red dots the size and shape of fingerprints. The next picture was of his back, the area just above his shoulder blades, the freckled flesh raw with what looked like carpet burn.

I'd investigated this kind of thing for years now, and this wasn't the worst I'd seen, but it was bad. Real bad. Someone had held this poor kid down by the neck and beat the shit out of him.

I flipped through the paperwork walking to my office. The initial report done by the cops was dated August of last summer, a little over a year ago. The police report, clearly written, stated an officer was called to the house on Kensington after a 911 call from Mrs. Denise Weller. The police arrived at the home at eight forty-seven p.m. to find Kyle badly beaten, and his father angry and intoxicated. I read the rest of the file once I reached my desk.

It seemed the whole thing started after Kyle was

92

"disrespectful." Daddy had been arrested, Kyle taken to Children's Hospital and then to DHS. I found the initial write-up that had been done the day after all this had happened, and looked for the name of the social worker.

Russell Sharp. My cubicle-mate had been the worker. No wonder Frank Weller had looked familiar. There was nothing to indicate Kyle had been placed in the State's custody, instead he was returned to his mother. Daddy had gone to jail overnight, then to court, ordered to substance abuse treatment for his drinking and to anger management classes. The whole family had been ordered to counseling. Russell kept the case open for a year, until this summer, before closing it.

I dumped the chart on my desk. Russell was out so I went back up to Michele's office.

"I see what you mean," I said as I entered.

"Did you see those pictures? Man, poor kid."

"You said it." More details of the case were coming back to me. I remembered Russell struggling over the decision to let Kyle stay home or not. DHS and Family Court always try to get kids back with their biological families if at all possible. Although Kyle had been badly beaten, his mom and dad had no other reports of child abuse. Dad had done everything asked, without any trouble. Those details had probably saved his family.

But Frank Weller had a temper, for sure. Could he have anything to do with Jean Chambless' death? Had there been some type of encounter between him and Jean? Some argument over the children? Frank hadn't exactly been forthcoming with any of this information. Maybe it was time to track down his wife, Denise.

Michele waved a hand in front of my face. "Hello?"

"Sorry. Just thinking."

"You want to go eat?"

My cell phone rang. "Hang on." I stepped out in the hall to take it. It was Detective Stringfellow. "Your boy never showed."

"What?"

"Kenny Thigpen. He never showed up here."

"Damn."

"Just wanted to let you know."

"Thanks." I poked my phone in frustration. Where had he gone and why was he suddenly avoiding the police? Was there something about our meeting that had scared him away?

Michele and I took my car to a chain restaurant a couple of blocks away. We ordered at the counter and took our plastic number to a table by the window. I asked Michele how her kids were doing.

"Samantha Chambless is all Kate's talking about. The other kids, too. It's gotten to the point where the school called in a few counselors in case any of the kids want to talk about what's happening."

"Is Kate going to go talk to someone?"

"I asked her, and she rolled her eyes at me. So I take it that's a no."

I laughed. "Thirteen. God help you."

"It'll all be over in just five short years when I drop her off at college. I swear, every time I open my mouth she looks at me like I'm a total fool."

"She's a good kid, though."

"She's a great kid, she's just a teenager."

"By the way, does she spend a lot of time on the computer?"

Michele shrugged. "Some. Not as much as her friends, I don't think. I set pretty tight limits on what she can do on it."

"What do you mean?"

"Oh, that's another sore subject. She gets angry at me every time we discuss it. All of her friends have accounts on Instagram and Facebook and Snapchat. She's not allowed."

"Why?"

"She's too young. It's the predators I'm mostly concerned about. What if some older man contacted her? Hit on her, or wanted to have sex with her? I'm not sure she's ready to handle that. And there's just a lot of mess that can go on sometimes."

"Like mean girl stuff?"

"Yeah, you know, name-calling especially. Stuff that spills over into the non-virtual world and can have an effect on her schoolwork. It's just best to stay out of it at her age. And the cell phone's another thing. I took it away last week when she didn't do something I asked, and you would have thought the universe was going to implode."

I laughed again. The waitress brought our sandwiches. I managed to avoid checking my cell phone for the entire meal. After it was over there were still no messages from Grant. As Michele and I returned to work, I decided I was going to see him, tonight.

In the meantime, I had to check on LaReesa. And get her some clothes. I called Royanne, who told me Reverend Jim had set aside a couple of things from the clothes closet at church and could provide a fifty dollar donation. I was grateful. It wasn't a lot, but it would do. I could chip in a twenty or so myself, and that would allow her to have more than one shirt.

I packed my briefcase, grabbed my purse and headed to the church first. The clothes and check had been left at the secretary's desk in a paper grocery bag, the clothes folded neatly and in pretty good condition. Two white polo shirts, one with a small brown stain on the sleeve, and one pair of slightly faded black pants. I left Reverend Jim a note of thanks and headed to the north side of town to Midfield Middle. The school was set in a valley; a series of low brick buildings, connected by tin-roofed walkways, with purple and white and pictures of knights everywhere. I checked in, and the secretary paged LaReesa to the office.

She was practically skipping when she arrived, her face again coated in way too much makeup. Her white blouse was unbuttoned just a little far down at the top, and was also too tight. Her black pants were clinging to her, too. We'd have to address that when we went shopping.

"Hey!" she sang out to me when she walked in the office.

"Hey yourself. Nice to see you in school."

"I told you I'd be here, didn't I?"

"Yep, and I'm just here to make sure you are."

"You get the money yet? For the clothes?"

"It's not a lot, but it'll get you some things. And I've got some uniforms, too, that are your size." I handed her the bag.

She glanced in the bag and grinned. "How much money?"

"Seventy bucks."

Her eyes lit up like it was Christmas morning. "Cool! When are we going?"

"Monday? After school?"

She nodded, then did something I never would have expected. She threw her arms around my waist in an impulsive, awkward hug. "Thanks."

I was touched. I hugged her back. "You're welcome. Now get on back to class."

I spent some time introducing myself to the principal at the school, getting the history of LaReesa's attendance and grades. She'd been in Midfield schools all of her life, and her grades were surprisingly good. Really good, in fact. Even this year, despite the fact that she'd missed a whole lot of days and was on the verge of being reported to Family Court for truancy. She was a smart girl.

After I finished at the school, I sat in my car trying to figure out what to do next. It was almost four, and the parking lot was emptying quickly. Frustrated, I checked my cell phone messages. Kenny Thigpen had not contacted me. I tried to call Grant on his cell and got his voice mail. I decided to call it a day and headed to Grant's shop in Hoover.

Vijay was manning the store. Grant, he informed me, was still on site. I asked him to have Grant call me and went home.

My little house seemed emptier than usual. I changed into shorts and poured myself a glass of Riesling. I was tuning in to the news on TV when my cell phone rang.

My heart skipped a beat as I checked the caller ID. Not Grant. Kirk's cell. I answered it.

"Good news. I tracked down a guy at a casino in Tunica who knew Jean. His name's Lloyd Adams, and he's going to meet with us at noon tomorrow. He'll meet us at the casino. What time do you want to leave?"

It would take about five hours to get there. "How about seven? That'll give us plenty of time to find our way around."

"Sounds good. I'll pick you up. Are you all right?"

"Why?"

"You don't sound good. You sound--"

"What?"

"Upset about something."

"It's nothing."

"Work?"

"It's nothing, really."

"Okay, then, I'll see you in the morning. Sleep tight."

"You, too."

I poured another glass of wine, watched a little news, and then wandered into my office. I woke up the computer, clicked on an icon on the taskbar and pulled up my instant messenger. Clicked HIGHTECH00 and typed hello.

Nothing. No response.

I checked my email, did an online crossword puzzle, and then remembered something Michele had said at lunch. I pulled up Google and entered "Instagram". Typed Samantha's various names along with "Birmingham Alabama" in the search box and was told I'd have to join the site to view profiles. Pass.

I went to Facebook. I had a page but never posted anything because I didn't have time. I entered Samantha's first and last name in the search box.

Several results appeared. Some without a picture, some with one. I scanned the pictures.

Bingo.

It was a pretty picture of Samantha, too, with her long red hair styled and her makeup perfect. She wore a lacy aqua top. I clicked on the link to her photos. The one I had from her bedroom was there, of her and her friends on the picnic table. There were a few more of her and Marci that looked like they'd been taken with a cell phone at school. In one they were laughing together, and again I could see blue lockers in the background.

I couldn't see her wall, just her basic information. I had to send her a friend request to see the rest. I had no idea if she had access to a computer or a phone that would allow her to get the request, but I sent it anyway.

One last thing. I pulled up Google again, then entered Samantha's names. Got over two million results for each of them. I didn't have time to surf through all those pages. How was I going to find out what Samantha had been doing on the web? According to Braden, Samantha had been chatting online, in the middle of the night. Where? And with whom? I wasn't skilled enough in searching to be able to find those sites.

But I knew someone who could help.

Chapter Fifteen

I called Grant again. Got his voice mail again. This time I left a message saying that I missed him and I had a computer question and would he please call me? Okay, I told myself after I hung up, that's it. I wasn't going to spend my days chasing after some guy who didn't want to talk to me. Right?

I had one more glass of wine and watched more TV until shortly after seven-thirty, when my phone finally rang. It was Grant.

"Hey. You off work?" I asked.

"Yep. Just got home. Did you need something?"

"I have a computer question, but I mostly want to see you. Can you come over?"

"Sure. Let me change clothes and I'll be right there." He sounded exhausted.

Thirty minutes later, he scooped me into a warm hug and held me there for several minutes. Into his chest I muttered, "I'm sorry."

"Me, too."

We held each other for several more minutes until he sweetly kissed my forehead, then my lips. I asked if he was hungry, made some salad and some sandwiches. We ate, then snuggled together on the couch, my head resting on his shoulder. "You said on the phone you had a computer question?" he said.

"Oh, yeah." I sat up and faced him. "I have a runaway teenage girl, and I wanted to know if there's any way to see what she'd been doing on the Web. The problem is I don't have her computer. It's missing."

"This is the teenager you're tracking tomorrow?"

I didn't want to talk about Kirk again. "Yes. Is there a way to do that?"

"Sure. You could get the records from her ISP. You'd need a warrant, though."

"ISP?"

"Internet Service Provider."

That sounded easy. "That's Charter."

"Then Charter could dump the traffic logs from the routers, and you look through the logs, looking for patterns."

"Patterns?"

"Yeah, the log will look like an IP address requesting something from another IP address. You'd have to go through and pull out all the sites most likely visited by a teenage girl. Study those patterns until you find the most likely source IP. Then you look in the DHCP logs, that's the Dynamic Host Configuration Protocol, and then--"

I was totally confused. "Whoa. Wait. You've lost me. In other words, it would be impossible."

"No, not impossible. Just very, very time consuming. But that's computer forensics. It's always like that."

"You do this, for your clients?"

"Sometimes. For lawyers, mostly, in civil cases. It's time intensive, but can be worth it. I'll be glad to help you if you can get the ISP records."

I lay back down on his shoulder and wondered how long that would take, and if it would be worth it.

"But the easiest thing would be to find the computer," Grant said. He ran his fingers through my hair and kissed my temple, then yawned.

"You ready for bed?" I asked.

He smiled. "Oh, yeah."

The next morning I gently kissed Grant's bare bicep, and eased out of the sheets. It was quarter to six, and I hadn't had much sleep. I took a hot shower and dressed, then left him a note telling him to help himself to coffee and anything in the fridge and I'd call him when I got back. I quietly slipped out of the house, locking the carport door behind me.

Kirk was right on time, his silver Infiniti stopping at the curb of my sloped yard. I fastened my seatbelt as he studied the van in my driveway.

"Well, well. Did we have a fun night?"

"Kirk—"

"Ha! Two seconds!"

"What?"

"I was timing you to see how long it took to say my name in that ever so special way of yours. Two seconds. And before you even said hello. That's a new record." He laughed.

"Kir. . .Oh, never mind."

He laughed again. "I brought you coffee. It's black, but there's sugar and stuff in the tray."

"Thanks. Black is fine."

Kirk wound his way out of my neighborhood as I sipped the hot Starbucks and tried to wake up. He drove to the road that led to Memphis, known as Corridor X. One day, I supposed, we'd have to start calling it I-22. Once we were on the four lane highway, Kirk looked at me. "Okay, we've got about five hours to kill. Tell me your life story."

I chuckled. "I don't have a life story."

"Sure you do. Everyone does."

"Okay, I don't have a very exciting life story."

"Where were you born?"

"Here, in Birmingham."

"Brothers and sisters?"

"One brother, Chris. He's a nurse in Orlando."

"And your parents are still in Birmingham?"

"My father is. My mother died of breast cancer when I was thirteen." I didn't want to be grilled, and turned it around to him. "What about you?"

"Born and raised in Richmond, Virginia. I'm the youngest of five boys."

"Oh, your poor parents."

"You said it. Being the youngest, I used to spy on my brothers for attention. I think that's why I became a journalist."

"Because you like to spy on people?"

"Exactly."

"So who are we going to talk to in Tunica, again?"

"Lloyd Adams. He's the Human Resources Director for the Lucky Clover Casino. He hired Jean a few years ago when she moved up there."

"He knows she's dead, right?"

"Yep. I called Stringfellow after I found this Lloyd guy and told him what I'd discovered and that we were headed over today. I think they sent someone over yesterday to see if anything in Mississippi might be connected to Jean's murder. I haven't heard whether or not they found anything out."

He glanced at his watch. "Hey, you mind if we listen to some news?" He flipped on the radio and pushed a few buttons until he found NPR. The broadcaster's voice had a soothing rhythm, and minutes into the headlines about the economy, I was fast asleep.

I woke up as the car slowed and braked. My head leaned against the window. I immediately reached up and wiped my mouth to make sure I wasn't drooling. I wasn't, much. I ran my fingers under my eyes and groaned softly.

"Good morning, sunshine. You must have had a really long night." He shot me a lecherous grin.

"Where are we?"

"Someplace in Mississippi called New Albany. We're about halfway there."

I checked my watch. Nine forty-seven. I needed more coffee and something to eat.

Another cup of java and a fast-food biscuit later, we were back on the road. The scenery for the next two hours wasn't much except farmland until we approached Tunica and Casino Strip Resort Boulevard. Several casinos were clustered together on the river. Kirk passed Harrah's and turned into the enormous parking lot of the Lucky Clover. The front of the lot held a huge sign, flashing dinner specials and upcoming shows. The building itself was faintly castle-like, and a valet in a white dress shirt and black tie with little green clovers on it took Kirk's keys and wished us good luck.

The casino had a large entryway, and a right turn led to the luxury hotel. We walked to the left and stood among the many rows of bright slot machines that chimed over the clanking of coins falling into metal trays. It was quite crowded for a Saturday afternoon.

"What now?" I asked Kirk.

"I'll ask for Lloyd." He nodded toward the change booth. I waited until he returned moments later.

"He's on his way." He held up a token embossed with a leprechaun and, of course, a four-leaf clover. "Feeling lucky?"

"Never."

"Really? You don't gamble?"

"I never win. Anything. Ever." I followed him to a twenty-five cent machine. He inserted the coin and pulled the lever. Nothing. He inserted the next coin and yanked again. Two dollars worth of tokens clanked into the tray.

"Hey! How about that?"

I rolled my eyes. "Figures."

A man in a striped shirt tapped Kirk on the shoulder. "Excuse me? You're Mr. Mahoney? I'm Lloyd Adams."

They shook hands and Kirk introduced me. Lloyd led us back to his office, a rather large one with soft green walls and a nice professional desk. He sat behind it and scratched the short beard on his face. "How can I help you?"

Kirk answered, "We're looking for information on Jean Chambless. Anything about her, really. The police are at a dead-end as to why she was murdered. Can you tell us a little about her?"

"I hired Jean a few years ago. At the time she was working odd jobs, and had been since Katrina destroyed the casino where she worked in Biloxi. We tried to hire as many of the poor folks from down there as we could. Man, what a disaster. Anyway, she dealt here after the storm. Poker mostly, and some Blackjack. She was real good at her job. Real quiet. Never late or irresponsible or anything. One of our better employees. I thought after she and Bobby got married she'd stay here in Tunica forever. I just can't believe she was killed."

"She was married?" I asked.

"Briefly, to Bobby Chambless. Nice guy. He's a local and he came in to play occasionally. That's how they met. He was head over heels, you know what I mean? He was crushed when she walked out."

"She left him?" Kirk asked.

"Yeah, I don't know why. We were all kind of surprised, you know? They weren't married all that long. And we all felt bad for Samantha. I think it was good for Sam to have a father. He kept her in line. I told the police all this stuff when they were here yesterday." He rummaged around in the papers on his desk, then wrote something on the back of one of his business cards. "Here's Bobby's address, out on Prichard Road."

"What does Mr. Chambless do?" I asked.

"Farm equipment repair, mostly. Combines, hay balers, that sort of stuff. He does okay, I think. Lot of business for him around here."

"Thanks." I took the card.

"I'm serious, I can't imagine Jean mixed up in anything that would cause her to be murdered. She just wasn't the type to attract trouble."

Kirk stood and offered Lloyd his hand. "Thanks so much for meeting us today, and for your help. We'll try to get some answers."

I shook his hand as well. He escorted us back out to the loud casino, which was growing even more crowded. Kirk stopped and put two quarter tokens in a slot machine and won eight dollars.

"You certainly seem to have all the luck." I said.

His blue eyes focused on me. "Not always."

He cashed out, and the valet fetched his car. He programmed his GPS system with Bobby Chambless' address, and exited the casino's lot. Mr. Chambless didn't live very far away. A few minutes' drive through the corn and cotton fields led us to an older farmhouse with a large metal shop behind it.

The wooden house looked like it was about a hundred years

old. It was tall and square, two floors and neatly painted white. I wondered how long the Chambless family had been rooted in this spot. For generations, maybe. Kirk knocked loudly once, then twice.

"Can I help you?" A soft voice said behind me. I jumped, and Kirk steadied me.

"Sorry," the man said. "Didn't mean to scare you. I was out in the shop."

"Are you Bobby Chambless?" Kirk asked.

"Yeah."

"I'm Kirk Mahoney, from the News, in Birmingham. This is Claire Conover. She's with the Alabama Department of Human Services. Can we talk to you for a second? It's about Jean and Samantha."

He looked older than Jean, at least by a few years. Thin brown hair and wide-set brown eyes. He wore a dirty T-shirt and jeans. He was thin. And strong, that was for sure. I guessed fixing combines, whatever those were, kept him in shape.

He opened the front door with a tan hand and brought us to a small sitting room. A worn beige sofa faced a television on a large entertainment center, and a collection of framed photos were on the many shelves. I noted several of Samantha and Jean. The walls were bright white and the place was remarkably clean, especially compared to its owner.

He gestured to the sofa. "Have a seat." He lowered himself into matching upholstered chair in the corner and fiddled with the buckle on his watch. "What can I do for you?"

Kirk and I glanced at each other, wondering who should proceed. Kirk cleared his throat and said, "I understand the police were here yesterday. They told you about Jean?"

Bobby's eyes filled with tears. "They said she was murdered. They asked me where I was that day. As if I. . .as if I could have. . ."

He covered his eyes with one hand and began to sob.

Chapter Sixteen

Kirk looked away to the floor, the walls, anywhere but at Bobby. Then he looked at me. "Well, so..."

I scowled at him, then moved to the chair across the room. I bent over and placed my arm around poor Mr. Chambless and patted his dusty shoulder. His head was now buried in his hands and he was shaking softly.

"I'm so sorry, Mr. Chambless."

He sniffled and wiped tears from his face. "I'm sorry."

"It's okay."

"I loved her. Jean, I mean. And Sam. Poor Sam. What's she gonna do without a mother? Or a father? She is such a good kid." He sniffled again.

"How long were you married?" I asked.

"Not long, about three years. The thing was, I thought we was happy. Then one day, out of the blue, she comes home from work and says she's moving to Birmingham, that she don't want to be married to me no more. She got offered a job over in Alabama, and that was that. She just took Sam and left. And I loved that little girl, too, I'll tell you. I've left her room with all her things just like she had it. Jean didn't even let her take any of her stuff." He took a deep breath, tears threatening again. "I couldn't believe it. Just like that, they was gone."

Kirk asked, "She got offered a job in Birmingham? It's my understanding the police haven't been able to determine where Jean worked."

"Yeah, the police said that yesterday. I don't think the place has a name. She worked in a poker place."

I looked at Kirk. Gambling was definitely illegal in Jefferson County, except for some ever-disputed Bingo machines and the dog track. We certainly didn't have casinos.

Bobby continued, "I reckon that's what you call them. It's a private sort of place, where men with a lot of money get together and play. See, this guy come in and played at her table here for a week. His name was the Admiral. That was all she ever called him. He liked her, I guess. Before he left he gave her a card with his name on it and a number, and told her to call if she ever wanted to come work for him. I guess it was a lot more money than she was makin' at the Clover. She said with that and the settlement check she could afford to go."

"Settlement check?" Kirk asked.

"Yeah. Jean inherited her parents' house in Biloxi after her mom died and it got flooded in the hurricane. She lost everything. She got some money from her insurance company, then the state paid her a bunch. All told, it was a lot, like a hundred thousand dollars. Excuse me for a second."

Bobby got up and left the room. We heard him climb the stairs, his footsteps echoing throughout the house.

I looked at Kirk, who had produced a notebook and was writing in it.

"Poker in Birmingham?" I asked.

"Sure. There's lots of gambling going on in our fair city, just not legally." He put the notebook back in his shirt pocket.

"I know there's a lot of sports betting, especially on football. I had no idea there were poker rooms. Did you know about this?"

"I've heard about one place, but I think there are several. They're not open to the public, you have to be invited to play, and you have to know what you are doing. Not for amateur gamblers, for sure. They're Texas Hold 'em tournaments, and usually for pretty big amounts."

"It must be if they can afford to hire dealers."

"Dealers, and girls for other things."

"Like prostitution?"

"Oh, I don't think so. I think the girls are there to wait on the players. Bring food and drinks and so forth. Not much different than the service you get at a casino, only on smaller scale, and much more intimate."

"And the cops don't know about this?"

He shrugged. "So what if they do? It's only poker."

"Yeah, but it's illegal."

He laughed. "So are a lot of things, but people do them anyway. Look, what's the harm? These are grown men, playing a game with their own money for fun. So what?"

He had a point. But this added a whole new dimension to Jean's murder. Could the fact that she was working in an illegal industry have anything to do with why she was killed? She'd pissed off the wrong person, for sure. Someone she worked with? A customer? Had she gambled herself and gotten into some trouble? And what about this Admiral? Was he just her boss? And what did Samantha know about any of this? Did she even know what her mom did for a living?

Footsteps echoed down the stairs again and Bobby re-entered the room, his red face scrubbed clean and a wad of wet tissue in his hand. "Sorry about that," he said. "It's just been a really rough couple of days. Do you want to see Sam's room?"

"Sure."

Kirk and I followed him to the narrow staircase, the polished wood worn in the center of each step. The upstairs had two bedrooms, both the same size, scuffed hardwood on the floor. Sam's room here was pink and white, geared for a much younger girl. Stuffed animals of every species crowded the tidy bed, and an empty aquarium stood by the door. Bobby stroked the top of the glass. "She liked fish. The police said Sam had ran away, is that right?"

"She did," I answered. "The police and I are looking for her. You haven't heard from her, I guess?"

"No, not since her and her mamma left. That was in December of last year."

"Did Samantha have a lot of friends here?"

He smiled, revealing teeth that were crooked and somewhat stained. "Oh yeah. There was always little girls over here playing. I put up a tire swing in the backyard. Hung it from a tree. They used to love that, Sam and her friends. Who's going to take care of her when you find her?"

"She's in the custody of the state. She'll probably go to a foster home."

He took a big, shaky breath. "Could she come and live with me?"

"That depends. Did you adopt Samantha, when you married Jean?"

"I did. I don't think her daddy was too happy about it. But he's in prison. Has been for a while."

"Not too happy?"

"To say the least."

So Bobby was her legal parent, and when and if she turned up, she'd be his. Unless her biological dad wanted custody now that he was out of jail. Then we'd have a custody fight. Was there one going on before Jean died? Did that have something to do with her murder?

"So her father relinquished his rights?" I asked.

"Yeah, I reckon that's the word for it. Finally. It took Jean forever to talk him into it. He was pretty angry about the whole thing. I don't know why. It wasn't like he was around much, anyway."

"Did he ever threaten Jean?" Kirk asked.

107

"I guess you could call it that. Mostly he just called her names. Ugly names, especially when he was drunk or high."

"Was Jean ever abused by him when they were married?"

"She told me he done hit her a couple times when he was on the drugs. That's one of the reasons why she left him."

Kenny hadn't mentioned he'd hit Jean. I wondered why. Was he embarrassed? I supposed admitting you were an abusive husband wouldn't be easy. Especially not to a total stranger. Kenny was angry, and couldn't--or wouldn't--control his anger. But did that make him a murderer?

Bobby let Kirk and me look around Samantha's room, and a quick check of the nightstand and closet didn't reveal much of interest. I considered getting the names of her friends here, but in the end didn't see the point. I doubted she had the means to get this far.

Bobby shut the lights off and walked us downstairs. I took some time to gather his contact information before Kirk and I said goodbye. His handshake was soft and gentle. I promised to keep in close touch.

Kirk eased the Infiniti out of Bobby's gravel drive onto the road. He checked the GPS for directions back to Corridor X and to Birmingham. I relaxed against the headrest and wondered whether Samantha had been happy in tiny Tunica, and whether she would be again.

"What are you thinking about?" Kirk murmured.

"Samantha. I hope she wants to come back here. I hope we can find her."

"You think she'd want to come back to live with Bobby? He's not the brightest bulb in the chandelier, that's for sure."

"Oh, he's nice though. And he really seems to love her."

"Well," Kirk said, "now comes the fun part."

"What?"

"Trying to find the Admiral."

"Think you can?"

"Sure. I can find anybody."

"You know, the scary thing is I believe you."

It was late by the time Kirk dropped me off at my house. He said he'd call when he found anything. Grant's van was gone, and the place was dark. I switched on a few lights and placed a quick call to let him know I was home. We were both yawning and half asleep by the time we hung up.

I put on a nightshirt, brushed my teeth and sank into bed. The pillow Grant had slept on last night still smelled like him. I cuddled it, and just as I was drifting off, my cell phone on the table sang its little tune. I fumbled toward it, hit "answer" and mumbled hello.

"Happy Saturday night. Hope you weren't doing anything fun."

Leah Knighton was one of the two caseworkers on the overnight unit. She used to work days with me before she transferred, and she was good at her job. A good soul. "Hey, what's up?" I yawned.

"I have a young lady here I think you know. Says her name is Sandy, and you're her social worker."

"She's at the office?"

"She just showed up at the back door. Literally."

"Her real name is Samantha Chambless. Her mother was murdered last weekend. For God's sake, tie her to a chair. I mean it. I'm on my way in."

Chapter Seventeen

I threw my clothes back on and sped through the empty streets to the office downtown. After signing in with the security staff, I rushed to Leah's office. I knocked softly on the door. She was on the phone and asked the caller to hang on, then punched a button and said, "I can take this across the hall." She pressed more buttons, then left me and Samantha alone.

She sat in a yellow plastic chair next to Leah's desk, her head down. It took all my willpower not to lose it. I wanted to yell. Things like where-the-hell-have-you-been and do-you-have-any-idea-how-worried-we've-been. But in the end I just took a deep breath and said, "Hi, Samantha."

Her gaze shot to me, her mouth opened.

I sat in Leah's abandoned chair. "Yes, I know that's your name. And I know you are the daughter of Jean Chambless, the woman who was killed this past weekend. I've also met your father, Kenny, and your stepfather, Bobby."

"Oh."

"They're both very worried about you. So was I. So are all of your friends. Braden, Marci, Kyle, Mr. Eddy at the school. All of them are very concerned."

She shifted in the chair. Her gaze was focused on the floor, fixed with the same traumatized look I'd noticed the first day I'd met her.

I studied her closely. Her hair was mussed, her makeup smeared and smudged. Her eyes were red and a little swollen, like she been crying recently. She wore the same clothes she'd had on earlier in the week, the lint-covered black sweatshirt now over the black T-shirt. Her red backpack hung on the back of the chair, and it was dirtier than before. She looked, I thought, worse for wear.

"Where have you been?" I asked, quietly.

She shrugged.

"On the street?"

Nothing.

I sighed and counted to ten in my head. "Samantha, the police really want to talk you about what happened to your mother."

She shook her head, faintly.

"Do you know who killed your mom?"

"I don't want to talk about it."

"Don't you want to see whoever did this caught? Punished?"

Her eyes filled. "Please, I don't want to talk about it."

111

"What's frightening you?"

She shook her head again, and quickly wiped away the tears.

"Bobby misses you."

She looked at me. Her expression brightened a bit. "You saw him? How is he?"

"He's very sad about your mom. Very upset. I think he misses both of you a lot."

"I hated that."

"Hated what?"

"That we had to go. My mom was so stupid, divorcing him. He was really nice. He took good care of us. I liked Tunica, too. I liked my teachers there. I wish we never came to this damn city."

"Samantha, do you know anything about where your mom worked?"

"Why?"

"I was just wondering if maybe her death had to do with what she did for a living."

"She was a poker dealer."

"Here, in Birmingham?"

"Yeah, but she wouldn't talk about it around me. You talked to my friends?"

"Yeah. Like I said, they're very worried about you."

She looked again at the floor. "Oh. What else did they say?"

"Not much else. Just that they wanted to know where you were. Are you hungry?"

"That lady, what's her name?"

"Leah."

"She got me some chips and a soda. I'm okay."

She looked exhausted. "Do you want to get some sleep?"

"I guess."

I gave it one more shot. "Samantha, if you know what happened to your mom--"

"I said I don't want to talk about it."

"The police really want to talk to you. There's a nice detective working on your mom's case, Detective Stringfellow--"

"No!" Her voice was high and sharp. "No! I'm not talking to the police!"

"Honey, you may not have a choice. Your mom was murdered."

She buried her face in her hands. "Just leave me alone. I want to go to sleep. I just want to go to sleep."

I didn't see any point in upsetting her further. I reached over and stroked her shoulder once. She flinched and pulled away. "Okay. I'll get the bed set up for you."

She followed me down the hall to Hotel DHS. I looked in the cabinet and found the same floral sheets she'd slept on before and the same pink blanket. I made up the cot again, and she lay down immediately, burying her head in the pillow. After a few minutes she began to breathe heavily, sound asleep.

For the millionth time, I wondered what she knew about her mother's death. Could the killer be someone she knew? Kenny, her father? He'd been in prison and had a history of violent behavior. And he was mad about the custody transfer. Not that he'd told me about it, I noted. I could see how a kid wouldn't want to send her own parent to jail. But Samantha didn't even know Kenny, really. Why would she protect him?

And what about Bobby? He could have had something to do with Jean's death. But he seemed to really love her. Maybe loved her too much to let her go. Who else would have wanted her dead? This Admiral guy? Someone else from her past? Someone else Samantha cared about?

Her shoulders rose and fell as she breathed under the blanket. I checked my watch and yawned. It was twenty after one. I shut the lights off and walked back to Leah's office. I flopped down on the chair next to her desk where Samantha had been sitting earlier.

Leah was off the phone. "She's asleep," I said. "I wish I was. How do you ever get used to working nights?" I yawned again.

She ran a hand through her short brown hair and laughed softly. "You just do. She say anything about what happened to her mom? Or where she's been?"

"Nope. She bolted from her foster home on Tuesday, been gone ever since. I have no idea where she's been, and she's not going to tell me."

"You think she knows anything?"

"I was just wondering that myself. If she does, why not say something? You'd think she'd want the killer caught."

Leah shrugged, her mouth frowning. "I don't know."

There were a lot of unknowns. I wished Leah a good rest of the night and went to the security station. I talked to Joel, the overnight guard. I explained about Samantha, about how she'd run away and asked him to keep a careful watch on her.

Back upstairs in my cubicle, I left Mac a message about the night's events. Then I had Stringfellow paged.

He called back a few minutes later. His hello sounded a little angry. I apologized for having to call him in the middle of the night.

"That's okay." He was yawning, too. "What's up?"

"Samantha's here. She's asleep."

"How'd she get there?"

"I don't know. They called me about an hour ago and said she just showed up at the door. She's messy and exhausted. She's sound asleep in one of the beds we have here. I've got the security guard watching her."

"What did she say? Where's she been?"

"She won't tell me. And she's refusing to talk to the police."

"Wonderful. Can you meet me in the morning? Maybe bring her to the station?"

"Don't you think that would be a little intimidating? I mean, she's already freaking out about talking to you. Why not do it here? Or someplace neutral?"

"I'll need to interview her here eventually, but maybe we can start slowly. I'll meet you at DHS at eight, okay?"

I agreed and said goodnight. I leaned back in my chair and studied the piles of papers and forms stacked on my desk. Now I had another problem, and that was where to put Samantha. I had serious reservations about sending her back to any foster home. I was afraid she'd run again. I would love to send to her a locked facility, but those were usually for kids diagnosed with a mental illness. She hadn't been. So a hospital or residential placement was impossible. Locking her in juvenile detention was also not possible since she hadn't committed any crime. And detention would just traumatize her further. I rubbed my sleepy eyes and decided to tackle those questions in the morning. Likely I would just send her back to Nettie, with instructions to lock and alarm the windows and keep a real close eye on her.

I got home a little after two-thirty, so tired I couldn't stop yawning as I changed again and fell into bed. I set my alarm for seven-fifteen and was dead to the world until seven, when the damn cell phone rang again. My eyelids were heavy as I struggled out from underneath my comforter and grabbed the phone. "Hello?"

"Look, just don't blow up at me, okay? It's not my fault."

"Leah?"

"I swear it's not my fault."

"What isn't?"

"She's gone again."

Chapter Eighteen

I rubbed my gritty eyes and tried to get my thoughts together. "Samantha ran again? Please tell me you're freaking kidding."

"I'm so sorry. I swear it's not my fault. I was in my office, packing up to leave. Joel was at the back desk, and the daytime security guy came in, and Joel was updating him. We think she went out the front door while all that was going on."

I swore. "I asked the damn guard to keep an eye on her. Specifically. Did you call the police?"

"I just did. We went out and looked for her, too. She just wasn't anywhere around. I'm so sorry," she said again. Leah said would inform the on-call weekend staff about what happened, just in case Samantha came back.

I hung up and tried to decide what to do next. Stringfellow was going to kill me. So was Mac. There wasn't much I could do. I could go to the office, but that wouldn't accomplish anything. If they hadn't found her, I doubt I could.

I paged Stringfellow, canceling our meeting and explaining that she'd run off again. He wasn't happy. Then I called Mac and told him everything that had happened. He wasn't pleased either, to say the least, to be disturbed on a Sunday morning with bad news.

I made a strong pot of coffee and browsed through the paper, all the time wondering in the back of my head if there wasn't something else I should be doing. I couldn't think what. Kirk didn't have an article in Sunday's paper. I fleetingly wondered what he was up to. Thought about calling him. Thought about calling Grant, too, but decided it was too early. For lack of anything better to do, I showered, then cleaned the house. I was mopping the kitchen floor when Dad walked in.

"Whoa."

"Oh, sorry." He tiptoed gingerly to the living room. I put the mop away and joined him, flopping down on my couch.

"You're being productive today."

"I'm just venting frustration." I told him about the case, and how Samantha had showed up then left again.

"Why?" he asked.

"Why what?"

"Why'd she leave?"

"That's a good question. So is why she came back."

"What did you say to scare her off?"

I hadn't thought about that. I replayed our conversation in my head. "I told her I knew who she was, and I knew her mom had been murdered. I told her I'd seen her friends and everyone was worried about her. I told her she was going to have to talk to the police about her mom's death. She wasn't real happy about it."

"Claire, you don't think—"

"That Samantha pulled the trigger?"

It wasn't the first time I'd considered it. It wasn't totally out of the realm of possibility. My mind went back to the autopsy report. Jean had been shot with a thirty-eight caliber. A very common revolver. Not too heavy or complicated. A thirteen year old could certainly figure it out. But where would a kid get a gun? Steal one, maybe.

The idea was ridiculous. Jean and Samantha's relationship didn't seem tumultuous. And what were the odds a tiny teen would steal a pistol, get her mother out to a deserted location and shoot her in the head? But if she had nothing to do with it, why would she run? Twice? And changed her appearance so drastically? And why wouldn't she want to talk to the police? Why wouldn't she want her mother's murderer brought to justice? And if she didn't kill her, who was she protecting?

"It's crossed my mind. I just can't figure out how she'd pull it off."

"Maybe she had help."

I buried my head in my hands. I didn't want to think about it anymore.

"I came over to see if you wanted to get some lunch," Dad said.

After some discussion, we decided on the Tip Top Grill. The restaurant was on the same street as Dad's house, and had the same gorgeous view of Oxmoor Valley. We ate outside on a cement picnic table. The heat of the day was peaking but the breeze from the valley made it tolerable. I ordered the cheeseburger, and my part-time vegetarian father had a grilled cheese sandwich and four bites of my burger.

After we finished, I sat with my chin in my hands and stared at the scenery. I could see the golf resort, red clay and construction supplies surrounding the luxury hotel, three-quarters of it covered in brick. Woods enclosed the entire property and some sections of the golf course were already sodded, the new grass a vibrant green. I wondered where in those woods Jean's body had been found.

And why there? Why were her remains in that location, and not at her home? Because it was isolated? No one would be around on the weekend, for sure. I had to admit, it was a good place to leave a corpse. If those kids hadn't been playing in the woods, it could have been months before she was found. Or never.

"Have any plans for the holiday tomorrow?" my father asked.

"Holiday?"

"Tomorrow's Labor Day. Didn't you know?"

"I forgot." Damn. I wanted to go back by Samantha's school tomorrow, but they'd be closed. And I promised LaReesa we'd go shopping after school. I'd have to pick her up at her house.

My father laughed. "One of these days you'll take some time off, I hope."

My father and I said goodbye and he went home. I sat in my car and decided what to do next. It was time to check in with Samantha's friends again. From the crest of Shades Mountain, West Oxmoor Road followed the steep hill into the valley and led to Braden's neighborhood. I turned onto his street.

Four vehicles lined the street in front of his house. I parked one lot down, trudged my way back to the Hawthorn's front door and rang the bell.

Don answered. He wore khaki shorts and an untucked red polo, and the bright green koozie in his hand was loaded with a bottle of Coors Light. His big smile faded when he saw who it was.

"Oh, Miss Conover. I wasn't expecting you. It's Sunday. It's a holiday weekend."

"I'm sorry to disturb you, Mr. Hawthorn. Can I talk to you for a second?"

"Sure. We haven't heard from Samantha. I've been monitoring Braden's communications, like you asked. He called and texted Samantha on Monday, asking where she was, and again on Tuesday, but that's pretty much it. She hasn't called or emailed here. That's why we haven't been in touch." He glanced behind him. "I'm sorry, we're having a cookout. I've got to get back to my guests."

"Samantha showed up last night at DHS."

"Oh, she did?" Was that disappointment or fear that crossed his face? "You must be very relieved."

"I was, but she's gone again."

"You're kidding."

"No, and I don't know where she might turn up. Possibly here. I wanted to give you and your wife a heads-up."

"Well, thanks for that, and we'll certainly keep an eye out."

Yeah, I thought, between the beer and the burgers. So nice he cared. I peeked around him. I could see through the foyer and into the high-ceilinged family room, where several adults milled around

117

the dark green sectional sofa, laughing and talking.

I tried to remember everything I'd seen the day I toured this house with Braden. I didn't remember any guns, but asked Mr. Hawthorn if he owned any.

"Guns, why?"

"Just wondering. If Samantha pulled the trigger, she would have stolen the murder weapon, and odds are it came from a friend's house."

"I don't own any, no."

More people gathered in the room behind him. Among them, I caught sight of a portly blond profile.

"Is that Frank Weller?" I asked.

"Yes, it is. Miss Conover, if you don't mind--"

I did mind. "Can I speak to him?"

"Look--"

"Please." I said it more like a command.

"Fine." He closed the door in my face. Moments later Frank opened it.

He had a beer in his hand, too, a sweating Bud Light in a yellow printed koozie. He saw me staring at it and looked uncomfortable. "Hello, Miss Conover."

"Sorry to disturb you. I'm checking to see whether anyone's heard from Samantha."

"No, no, we haven't. I checked Kyle's cell phone, as you asked, and I didn't find and messages or texts from her. Checked his email, too, and there was nothing. Sorry." He moved to close the door again.

That pissed me off. A thirteen-year-old girl was missing, very likely in danger, her mother murdered, and these people acted like it was a minor inconvenience. I'd had it.

I stuck my foot in the door and snapped, "Mr. Weller, I'm so sorry to bother you, but I'm very worried about her. She showed up at my office last night, highly distraught, and now she's run off again. This is very serious. Is your wife here?"

"No, she's not. I told you, Kyle hasn't heard from Samantha. I don't know how else I can help you." He was getting angry, too, which fueled my anger even more.

"Is he here? Kyle?"

"No, he's at home. He's on restriction."

I knew I shouldn't have said it the moment I opened my mouth, but out it came anyway. "I suppose that's a better way of correcting his behavior than beating the shit out of him."

118

Chapter Nineteen

Frank Weller's eyes went wide. He turned quickly to make sure no one had heard me. He stepped outside and pulled the door closed. Then he took an aggressive step toward me.

The image of Kyle's badly beaten face flashed through my mind. I hoped I wasn't next. I stood firm.

He towered over me. "You little *bitch*. You don't know anything about it."

"I've seen the pictures. I know what you did to your son. I know you've been through alcohol treatment, yet here you are drinking beer. What else do I need to know?"

"My case with DHS is closed."

"But can easily be reopened."

I watched as the struggle of whether or not to back off played across his face. He stepped away and switched tactics.

"Miss Conover, I don't want that to happen. I'm sorry. I'm not trying to be difficult. Kyle and I went through a hard time last year. Things are better, I promise. I've got the drinking under control. And I haven't hit him again. No one here knows what happened between me and Kyle. No one knows I've got a DHS record."

"Really?" I said with disbelief. "How'd you pull that off?"

"Denise and I told everyone that Kyle had gotten into a fight at football practice. It's not something they need to know. Please?"

I really didn't care. "Mr. Weller, I'm just very worried about Samantha right now, and none of the adults who knew her seem to give a damn about where she is or what she's doing."

"What else do you want me to do?"

"Just keep an eye out for her. Talk to Kyle about her, okay? And let me know if anything comes up."

"I will."

As he turned to leave, I said, "Mr. Weller, do you own any guns?"

"I have two hunting rifles, a Winchester thirty-thirty and a Remington thirty-aught-six."

"Where are they?"

"Locked in a safe in my basement."

He eased through the Hawthorn's front door and back to the party. I knew exactly where I was headed.

The afternoon sun was bright and the sky clear as I drove down Lakeshore and then Kensington. No cars were in the Weller's driveway, and I wondered again where Denise was. She sure didn't spend a lot of time at home. Or with her husband.

Kyle answered the door after I rang the bell. He looked older than in the photos I'd seen of him recently. His hair was a little longer, his facial features a little sharper and more mature. A soft fuzz of light hair grew on his chin. The cut near his eye had healed well, the scar just a faint white line.

"Hi," he said.

"Hi, Kyle. I'm Claire Conover, and I'm with DHS. I've got custody of your friend Samantha Chambless."

He nodded. "You wanna come in?"

I followed him into the house, through the arched doorway to the same white sofas where I'd first talked with his father. The resemblance between them was there, he was blond and bulky like his dad. I imagined it served him well on the football field. He sat down on one of the couches and asked, "So Sam isn't back?"

"She was back for a little while last night, just for a few hours, but now she's run away again. You haven't seen her? Heard from her?"

"Nah." He chewed the corner of one of his nails. "I mean, I like Sam and all, but she's really more my girlfriend's friend, you know?"

"I've met Marci. She said she hasn't heard from her either."

"Nope. She's real torn up about it."

"We all are."

I stood and began to wander the room a bit. Studied a pretty basket and a vase of fake flowers on a shelf in the corner.

Then, quietly, I said, "I saw your DHS record." I faced him, to see his reaction. He was embarrassed, not making eye contact, staring at the floor, and turning a faint shade of red.

"Oh."

"Your dad really bashed the hell out of you."

"I know."

He didn't want to talk about it, but I pressed on. "Are you guys getting along okay now?"

"Not really."

"Has he hit you again?"

"No."

"Do you have a plan if he does?"

"I wish he would hit me. I'll call the cops on his – on him. I'd love to see him locked up in jail. Forever."

Poor Kyle. It was going to be a long four years before he could move out. To college, to anywhere. And that was if he could stay on the right track until then. So many kids from abusive families wound up in detention, or worse. My heart went out to him. I wondered if there was anyone else around to help keep him safe.

"Is your mom home?"

"She doesn't live here anymore."

"Since when?"

He stood and started to pace quickly, all the pent-up anger evident. "She moved out about three weeks ago. She moved up to north Alabama, to Muscle Shoals. I want to go live with her, but Dad won't let me. He says he can manage me better. Ha! Beating the sh— crap out of me, that's how he manages." He took a deep breath. "He's a bastard, and I hate him."

Whew. "Did you tell Russell this? Your social worker last year?"

"No."

"Why not?"

"I wanted to stay here. I didn't want to live with some strange family. I wanted to stay with my mom. I told Russell I wanted to go home."

"Did your dad abuse your mom, too?"

He winced at the word. "Sometimes. He'd slap her, but mostly he was mean to her. Yelled at her, called her names. I was always afraid he'd really hurt her, you know?"

I knew. I'd met way too many thirteen and fourteen year olds who felt they had to be the protector, the responsible one, the man of the family. "Why'd she finally leave?"

"Because he's a prick. I just want to go live with my mom."

"Tell her to file for custody."

He shook his head. "She doesn't have the money right now. She wants to get a divorce, and that's going to take all the extra money she's got."

I got a card out of my purse. "Kyle, here's my number. If you just want to talk to somebody, you can call me, okay? Or if anything happens with your dad, or you feel like you're in danger. I also need you to call me if Samantha gets in touch with you. I mean, even if you think it's no big deal. Even if she just calls to say hello."

"Do you think Sam's okay?"

"No, I don't. Her mother was murdered. I think she knows more about what happened than she's told us. The police want to talk to her. She could be in real danger. She didn't say anything to you about being afraid? About any trouble her mom might be in?"

121

"No. She would have told Marci, if anybody."

"Samantha had a computer, right?"

"Uh-huh. A laptop."

"Do you know where it is? The police couldn't find it after Jean was killed."

He shook his head and nibbled on the corner of his fingernail again. "I don't know. I don't know where it is. Marci might."

"Do you ever talk to Marci online? Or to Samantha?"

"We post on each other's walls on Facebook and stuff. Do you want to see her page?"

Oh, hell. Why hadn't I thought of this sooner? Of course her friends would have access to her page. "I'd love to."

I followed Kyle upstairs to an office on the second floor of the house. A desktop computer with a large flat-screen monitor sat on a modern black desk. Kyle hit the button to boot it. "I'm on restriction. I'm not allowed to use the computer, but since it's for you..." He shot me a small sneaky grin.

I smiled. He pulled up his own Facebook page. His picture, taken with a cell phone, showed him on the bench at a football game. He was looking over his shoulder with a big bright smile for the camera, and was dressed in pads and a royal blue and white jersey, number thirty-seven. His hair was damp with sweat.

"Cute picture," I said.

"One of my friends took that right after we scored last week." He was reading the latest comments on his wall, then moved the cursor to a smaller picture on the bottom left corner of the page. "That's Sam." He clicked it.

A larger version of the picture I'd seen at my house loaded on the screen. I didn't let on I'd seen it before, instead I said, "Oh, wow."

"Yeah, she had that done professionally."

She was beautiful in the picture, I noted again. Her hair was one length, softly styled, some of the wavy dark red strands draped over her shoulder. Her eyes were big and chocolate brown, and her makeup was well applied and enhanced her appearance. It covered the freckles. The picture was a head shot, and she looked at the camera straight on. I could see the top of her blouse, aqua colored and lacy, around her neck. The jewelry she'd worn when I'd met her was missing. Her relaxed lips were parted slightly, showing a bit of straight front teeth. She looked, I realized as my stomach turned a little sick, very grown up.

"Doesn't she look hot?" Kyle asked.

"She looks a lot older than thirteen."

"Isn't that the idea? Sam wants to be a model. She's done some modeling work before."

"She did?"

"She said she was in some advertising campaign when she lived in Mississippi and had done one here, too."

"Do you know with whom?"

"Nope. I think she wants to move to New York after we get out of high school. Maybe even before then."

I read the comments on her wall. None of the comments were long, or said anything much. There was some discussion about a history quiz and tryouts for band. Nothing had been posted in the last week.

"Could we leave her a message?" I asked.

"Sure." He selected a box. "What do you want to say?"

"Nothing much. Just tell her Claire's here and please call me."

He pecked, "Hey, Claire wants to hear from you. Hope you are okay. Come home soon."

It wasn't as insistent as I wanted it to be, but it would do. "Thanks," I said.

"No problem. You mind if I check my email? Maybe Sam emailed me, you know?"

I grinned. "Yeah, of course. That's important."

He checked it and answered a message from his mother. I made a note of her email address. It started with Dwellermom. He said he was on restriction again and would try to sneak a call to her later. He had one from a friend on the football team, but nothing from Samantha. "Sorry," he said.

"That's okay, I'll check with Marci next. Maybe she's had better luck."

"Yeah." He shut down the computer, surveying the desk to make sure he hadn't left anything around the computer, and that it looked just as his dad had left it.

I thanked him again for his help and he walked me toward the door. As we crossed the living room, he stopped behind me. I turned around.

He looked uncomfortable suddenly. I wondered what was up. "What's wrong?"

"You seem pretty cool."

I laughed. "Thanks."

"If I tell you something, will you promise not to tell anyone?"

Uh-oh, I thought. Usually when kids asked me that question, it

123

meant I was about to see bruises, or worse. "Kyle, as much as I would really love to make that promise, I can't. If your dad has hurt you—"

"He hasn't."

"Is it about Samantha?"

"Not really. It's about her mom."

"What about her?"

He hesitated.

"Come on, Kyle, please."

"My dad was having an affair with Sam's mom."

Chapter Twenty

Holy cow. "Your Dad? With Jean Chambless? You're sure?"

I sat down on the sofa again. Kyle joined me.

"Yeah. I don't know how long they've been sleeping together."

"How did you find out?"

"I caught them." He hung his head. "I found out about a month ago. It was right before the school year started. I had football practice. One Friday practice was cancelled because my coach had some family emergency. I caught a ride home with one of the high school guys. Miss Jean was here." He nodded toward the hallway. "She was coming out of my parent's bedroom. She was buttoning her shirt. My dad was right behind her, putting on his belt. The bastard. He was so embarrassed."

"What did they say?"

"Miss Jean didn't say much, just hello, then she practically ran out the door. Dad said not to jump to conclusions, that it wasn't as bad as it looked. Whatever. He even bought me a new I-pad to keep me quiet. Didn't work. I told my mom."

"That must've made him mad."

"Like you wouldn't believe." He gave a wry grin. "And he couldn't hit me, because I told him if he did I'd call Russell and have him arrested again." His expression saddened. "So anyway, that's why my mom left."

"Because of Jean?"

"It wasn't the first time my dad cheated on her but this time she was really pissed. Said she'd had enough and moved out the next week."

God, this poor kid. As if breaking up his parents' marriage needed to be on his conscience on top of everything else. "Are you sorry you told her?"

"No. She had to get away from him. He's such a jerk. I just miss her, that's all."

I scooted over and gently put a hand on his arm. "You've really been through it, huh? Did you tell Samantha?"

"Yeah. She was pissed, too. She was already real mad at her mom for divorcing her stepdad and all. And now this."

"I'm so sorry."

He shrugged. "Are you going to tell the cops?"

"Kyle, I have to. Do you think your dad had anything to do with Jean's death?"

"I don't know," he mumbled.

"Your father has a temper, that's for sure. I've seen the evidence. Jean was killed with a thirty-eight. Do you know if he owns a pistol? A revolver?"

"He just has hunting rifles, as far as I know." He looked at me and I could see in his eyes all the hurt his lousy father had caused. "And there's one more thing."

"What?"

"You know the new golf resort, the one where they found Miss Jean's body?"

"Yeah."

"My dad's building it. His company. Wellstone Construction."

God Almighty. I ran a hand over my eyes. Damn you, Frank Weller. He was up to his eyeballs in everything to do with this case, and had told the police none of it. Nothing about his affair with the victim, nothing about his access to where her body was found. I was going to have to tell the police. Now. I looked at Kyle.

"I know," he said. "He should've gone to the cops. But my dad's real nervous about what this could do to his company's reputation. It's bad enough that a body was found so close to the resort. I heard him talking to somebody about it on the phone. He said if anyone finds about him and Jean, it could be awful. And things have been bad enough with the economy and everything. There was a long time when he didn't have any work at all. This golf resort has really saved Wellstone. Not that I give a damn."

Maybe you don't, but your dad's company is the money for your next supper. And the roof over your head, and the fees for football and cash for school clothes. Plenty of kids were wondering where their next meal was coming from these days, and it looked like Kyle was one of them. It put a new spin on everything. What if I did go to the cops and told them what Kyle had told me? What if Frank had killed Jean? What would happen to Kyle? He'd go live with his mom, I guessed. If she could afford to keep him.

"Kyle, I have to tell the police."

"I know."

"Your dad had the opportunity, maybe even the motive."

"I know."

"I'm sorry."

"It's not your fault my dad's an asshole. I needed to tell someone. I just didn't know who to talk to."

"There's a very nice guy investigating Jean's murder. Detective Stringfellow. He's very levelheaded and fair."

"Okay."

"Are you scared about talking to the police?"

"Yeah, in a way. If my dad finds out what I told you—"

"You're afraid he's going to beat you up again?"

He nodded. "A little."

"Just don't say anything to him. I'll talk to Stringfellow and explain the situation. Stringfellow can make it look like the police found out some other way. Maybe he could say they found something in Miss Jean's townhouse. His phone number, or something."

"You think they'd do that?"

"I hope so. Let me check. But for now, just don't say anything to anyone, okay? And you've got my card if you need me."

Kyle walked me to the door, giving me a nervous wave as I walked to my car. He should be scared, I thought. I would be. He had a father who had a temper like a starving lion and was way over his head in something very dangerous.

I sat in my car for a few minutes, trying to decide what to do. My cell phone beeped from inside my purse. I had messages, two of them.

Both were from LaReesa. The first one said, "Hey, Miss Claire, you were gonna pick me up from school tomorrow but we ain't havin' school. Can you pick me up at my grandma's? Call me." She left a number. The second message was much the same, left just a few minutes ago. I pulled out of the Weller's neighborhood and called her back. I told her I'd pick her up tomorrow around eleven and we'd do lunch and shopping.

I drove down Lakeshore, checked the time on my dashboard clock. It was almost four. I steered the Honda to Marci's house, near the university.

The neighborhood was quiet today. I parked in the Silva's long driveway and walked to the front door. I couldn't hear anything inside. I rang the bell. No answer.

An attached three-car garage sat at the left end of the house, the wide doors facing the street. The rectangular windows were fairly high, and I stood on my tiptoes to look through them. Two of the cars were missing. Next to one of the empty spaces was a large white Mercedes M-class. I went back to the house and peeked in the narrow windows around the door. All the lights were off. Maybe they'd gone out of town for the weekend. If my daughter's best friend was missing and her mother had been murdered, would I have left? Gone to the beach for some fun and sun? What the hell was with these people?

127

I went back and sat in my Honda again, rested my chin on the steering wheel. I was out of options, and decided to go home.

My answering machine had several messages. The first was from Grant, wondering what I was doing tonight. A second from Royanne asked the same thing. The third was from Kirk. All it said was, "Call me, I've got a lead on the Admiral."

I called him back first.

"What have you been up to?" he asked.

"Promise it's off the record? For now?"

"Sure."

I filled him in on my night, about Samantha's coming back and leaving again. Told him about my visit to the Hawthorn's party and then to Kyle's house, and about Frank and Jean's affair and my plans to call Stringfellow.

"Man, poor kid," Kirk said when I finished.

"Yeah, what a mess, huh? And Frank Weller hasn't told the police any of it. You said you had a lead on the Admiral?"

"I think so. I called a friend who's played poker at a place here. He likes to bet the big bucks. He's never been to a hall run by anyone named Admiral but he's going to ask around. He said most of the guys who run these halls don't go by their real names. His guy's nickname is Skeeter."

"Great."

"Yeah, so I'll let you know when I hear something. You doing anything for Labor Day?"

"I don't know."

"No plans with Minivan Man?"

"Probably. I'll call you."

I called Royanne back. She was going to her parents on Monday and asked if I could come by her office Tuesday and pick up some clothes for LaReesa's cousins. I thanked her and said I would. I called Dad and chatted with him for a minute about my afternoon, then called my brother Chris in Orlando.

I was ready for a drink at five-thirty. On impulse, I dialed Russell's number. I felt guilty. My poor cubicle-mate was so broken up over his boyfriend Heinrich's return to Germany and the fact that their relationship wasn't working out. I had done so little to help him through it. He needed support and someone to be there for him, and I'd fallen down on the job.

He was working out when I called, but agreed to meet me in thirty minutes at a bar called Fuel, in the Lakeview area near downtown. I'd been there several times with him. The place had been a gas station in the nineteen-thirties, and its homage to its heritage could be found in the pictures of antique cars on the pub-like walls.

Russell had found a table on the patio in front by the time I arrived. He was still dressed in his workout attire, a white T-shirt over a pair of long red and white shorts. He was sipping on a glass of white wine, his keys on the table. The afternoon sun was blazing and it was hot.

We said hello, and I fetched my own glass of cool Riesling from the bartender manning the long, wooden bar inside. I joined Russell at the round wrought-iron table with a sigh, and slumped back in the chair.

"Long day?" he asked.

I made sure no one could overhear us. Only one other couple sat on the patio, and they were far away. I told him what was going on with Samantha's case, about how she'd shown up on Leah's shift the night before and left again. Then I told him about Frank and Kyle's involvement, and the fact that Frank hadn't told the police about his relationship with Jean.

He scoffed. "Like, I'm totally not surprised."

"Really?"

"That was the whole name of the game with Frank Weller. How much can I get away with and not have to face the consequences? He's an underhanded scumbag."

"But he did everything you asked, right? I mean, you recommended Kyle be placed back with him."

"Yeah, but he was one I had to watch. I mean, he did everything I asked--alcohol treatment, counseling and all--but I had the feeling it was because I was watching, you know?"

"Yep, but a lot of our clients are that way."

"I know, but he was particularly bad. Wanted to do the bare minimum and then have me go away."

"He's drinking again."

Russell's wine glass stopped at his lips. "When?"

"Today. He had a beer. He said he's got it under control."

"Damn it."

"You think I should reopen his case?"

He rested the cool glass on his cheek and thought for a minute. "I don't know. Kyle said he hasn't been hit, right? So we wouldn't have grounds to open an abuse case. Neglect, maybe, based on the drinking. But I doubt it. Nobody's made any reports about neglect."

"I think I'll run it by Mac on Tuesday."

"That's a good idea. Maybe I shouldn't have returned Kyle home."

"Don't say that. It's not your fault. The family did everything you asked them to. And the Judge agreed with you."

"Yeah."

"I'm worried to death about Samantha. Where could she be?"

"She's not at one of her friend's houses?"

"Not that I can tell. She showed up out of the blue at the office on Saturday. I have no idea how she got there or where she'd been. She refused to talk to the cops and bolted again. I've looked at all of her friends houses. I've looked everywhere."

Wait. No, I hadn't.

Chapter Twenty One

I grabbed my cell phone.

"What is it?" Russell asked.

I started to dial 411, then remembered something. "Russ, do you know the name of the principal at E.W. Dodge?"

"Mr. Eddy."

"Yeah, but what's his first name?"

"James, I think."

I dialed information and asked for James Eddy's number. He wasn't listed. I didn't blame him. If I were a middle school administrator, I wouldn't have a listed number either. The prank calls from the kids would have been horrible.

I dialed Michele's house. Kate was a student at Dodge. I hoped she had a school directory or some way to reach him. He wasn't home, and I didn't leave a message. Finally, I dialed Kirk's cell.

"Yo," he answered. "I haven't heard anything yet."

I could hear a crowd of people talking in the background. A girl near him giggled.

"Where are you?"

"Hanging out with some friends."

I wondered who the girl was. Wondered what their relationship was and what she looked like. I focused again, and said I needed James Eddy's phone number.

"Why?"

"Samantha's school is the only place I haven't looked for clues to where she could be."

He laughed. "Most kids run away from school, not to it."

"Can you get the number?"

"I'll call you back."

I sipped another glass of wine and caught up with Russell while I waited. Heinrich still had no plans to come back to Alabama, and Russell was learning to live with it. Not that it was easy. Twenty minutes later, my phone rang.

"Here you go," Kirk said, and read me seven digits.

"You're amazing."

"Thank you. What's next?"

"I'm going to see if I can get him to meet me at the school."

"Call me and I'll meet you there."

I dialed Mr. Eddy's number, hoping he was home. He was. I heard his young daughters playing in the background. I told him I needed to meet him at the school ASAP. He said he could be there in thirty minutes. I called Kirk back and we agreed to meet at the school.

I said a quick goodbye to Russell and sped to Dodge. The sun was sinking in the west, turning the sky a glorious pink. The parking lot was empty except for two school buses. I waited by the front doors. Kirk got there minutes after I arrived. He was dressed in long khaki shorts and a faded green T-shirt from Hilton Head Island. His tan skin was slightly sunburned.

"What's up?" he asked.

"Samantha hasn't shown up at any of her friends' houses that we know of. What if there's some clue here?"

"What makes you think that?"

"I don't know. It's the only place I haven't looked."

Mr. Eddy rolled up in a silver Toyota Camry. He carried a huge ring of keys. I tried to avoid introducing Kirk. The last thing I needed was anyone to find out we were hanging around together. As he unlocked the heavy door, I asked Mr. Eddy, "Did the police search Samantha's locker, by any chance?"

"Yeah, they did. They didn't find anything."

That was disappointing. I was sure they hadn't searched it. Now I felt like I'd wasted Mr. Eddy's time. But I wanted to look anyway. "Can you open her locker for me?"

"Sure."

"What are we looking for?" Kirk asked.

"I don't know. Any hint about where she is. I'm surprised the police thought of this. I doubt we'll find anything either, but I have to check."

Mr. Eddy led us down the main hall to locker number 126. The lockers were stacked in twos, and Samantha's was on the bottom. It had a combination lock for the kids to use, but a keyhole was in the middle of the knob that turned. Mr. Eddy fished around on his massive key ring again until he found the one that fit and opened it.

"There you go. I think I'll go check on some things in the office, if you don't mind?"

I didn't. I sat down on the dirty tile floor and started to go through the locker's contents. Kirk sat down and leaned his back on the royal blue metal door next to me. "If the police have already been here, don't you think this is pointless?"

"Maybe."

I picked up a red binder, evidently her World History notebook. I flipped through it, finding little but a lot of notes about the Roman Empire. I picked up the next one. Language Arts.

Didn't find anything there either. I went through Earth Science and Pre-algebra binders, then through the textbooks. Nothing. I closed the locker door, sat with my back against it, and closed my eyes.

"Sorry." Kirk said.

"There's no notes."

"What?"

"No notes. Didn't you ever write notes to your friends in middle school?"

"No."

"Really?"

"Well, maybe, if a girl insisted."

"Exactly. My friends and I wrote tons of notes to each other in class. Then you'd fold them special, with that little tab you had to pull to get it open, and pass them to each other in the hall between classes. My locker was always full of them."

"Kids today text each other on their cell phones instead."

"Yeah, and Samantha's cell phone is missing, too. She didn't have it with her either time she was at my office, and it wasn't in the townhouse." I had an idea. I opened my eyes and stood, brushing off my shorts. "Let's go find Mr. Eddy."

He was typing at his computer. "Find anything?"

"No, but I have another favor to ask. Did the police check Samantha's friend's lockers?"

He thought for a second. "You know, I don't think they did."

"Can you open them for me?"

"Sure." He grabbed the keys again. "Where do you want to start?"

"With Braden Hawthorn's, I think."

He checked a file on his computer to get the number, then led us to locker number 178. This one was on the bottom row as well. It was a mess, full of loose papers and books haphazardly stacked on top of one another. I went through everything. No notes from Samantha, or any clues to where she might be. I looked at Mr. Eddy.

"What about Marci Silva's?"

We returned to the office and he checked the computer again. We went to locker 117, two down from Samantha's but on the top row. Mr. Eddy opened it.

Marci was a lot neater than her friends. Textbooks were lined up in a row, with her notebooks placed on the shelf above. Everything was color-coordinated. I looked at the textbooks first, and tucked in between Language Arts and Earth Science was a surprise.

A laptop. I glanced at Mr. Eddy, who raised his eyebrows. "Those aren't allowed," he said, "unless they have special permission. And I don't remember giving Marci permission."

I extracted the computer. It was black, with a silver stripe across the center of the top. DELL was circled in the middle.

"Something tells me this is an XPS," I said.

"Think it's Samantha's?"

"I'm almost sure of it."

I pushed the button to turn it on. Nothing.

"Battery's dead." Kirk said.

I put the laptop aside and began to pull books out of Marci's locker. I went through all of them, but didn't see any notes or anything important. I put them back they way they were, and pulled out the three-ring notebooks, one at a time.

Marci had good grades. Spectacular grades, in fact. All A's, from what I could see. I commented on it.

"Oh, yes, Marci is one of our best students. I hate to think that she's involved in all this. She has a bright future," Mr. Eddy said, "if she can stay on the right path."

The third notebook I opened, a white binder with MARCI outlined in sparkly little heart-stickers on the front, had a cell phone tucked into the front pocket. It was a red Nokia, flip style. I opened it and punched the power button. Nothing there, either.

"Another dead battery," Kirk said.

I was willing to bet a year's salary that the phone was Samantha's, too. It had been in Marci's possession the whole time, and she hadn't told anyone.

I needed to get with Stringfellow. These items might now be evidence, and I didn't want to screw up anything should the case ever go to court, if anyone was ever arrested and charged for Jean's murder. Especially if that person was Samantha. I pulled out my own cell phone.

I told the person who answered at the Homewood police station I needed to talk to Jonathan Stringfellow urgently and gave them my number, and they said they'd have him call me. I closed Marci's door and leaned against the locker.

"Should you have done that?" Kirk asked.

"What do you mean?"

"Well, what if Stringfellow just marches in here and takes everything?"

"You think he'd do that?"

"I'm almost sure of it. What's to stop him? It might be

134

evidence."

"Then let's get out of here."

We said goodbye to Mr. Eddy and thanked him for his help. I asked him not to say anything to Marci when she arrived at school on Tuesday. I wanted to see the reaction from her, and her friends, when she discovered the computer and the phone were missing.

As we walked out the glass front doors, Kirk asked, "Where are we going?"

"Somewhere where we can see what's on the computer and cell phone."

"And where would that be?"

I pulled out my cell phone and speed-dialed Grant.

"Hey you," he answered.

"I need you to meet me at your shop as soon as you can get there."

"Sure. Why?"

"I'll explain when I see you."

"Okay. Is anything wrong?"

"No, I'll see you in a few minutes." I hung up.

Kirk grinned. "So we're going to see Minivan Man, huh? I can't wait to meet him."

God help me.

Chapter Twenty Two

Kirk tailgated me the whole way to High Tech., and it annoyed me.

"You drive too slow," he said as he exited his Infiniti.

"You were almost in my trunk, for God's sake."

I carried the computer and the phone to the glass front door, the smell of coffee in the air from the Starbuck's next door. Grant hadn't arrived yet. My cell phone rang. I handed the stuff to Kirk and checked the caller ID.

"That's Stringfellow."

"Don't answer it."

"Why?"

"Let's just see what we've got first, okay?"

"I don't know—" It rang again and again. I hit ignore, and felt really guilty. "He's going to be furious."

"Just tell him you didn't hear it ring." He handed the laptop and the phone back to me.

"You are so sneaky."

He winked at me and smiled. Grant's van pulled into the parking lot. He looked good, in an olive green pocket t-shirt and jeans. The shirt complemented his eyes.

I was dreading this moment. "Hi," I said to him.

"Hi." He bent down and kissed me on the lips quickly, which surprised me. Grant was an affectionate guy, just not in public. Then he focused on Kirk. I swear Kirk was trying not to stand on his toes. Grant towered over him by at least four inches.

"Grant, this is Kirk Mahoney. Kirk, Grant Summerville." I wanted to get in the store and get going on the computer.

Grant pushed his glasses up on his nose and offered Kirk a hand. "Hello. I've heard a lot about you."

"Same here." The handshake was firm. Please, God, help me get through this, I thought.

Grant opened the door and turned on the lights. I put the laptop and the cell phone on the long counter that separated the sales floor from the back. Grant had trestle tables lining the back wall, all covered with computers of various types and in different stages of repair.

"What's up?"

I pointed to the laptop. "I need to know what's on this computer. The battery's dead, though, and I don't have the cord."

"I'm sure I've got something. Hang on." He went to the storage room in the back corner.

"Nice guy," Kirk said, browsing a rack full of computer games.

"Yep."

Grant returned with a worn, off-white cardboard box. He placed it on the counter and looked at Samantha's laptop. "Dell XPS Studio 16," he muttered, and glanced at the port on the back. He searched in the box for a minute and said, "Aha!"

"Got it?"

"This should do it." He pulled out a black cord that was neatly wrapped. "You want to come back here?"

Kirk and I joined him behind the counter. He sat at one of the tables that had a power strip and some other computer equipment on it, and plugged everything in. He pushed his glasses up again, and turned the laptop on.

The Windows logo glowed on the screen as it booted. Grant pulled up the main menu and typed a few commands. "Okay, he said, "What are we looking for?" he asked.

"I'm not sure. The computer belonged to the woman that was murdered last week, and her daughter. I'd like to know what's on the hard drive, and what websites she's visited. Can you do that?"

"Sure. Easy."

He glanced through the hard drive's menu. There was a file labeled "Samantha" that contained a couple of projects for school. Her mother had some files, too, of financial stuff and the contract for the purchase of the townhouse. As we looked through all of it, my cell phone rang again. Stringfellow, J was on my caller ID.

"Hold off," Kirk said.

"No, I have to answer this time." I excused myself and went to the front of the store.

I told Stringfellow I had a lot to discuss with him, and that we had found Samantha and Jean's computer. I gave him directions to High Tech, and he said he was on his way.

Kirk was peeved when I returned the area behind the counter and told him Stringfellow would be here soon. "Great," he said. "I just hope we find something useful before the computer's gone."

The rest of the hard drive didn't reveal much. A few pictures, some of Samantha and Jean at a beach, and a few of Samantha and Marci. Grant checked the email account. There were a few from some women that I assumed were friends of Jean's, mostly jokes and pictures making the rounds on the Web. Some ads, from Pottery Barn and a women's boutique.

Then, something from Frank at wellstoneinc.com. "Wait," I said, "Let's look at that one." He pulled it up. It was a reply from an email that Jean had sent him. Grant scrolled down to view the first email, from jrchambless at charter.net, from the last Thursday in August. The day before she was killed.

"Admiral found out. He's pissed. He fired me."

That was all it said. Frank's response was next, later that same day.

"Jean, I'm sorry, but there's no way I can hire another person right now. I don't have the money. I hope you understand."

Then, Jean's reply, almost immediately.

"I understand that the whole damn thing was your idea. Your bad idea. And now I'm fucked. Screw you, Frank."

That was the last message.

"I guess they broke up," I said.

"You think?" Grant said.

So now Frank had a motive for Jean's death. If being told screw you counted as motive. And here was Admiral's name again, and he was angry at Jean. What on earth had she done to her boss? Something so bad he'd want her dead?

Grant pulled up Internet Explorer and hit the control H.

"What are you doing?" I asked as a side menu popped up. It was divided by weeks.

"Seeing what websites they've been to. I can do it one of two ways. I can go to the history, which is what I'm doing now, or I can look at the cookies. See here," he clicked on "Last week" and pointed to the screen and a long list of websites. "She's been to Yahoo, Google, and here's some links to CNN. Pogo. That's a game site. Some links to Myspace and Facebook. Huh," he said.

"What?"

"This one is a bit weird." He pointed to another link. It said bu2fulls.com. "Someone's been there a few times."

"Beautiful ones dot com," I sounded out.

"Sounds like a porn site," Kirk scoffed.

"Yeah, it does." Grant typed in the name. "Well, here goes."

The website had a light tan background. Beautiful Ones Modeling and Talent Agency, said the title, in a fancy pink font. About twelve thumbnail-sized images of girl's faces crowded together in a grid near the center of the screen. They looked to be all ages, from teens to young adults, and even some older women. Below them was another, smaller grid of boys and men. Grant clicked one of the girls, and four pictures filled the screen.

First was a head shot. She looked about twenty, and was dressed in a red top with spaghetti straps. Her blond hair was thick and one side was tucked behind her ear. Her blue eyes were nicely made-up. She leaned forward, her lips covered in bright red lipstick and parted slightly in a cute grin. Next to that picture was one of her face and torso, in a printed red top. The next row showed her in a fancy, strapless red dress, spotlights shining on her and showing off her tan. Last in the group was a bikini shot. Red, of course. She relaxed on a lounge chair by a pool. "Rubie" was the caption under the picture. They were all good photos. Professionally done.

Grant navigated back to the home page and clicked on another girl's face. The head shot of the girl showed her in a white t-shirt. In the next, she waved playfully at the camera, her long brown hair flowing over her shoulders. She was dressed in a medley of white outfits, and her name was "Angel", according to the caption.

Back at the home screen, I spotted a picture I wanted to see. "Click on that one, please."

A large version of a picture of Samantha filled the screen, along with three others. Her head shot was the one I'd seen on her Facebook page, in the lacy aqua halter top. The next photo was her in a blouse of the same color, with long flowing sleeves. The turquoise enhanced her features, especially her auburn hair. The lighting was soft. Innocence and beauty all in one.

The third photo was Samantha in a long dress, haltered with rhinestones at the top and the same blue-green tone. For the swimsuit picture, she knelt in a pile of white sand, and the pose accentuated her long torso and limbs. The bright aqua bikini she wore was low cut, the tops of her new breasts peeking out. The bottom of the bathing suit was tied on the sides and sat high on her hips, which were dusted with the sand. A palm frond was to her left, a beach ball on her right, in front of a painted blue-sky background. It was inappropriately sexy, particularly if you knew her age. "Sandy" was the caption under the photo.

"Wow," Kirk said. "She's hot."

I reached over and slapped him, hard, on the shoulder.

"Ow! What the hell!"

"She is **not** hot! She is thirteen years old!"

"No way! That's Samantha?"

"That's her, you sick bastard."

He leaned in closer, squinting at the screen. "She sure doesn't look thirteen."

"She sure doesn't." Grant ducked in the chair. "Don't hit me."

"No," I agreed. "She really doesn't. I wonder who took that picture and how it got here?"

He returned to the home screen. I spotted another picture. "Grant, let me see that one." He clicked the thumbnail image.

Four professional pictures again. The headshot was particularly good. The third picture in the set showed the girl in a slinky red dress, the satin tight on her curvaceous hips. She was tall, with long brown hair and flawless tan skin. In the fourth photo, she looked like she was dancing, arms in the air and a bright smile on her young face. On her head was a large red headdress, with lots of feathers. Her bikini was red, too, draped in a ton of beads and a fringe of shiny ribbon. A set behind her showed a float crowded with more partygoers. "Doce" was her caption.

"Ooh la la," Kirk said. "I love Carnival."

I raised my hand to hit him again.

He flinched. "What?"

"That's Samantha's best friend. Her name's Marci. She's also thirteen."

"Damn," Kirk said. "She'd almost be worth the jail time."

"Knock it off."

"What kind of name is Doce, anyway?" Kirk asked.

Grant pronounced it correctly for him. "It's the Portuguese word for sweet."

"Oh, well then, it fits."

Grant returned to the home screen. Underneath the cluster of photos was an invitation to contact Beautiful Ones Modeling and Talent for more information on their models. They offered in-house photography and makeovers, as well. There was an email address only.

I said, "Samantha's boyfriend told me she did some modeling locally. I guess this is her agency. Maybe I can get in touch with someone there and see if anyone's heard from her." I borrowed a pen from Grant and wrote down the email address, info@bu2full5.com.

Grant scrolled back to Samantha's four photos and clicked on the one of her in the bikini. An even larger version of it filled the screen. She had the body for it, I had to admit. And the height. Even at her age. And I never would have guessed she was thirteen from that picture, if I didn't know her.

Suddenly, from behind us, a man's voice rang out. "What in the hell are you all doing?"

Chapter Twenty-three

I whirled around, startled. "Detective Stringfellow!"

"Uh-oh," Grant muttered. Kirk looked sheepish.

"What's going on?" the detective asked.

I motioned for him to follow me outside. Grant and Kirk went back to studying the photos, looking at the girls.

"We found Jean's computer," I began, once we were outside on the sidewalk.

"Yes, you said that. So you decided to use it to surf porn?"

"It wasn't porn. That was a picture of Samantha." I paused. "I'm not exactly sure where to start. Samantha did some modeling here in Birmingham, and we think that's the agency she used. I'm going to contact them to see if they've heard from her. But that's not the most important thing we've discovered. Jean Chambless was having an affair with a man named Frank Weller. He owns the construction company that's building the golf resort where her body was found."

"How do you know that?"

"From his son, Kyle. Kyle is a friend of Samantha's. He's one of the boys from those pictures in Samantha's bedroom. Only here's the deal, Kyle can't be involved. You've got to promise me this information won't be traced back to him."

"Whoa, whoa. Slow down. I can't promise anything yet."

"Please? His father has a horrible temper and I'm very concerned for Kyle's safety."

"Frank Weller has a DHS record?"

"Oh, big time."

"I see. Would my department have a record of Mr. Weller's behavior?"

"Yep. So, by the way, would Children's Hospital. And the Jefferson County Family Court."

"I'll check on that. And I think I can swing it so that Kyle's not involved."

"Thank you. There's more." I told him about finding the computer in Marci's locker at school, and the angry email between Jean and Frank and her mention of Admiral. "She said Admiral was mad at her. We think he was her boss."

"Yeah, we sent someone over to talk to her ex-husband in Mississippi. He told us that's who she worked for."

"Any idea who this Admiral might be?" I asked.

"Nope. We used to have one of those poker places here in

Homewood, but we shut it down. I've got word out to some folks on the city department and the Sheriff's office, asking who he might be, but no response yet."

"Kirk is trying to track him down, too, but hasn't had any luck yet either."

"That's the guy from the newspaper, right?"

"Right. The other guy is my boyfriend, Grant Summerville. He owns this place."

"Anything else?"

"We found a cell phone, too. I think it's Samantha's. We haven't looked at it yet."

The detective took a deep breath in frustration. "I was hoping I could get some of this investigation done without it being in the paper."

"Kirk's a reasonable guy. I bet he'd hold the story for a while, if you asked him to. As long as he gets to report it eventually."

"And I'm going to have to haul this Frank Weller in for questioning. Now."

"How long will that take?"

"Two hours, maybe longer. Depends on what happens. Why?"

"I'm just trying to see if I need to find a place for Kyle to live. I know he wants to go live with his mother in Muscle Shoals. Her name's Denise."

"I need to talk to her, too."

"Why?"

He gave me a small grin. "The woman her husband was sleeping with winds up dead in the woods. I'd say that makes her a suspect, wouldn't you?"

Shit. I hadn't thought about that. It sure would. Muscle Shoals was only two hours away. It would be no trick for Denise Weller to come down here and commit murder. Kyle had mentioned how angry she was about Frank cheating on her. Again. She'd had enough. Was she mad enough to kill Jean? I bit my lip. I wondered if Kyle suspected his own mother of murder.

Stringfellow said he wanted to go in and monitor what Kirk and Grant were doing. I followed him back into the store and behind the counter.

Grant was doing something to Jean's computer. He had a screwdriver out and was putting something back in the bottom of it. He finished tightening the screw, flipped it over, and showed Detective Stringfellow the pictures of Samantha and Marci.

"Can we see that cell phone?" the Detective asked.

144

"The battery's dead." I said.

"I'm sure I've got something that would work," Grant said. He went back to the tea-colored box and found an unwrapped cord. "This should do it."

He brought the cell phone to the table and plugged it in. It chirped a little tune and soon the main screen appeared. There was a photo behind all the icons on the screen. Samantha and Marci, arms around each other's shoulders, making silly faces. Suddenly, I was nearly overwhelmed with sadness. These poor kids, dealing with a dead mother and a missing best friend.

I peered over Grant's forearm and looked at the small screen. He read the highlights. "There are six text messages, and at least one voicemail." He hit the button for the voicemail, and put the sound on speakerphone.

"You have eight new messages," an electronic female voice said. "First message."

"Hey Sam, it's Mom. I can pick you up after my job interview. Should be about six thirty. Love you." The message ended. The electronic lady's voice said, "Received Friday, August twenty-eight at four thirty nine p.m. Press seven to delete. Next message."

It creeped me out, hearing Jean's voice. It was a pleasant voice, too, and the care she felt for Samantha was evident. She didn't sound distressed or worried at all. The anger she'd written to Frank the day before wasn't in her voice. I bet she had no idea that she was going to be shot in the head within forty-eight hours. And now she was gone. I felt a lump rise in my throat and controlled myself, quickly.

The next message played. "Hey, where are you? Call me."

Marci. The female voice told us that it had been received Friday night at eight twenty three. She said the delete cue again, and then the next message came on. "Hey girl, it's Pat. Give me a buzz. Bye." The message was left Tuesday afternoon, September first, at three ten, the day I'd gotten custody of her.

Pat was a man. A grown man. Why was he calling a thirteen year old girl? Worse case scenario, it was someone she was seeing. Dating seemed like a foolish term for it. Someone she was sleeping with, maybe? Someone she had met online, thanks to those pictures? The creeped-out feeling got worse.

"Who's that?" Kirk asked.

"Good question."

"Her dad, maybe?" Grant asked me.

"She has two of them and they are Kenny and Bobby. But the

145

guy she called from the gas station, wasn't he named Pat?"

Stringfellow said, "Yeah, Patrick Merrick."

"Let's check her contact list." Grant said.

Grant pushed the button. First names appeared, and they included Braden and Marci, Mom, and then, Pat.

"Here we go," Grant said. He hit another button, and the number appeared. It was the 910 prefix, the same number Samantha had called from the gas station.

"Well," I said. "That looks familiar."

"It sure does," Stringfellow said. "Hell, it's the same damn guy. And he said he had no idea who she was."

"He lied," I said.

"I want to talk to him," Stringfellow said.

Grant pushed the button to dial the number and we all listened. He got the same voicemail I got when I'd called the number from the gas station. Grant handed the phone to Stringfellow, who left a stern message to call him about Samantha Chambless. He left his number.

"We'll see what happens," he said, after he hung up. "I'll see if I can get more information on this Patrick Merrick guy."

We went back to Samantha's voicemail. The next message was Braden, asking her to call him. That one was Wednesday, the day after she'd disappeared on me the first time. The next four messages were also from Braden, his tone of voice increasingly worried with every one. The text messages were all from him, too. Marci hadn't called or texted, I noted. She knew Samantha wouldn't receive any of the messages, because her phone was locked in her locker.

Lots of questions, I thought. And every time we answered one, another popped up. I ran a hand over my eyes and sighed.

Then I said, "Oh, Grant, the detective needs to see Jean's email, too."

He brought up the account, and Stringfellow read the exchange between Frank and Jean. "I'll need the computer and the phone," he said when he was finished. "And I'm bringing Frank Weller in for questioning."

I had to admit, it seemed like Frank was the most likely suspect at this point. Jean's body had been found close to his work site, and he hadn't told the police anything about his relationship with her. He should be very nervous, I thought. I would be.

"Detective, when will you be picking him up?" Kirk asked.

"As soon as I can find him."

"Mind if I tag along?"

"I can't stop you."

I gave the detective the Weller's address on Kensington, and he promised to keep Kyle out of it if he could. Grant unplugged the computer and phone and handed them over.

Kirk bent down like he was going to kiss me on the cheek, but then glanced at Grant and stopped. "Bye," he said, and quickly followed Stringfellow out the door.

I felt totally defeated and a little sorrowful. I leaned against the long red counter that spanned the length of the store, folded my arms and stared at the floor.

Pat/Patrick was bothering me. Who was he? He was evidently who Samantha had run to when she left Nettie's. He was certainly old enough to drive. I wondered if he owned a blue SUV. My head was spinning with all the unanswered questions.

Grant walked over and put his arms around me, drawing me into a hug. He kissed the top of my head. "You okay?"

"A little sad, for some reason. I think it's from hearing Jean's voice."

"Yeah, that's understandable."

"What a mess. Poor Jean. And Samantha and Marci, too. And I'm concerned about those pictures. Especially the ones in the bikinis. I know it's not exactly porn, but I'm afraid someone is taking advantage of all those young girls. And I'm mad that Detective Stringfellow had to take that computer and cell phone. I'm not sure we saw everything on it. We may have missed something."

"No worries."

"What do you mean?"

He nodded to a yellow box on the table, next to another laptop. I knew the laptop was his. "I made a forensic copy," he said.

"A forensic copy?"

"Of her computer. It's all on there."

"Really?"

"Yep. All the files."

"When?"

"While you were outside with the detective. There wasn't much on it, so it didn't take long."

I smiled. "I love you."

He laughed, then suddenly turned serious. "Really?"

Oh, my God. What the hell had I just said?

Chapter Twenty Four

I felt the blood rush to my feet. I'd said it as joke. Sort of. I really did care for Grant. But was I ready to be in love? Whatever that meant? Commitment, for a start. I began to panic, and he saw it.

"I'm sorry," he said.

"No, no, I do mean it. I think."

He laughed and kissed me on the top of the head again. "Well, I love you, too, I think."

"Let's just leave it at that."

"Deal. Are you hungry?"

It was past suppertime. We decided to go to Grant's place and order pizza, the number one food group in his diet. I was getting used to it, but envied the fact that he could eat like this every day and never gain any weight.

I spent the night and slept late. Grant woke me up with a hot cup of coffee and a kiss. I rubbed my eyes and asked, "What time is it?"

"Ten minutes to ten."

"Oh, damn." I took a gulp of coffee and crawled out of the sheets.

"What?"

"I have plans with someone."

"I see. So it's wham-bam-thank-you-sir."

I laughed, walked to his bathroom and put toothpaste on my toothbrush. "It's one of my clients. In a way. Really cute thirteen year old girl, and she and her family are going through a rough time. I scrounged up some money and promised to take her shopping for school clothes."

"That's sweet."

"What are you doing today?"

He shrugged. "My parents rented a house up at Smith Lake, so I'm not seeing them today. I guess I'll catch up on some work. I'm going to go through all those files that I copied yesterday from your client's laptop, see if I can find anything else. I doubt it, but I'll give it a shot."

"Do you have today's newspaper?"

"It should be downstairs in the box."

"Will you run and get it for me?"

I showered quickly while Grant got the paper. I towel-dried my hair and threw on my clothes from yesterday. I needed to bring a few outfits over here, since I was spending the night more and more frequently.

When I finished dressing, the newspaper lay on the bar that separated the kitchen from the living room. Grant was looking at the front page. "It's a good article," he said, and passed it to me.

SUSPECT QUESTIONED IN GOLF RESORT MURDER, the headline said. The color picture underneath showed Detective Stringfellow and Frank Weller walking into the Homewood Police station. He wasn't in handcuffs, I noted, so he wasn't in custody that I could see. Yet.

I skimmed the article. Kirk had included a brief bio of Frank, from his background in construction engineering to his founding of Wellstone eleven years ago. He quoted "sources"-- and I guessed that was me--who revealed his relationship with Jean Chambless, and said that Denise Weller, his soon-to-be-ex-wife, refused to comment when contacted by the paper. His history of arrest for assault was covered, briefly, but with no mention of Kyle. That was good. Kyle's life was difficult enough already without it being in the media.

I kissed Grant goodbye quickly and sped up Shades Mountain to my neighborhood. I fetched my own newspaper out of the yard before throwing on some clean jeans and a pink t-shirt. I sped, again, to Midfield, and was only about ten minutes late picking up LaReesa at her grandmother's.

"You're late," she said as she opened the door.

"I'm sorry, I overslept. Forgive me?"

"I guess."

The inside of the house was chaotic. DeCameron was in the living room with the mismatched sofas, in nothing but his diaper and playing with a plastic car that was emitting a loud siren. Two girls, still in their pajamas, were in the dining room chatting happily. Little plastic beads were scattered all over the table. They were threading them on white string. DeCora and DeCaria, I remembered. DeCora, the six year old, showed me the colorful half-necklace she'd constructed with pride. DeCaria was helping her, she told me. They were both really cute girls.

"Where's your grandmother?" I asked.

"She's in her bedroom, watching her stories," DeCaria said.

"I need to talk to her."

LaReesa went and got Estelle, who was in the blue housecoat again. She nodded to me in greeting. I told her that LaReesa and I were going shopping and I'd have her back around three. I told her I thought I had some clothes for the other children that might fit, and if it was okay, I'd bring them by tomorrow afternoon. She said fine and went back to her room. I had the feeling that LaReesa had woken her up, and she was going back to sleep. At any rate, she wasn't exactly thrilled to see me.

LaReesa and I headed for the suburb of Hoover and the Galleria Mall. The area around the shopping center was crowded with just about every retail outlet imaginable, it seemed. I asked her what she wanted for lunch.

"Barbeque."

"Okay." Interesting choice. I would've expected a hamburger. There was a Jim 'N Nicks restaurant just down the street, and minutes later we were seated in a booth. LaReesa was smiling as she studied the menu.

"I ain't never ate here before."

"It's great food." I studied the salads. After the pizza last night, I had to be good. We ordered and as the waitress brought our drinks, my cell phone rang.

Kirk. I answered it.

"My friend called and he's found the Admiral."

"Really?"

"Yep. Real name's Ari Levi. He's a young guy, too, like twenty-four. Supposed to be a hell of a poker player. Plays in some of the national tournaments, the ones you see on TV."

"Why is he called the Admiral, then? I thought he'd be someone from the Navy."

Kirk laughed. "It's a poker term, apparently. Full houses are also called full boats, and if you have a lot of full boats--"

"You're an Admiral. Got it."

"Right. Anyway, his place of business is in Vestavia Hills, off Highway 31. It's closed tonight because of the holiday, but my source says there will probably be a game tomorrow night. Do you want to go?"

"Do you honestly think they'll even talk to us?"

"I can be pretty forceful, if I need to be."

"They could be murderers, Kirk, I don't know--"

"Chicken."

"Fine. What time?"

"I'll pick you up at eight."

"That late?"

"My friend says the games don't start till eight-thirty or nine. That way there's time for everyone to tuck the kids in bed before heading out to blow the mortgage."

I groaned. I wasn't looking forward to this. I told Kirk I'd see him tomorrow and hung up.

"Who could be murderers?" LaReesa asked.

"What?"

"You said some folks could be murderers. Who?"

"Oh, don't worry about it. It has to do with that missing girl I was asking you about when we first met."

"Did you ever find her?"

"Briefly, then she disappeared again."

"You think she's dead?"

"I hope not."

LaReesa played with the straw in her Coke. "Why'd she run away?"

"Her mother was murdered last weekend. That probably had something to do with it."

"That sucks."

"Yes, it does."

She slurped soda out of the bottom of her straw, then said, "I've thought about runnin' away."

"When?"

"All the time."

"Why?"

She shrugged. "I dunno. I gets mad at my grandma sometimes. Real mad. Like when she hits me and stuff. And my mom wouldn't care if I left. Sometimes I think she'd be better off."

"Better off if you weren't around?"

"Yep." She loaded some ice in her straw and ate it.

I took a sip of my iced tea and thought about that for a minute. Poor kid. What must it be like to think that nobody wants you? Nobody loves you? "I think they'd miss you."

"Nope." Crunch, crunch.

"*I'd* miss you."

LaReesa smiled.

"Where would you run to, if you ran?"

She shrugged again. "I dunno. Lots of places to go."

"Is there?"

"Sure. My friend's houses, maybe. Or there are things I could do."

"Do?"

"For money."

My stomach sank. "Like what?"

"Sell drugs."

152

"Seriously?"

"Sure. Dealers are always looking for kids to do that stuff. Keeps them outta jail, and kids never get no real long sentence."

"Yes, they do."

"But you're out when you're twenty-one. And it's just weed. And some pills. Ain't no big thing."

"You haven't sold drugs. Please tell me you haven't sold drugs."

"Just once or twice. It's no big deal. Good money, too. It helps my mom."

"Does she know where the money comes from?"

"She don't ask."

I closed my eyes. LaReesa's revelations were about to force me to open a DHS investigation. For real, this time.

"Anyway," she continued, "that was a while ago. I ain't sold nothin' in a long time."

"Good."

The waitress brought LaReesa's pulled pork sandwich with onion rings and my Pig in the Garden salad. LaReesa scowled at mine. "Mine looks better."

"Sure does," I said, and stole an onion ring off her plate.

"Hey!"

We ate for a few minutes. Then I said, "Look, we need to talk about this shopping trip."

"Okay. Where are we going?"

"I figured we'd start at Wal-Mart or Target. We can get the best deals there."

She wiped barbeque sauce off her lips. "Okay."

"You have seventy dollars. That's it. And I want you to get clothes that fit well. Maybe even a little big, so they'll last a while."

She rolled her eyes at me. "You sound like my mother."

"Thank you. I'm serious. You shouldn't wear things that are too sexy or too tight to school."

"It all has to be school clothes?" She looked so disappointed.

"We'll see. But the school clothes have to fit appropriately, agreed?"

"Okay."

I paid the check and we started at Wal-Mart. We found several cute short-sleeved white shirts, some polo-style and some button-down, on sale. Found four pairs of pants, two black and two navy, that fit well for a great price. I told LaReesa she could pick out a non-school outfit of her choice, and found a chair near the dressing

153

rooms.

My cell phone rang again as I waited for her. Grant.

"Hey," I answered.

"Hi sweetie. How goes the shopping?"

"We're doing well. Almost done. What are you doing?"

"I'm at High Tech. I was getting some work finished, but I'm about to start looking at your client's computer stuff. Just to make sure we didn't miss anything."

"Is there any way to figure out who owns that website? Where her pictures are?"

"Um, maybe."

"What's that mean?"

"All websites are supposed to be registered, but sometimes it's an agency and we won't get too much information."

"I don't understand," I said. LaReesa appeared from the floor, a bright pink shirt draped over her arm and another big smile on her gap-toothed face.

"It might be some company," Grant said. "There's no way to get the real owner's name from that source."

"So how do you find out who runs it? I mean, what if it was pornography, or something worse? You'd think there'd be a way."

"There is a way, young Padawan. Be patient. Can you come here when you're finished?"

"Yep, see you in about an hour."

Grant and I hung up, and LaReesa asked, "Can I try this on?"

"Sure."

The outfit was cute, a short-sleeved graphic pink hoodie and a pair of white Bermuda shorts. She decided to get it and we checked out and loaded all the stuff onto the back seat of my Honda Civic.

"Thanks," LaReesa said, once we were on our way back to her house.

"You're welcome."

"Who were you talking to, back there?"

"When?"

"On the phone, when I walked up."

"My boyfriend."

"Ooo-ooh," she said, and made kissing noises.

"Yeah, yeah."

"Why were you talking about porn?"

"Were we?"

"Uh huh."

I'd have to watch my mouth around LaReesa, I thought. She

154

didn't miss anything.

"You didn't answer me," she said.

"I know."

"Well, why? You into that?"

I laughed. "No. We were just talking, that's all."

"Porn ain't no big thing, you know."

Chapter Twenty Five

It was all I could do not to slam on the brakes in the middle of the interstate.

"What!" I said, loud.

"Porn ain't no big thing. I don't know why everybody gets so weird about it."

"Of course it's a big thing."

"Why? It's just your body. Nothing to be 'shamed of."

"LaReesa--"

"What?"

How was I going to do this? How would I explain modesty and privacy to a girl who'd never had them? "Putting sexy pictures of yourself on the Internet can have serious consequences. You never know who's going to see them, And it could be dangerous."

"Whatever."

I felt like I was trying to cross the generation gap without a rope.

"I've had sex. It's no big deal." LaReesa continued.

For some reason that confession didn't surprise me. "I hope you were careful. Sex is one thing, babies are another."

"I was careful. I don't want a baby."

"Good."

"I just don't see why everybody freaks out about it."

"It's just a big decision, that's all, to be sexually active. I hope that you'll always be careful and use a condom."

"Now you sound like a social worker."

I laughed, and turned onto her grandmother's street. I helped LaReesa unload everything and watched while she carefully hung it up in a meager closet in her bedroom. There wasn't much room. She shared the bedroom with both DeCora and DeCaria, and the small room was crowded with a dresser, a set of bunk beds and another single bed. Her third of the closet wasn't much, but she managed to get it all in. I didn't see Estelle at all.

I said goodbye to LaReesa and said I'd be by tomorrow with some things for her cousins and headed to Grant's shop. I stopped by the Starbuck's on my way in and bought us both a couple of tall lattes. He unlocked the door for me when I knocked with my elbow, hands full of coffees.

"Thanks," he said, taking the hot cup from me.

"You're welcome. Any luck with the laptop's contents?"

"Not much so far. Most of it we've already seen."

"Damn."

"I didn't think there'd be a lot of other stuff on it."

"You said we could trace that website, though?"

"Yep, come on."

I followed him to the back of the shop with my cup. He sat in front of a machine on one of the tables. The area around it was scattered with CD ROMs and papers with instructions on them. "Grab a chair," he said, shoving some of the junk aside.

I scooted a folding metal chair over from a corner. Grant brought up whois.com and chose to do a lookup. He entered the Beautiful Ones website address, and a numeric security key, and hit "search".

A page of information appeared. Most of it was legal jargon that I didn't even try to understand. "That's what I was afraid of," he said. "Nothing there."

"Damn."

"Wait, though. I've got an idea."

He pulled up the command prompt, and on the black screen typed "tracert www.bu2fulls.com"

"What's that?" I asked.

"I'm trying to get the IP address."

Five columns of numbers and letters appeared. I didn't understand any of them, but it was clear Grant did. He pulled up an internet browser and entered www.whatismyipaddress.com.

"What—"

"Hang on." He clicked IP Lookup and entered the numbers from the command prompt into a search box, and then said, "Bingo."

"What?"

"Look." He scrolled down the page. A section was labeled "General Information" and it held the name of a company, Keepers of Time Photography. There was even a map. It was local, and the address was close to the southern area of Birmingham, near Redmont. The same area where mysterious Patrick's business was located. I'd bet it was the same place. "It's not an individual name, but at least it's a start."

"True." I wrote the address down on a Post-it from Grant's table. "I think I'll head over there."

"I doubt they'll be open. It's a holiday. And it's late."

He was right. It would have to wait until tomorrow. I let out a frustrated sigh.

"Hey," he said, slipping his arm around my shoulders. "What

say we go to your house and grill some burgers, maybe? You need to relax a while. There's nothing more you can do today, anyway."

"You're right. You mind if I ask my father to join us?"

"Of course not."

Grant locked High Tech and followed me to the Piggly Wiggly in my neighborhood, where we stocked up on beer, ground beef, buns and all the stuff to make potato salad and baked beans. I bought a box of veggie burgers for Dad, and called him on my cell phone. He agreed to join us for dinner. We got to my house about five o'clock, and by the time the burgers were ready to go on the grill, Dad arrived.

It was a lovely evening. The temperature had moderated a little and it was in the high sixties. The three of us ate at the table on the back patio, watching a parade of birds peck at the sunflower seeds in my feeder in the twilight. I sipped a Michelob and wondered numerous times where Samantha was. I hoped she was under shelter, and that it was not just a bridge somewhere.

Grant stayed until ten. Dad left about the same time. I spent a little time catching up on emails and bills before hitting the sack.

Tuesday I was slammed. Two emergencies, one involving a kid who had blown his placement, and another new case involving two little ones I had to take into care from the hospital, a drug-exposed newborn baby and a toddler. Foster homes were filling up fast and it was difficult to find a place to put them. By November, it would be nearly impossible. Russell was sweet, agreeing to deliver the kids to their foster parents in the afternoon so I could get to E.W. Dodge.

I got there just after lunch. Mr. Eddy greeted me. I asked him if Marci was in school, and she was. He hadn't spoken to her yet. He sent an office aide to get her out of class and let me use his office to talk to her. I sat in one of the chairs and waited.

She knocked gently on the door and peered in at me. She looked nervous, to say the least. Her eyes were tired, like she hadn't slept. Her graphic t-shirt and jeans were wrinkled. I motioned her in and asked her to sit down.

She sat on the edge of the chair, playing with the ends of her hair. "You remember me?" I asked.

"Sure."

"I went by your house this weekend. Did you and your family go out of town?"

She nodded. "We went to Atlanta for the weekend. You haven't found Sam yet?"

"No. But I'll tell you what I did find. Her computer, and her

159

phone. In your locker."

She stared at me, surprised. "You? You have them?"

"Why didn't you tell me you had her computer and her phone?"

She shrugged. "I don't know."

"How did you get them?"

"Sam gave them to me last week. On Friday. Her mom was mad at her and was going to take them away. For good. She asked me to hold them for her until things calmed down."

"What was her mom mad about?"

"Just stuff. You know."

"What stuff?"

"Just stuff. Can I have them back?"

"The police have them now."

She bit her lip and looked away from me, her big brown eyes filling with tears. "Why? Why'd you give them to the cops?"

"I had to. They might be evidence. You can see that, can't you? What's on them that's got you so worried?"

"I don't know. Nothing."

"Is it something to do with that modeling agency? Beautiful Ones?"

"No. It's nothing, really."

I didn't believe her.

"Can I go back to class?" She wiped her eyes with her fingertips, wiping away a bit of mascara. "Please?"

"Marci, if you know anything--"

"I don't! I have to get back to History." I could tell it was taking a lot for her to hold it together. "Please?"

"You still have my card?"

"Yes."

"Please call me if you hear from her, okay?"

"Sure." She left the office and Mr. Eddy joined me.

"What's up? She was bawling on the way back to class."

"I don't know. She's upset about something. I'm not sure what, specifically."

What was that all about? Was she upset about the computer and the cell phone being gone? What was on them that would have her so distraught? Or was it about Samantha, and the fight she'd had with her mom over the computer and phone? Could that be the reason for Jean's murder, and Marci knew it? People had been killed for less, I guess.

I thanked Mr. Eddy for his time and the use of his office and went back to my office to finish working on the two cases from this morning.

At four-thirty, I sped the few blocks to the Birmingham Financial Bank and took the elevator to Royanne's twelfth-floor office. I was jealous of her workspace: a large office with pretty gray-blue walls and comfortable upholstered chairs for her guests. And she had a whole wall of windows overlooking the city to the south. It was so unfair.

"Hey," I said, knocking on the door.

"Hey. I was starting to wonder if you were going to show up." She rose from her desk and grabbed a large white garbage bag from behind it. It was stuffed full.

"Sorry. Been busy."

"This is what I was able to dig up from the kid's closets and the daycare. I hope it's helpful."

"Thanks." I went through it. A lot of the items would probably fit DeCora. A few of the things looked to be DeCaria's size. There were several white t-shirts for DeCameron, too, and a pack of diapers.

"I'm sure they'll appreciate it," I said, packing it all back in the plastic bag. I walked over to the windows and gazed at Vulcan, our naked statue of the god of the forge on top of Red Mountain. He held a spear in his right hand, pointing up to the mass of cumulous clouds above. They were getting darker. It was going to rain.

"You okay?" Royanne asked.

"Yeah," I said, yawning with a hand over my mouth. "It's just been a long day." We chatted for a few minutes about what we'd done over the weekend, and agreed to do lunch as usual on Thursday before I gathered the white bag and took it to my car.

I got to LaReesa's about five thirty, just as it started to sprinkle. I could smell dinner cooking, and it smelled good. Like bacon. Estelle nodded to me from the kitchen and I walked back to tell her I'd brought some clothes for DeCora and DeCaria. She thanked me and called them from their room. We were trying things on in the living room, with LaReesa watching, when my cell phone rang.

Kirk. I stepped outside to the front porch to take it.

"We still on for tonight?" he asked.

"Yeah, that's fine. Eight, right?"

"Right."

"We got a little more info on Samantha's recent activities," I said. "Grant was able to trace that Beautiful Ones website to a photographer near Southside. His place is on Pawnee Avenue. I was going to go check it out today but got buried at work."

"What's it called?"

"Keepers of Time Photography. I wouldn't be surprised if it was owned by someone named Patrick Merrick. I'm guessing he might be the one who took the pictures of Samantha and Marci. Who knows, maybe he's heard from Samantha."

"That's a long shot."

"It's the only shot I've got."

I told Kirk I'd see him at eight and hung up. As I turned to go back in the house, I noticed the front door was cracked. LaReesa had been listening in.

She was near the door when I entered. "What's up?" she asked.

"Nothing."

"Was that about that missing girl?"

"Yep. I've got to go." I said goodbye to Estelle and all the girls and headed home. I showered and put on jeans and a yellow top. I had no idea what the dress code was at these places. I decided I was too casual and put on a dress. Then changed back again. I was nervous, and needed to calm down.

I ate a leftover burger and was ready when Kirk arrived. He was in jeans, too, which made me feel better. He opened the car door for me and we headed for Vestavia Hills, down the mountain and to the east.

It didn't take us long to get there. The building stood alone, hidden by plenty of trees, behind a sports-and-outdoors place. The neighboring buildings weren't very visible. Kirk parked his Infiniti in the small lot. I locked my purse and phone in the trunk of his car and we crossed the tarmac to the front door. No signs were present, no clue to what the place was. But I'd been here before and was struggling to remember when and why. I mentioned it to Kirk.

"It used to be Vincenza's, the Italian restaurant."

"Oh, yeah." I'd eaten there once. The food was expensive and not great. It made sense that they'd gone under.

The glass door was well lit, and a makeshift foyer had been constructed around it out of two-by-fours and unpainted plywood. Mounted to the top of the homemade wall that faced us was a small white camera. That was all I could see.

Kirk reached toward a small doorbell to the right of the door, and glanced at me. "Ready?" he asked.

"I guess."

He rang the bell.

Chapter Twenty Six

Nothing happened.

We waited, then Kirk leaned over and rang the bell again.

"Well?" I asked.

"Wait."

A man appeared, dressed in worn denim shorts and a faded black t-shirt. He was young and trim. His black hair was shaved close and his skin was a dark tan. His eyes were a light hazel. The eyes threw me off. They were very light for his face and met us with an intense gaze. He produced a key and unlocked the door before opening it a crack. "Help you?"

"We're looking for Ari Levi."

"That's me."

"I'm Kirk Mahoney, from the *News,* and this is Claire Conover from DHS. We'd like to talk to you about Jean Chambless."

"I've no interest in talking to the *News.*"

"I'm just gathering a little information—"

"No." He started to close the door.

"Wait!" I cried, grabbing the door handle. "Please. I've got custody of Jean's young daughter, and she's missing. It's very important that I talk to anyone who might know anything. Whatever you say doesn't have to go in the newspaper."

I shot Kirk a look. He opened his mouth, then closed it, then nodded. I knew he was furious at me.

Ari thought about it for a few seconds, then opened the door. "Put nothing in the paper. I'm serious."

"You have my word," Kirk said, and narrowed his eyes at me. Boy, was I going to get it later.

"Thanks," I said, as he held the door open for me. Kirk and I followed him through the gap in the plywood screen, which led to a large room. The last time I'd seen it, it had been filled with white-clothed tables, a Tuscan burnt orange on the walls and industrial brown carpet on the floor. The orange was still there and the carpet was much more worn. The dining tables had been replaced by poker tables. Seven of them, large and oval, with green felt over the tops and black padding around the edges. Small vinyl-covered chairs, also black, surrounded each one.

I stopped for a second to inspect the room. I couldn't remember what had been on the walls previously. Now there were gambling-themed posters framed in black. One from the movie *The Cooler*, with William H. Macy and Alec Baldwin, and another of

Rounders with Matt Damon.

I could see through to what used to be the kitchen, too, since the doors had been removed. In front of a long metal prep table, a woman worked. It looked like she was making sandwiches. Bottles of beer and liquor stood in rows on a table to the right, with a large bowl of ice. Plastic glasses stacked were beside it.

Kirk halted beside me. "What?" he whispered.

"I don't know. I thought it would be more subtle."

Ari went to one of the tables. Poker chips were stacked next to one of the stations and some cards were next to them. Ari rested on the edge of the table, his butt on the black padding, and pulled a plastic chip out his pocket. He played with it, rolling it back and forth over his fingers. "What is it you want to know?" he asked.

I said, "We were told Jean Chambless used to work here. Is that true?"

He nodded.

"What did she do?"

He shrugged. "Dealt games. Served food and drinks."

Much like the lady in the kitchen now, I thought. I wondered who she was, and if she'd known Jean. "She was fired, is that right?" I asked.

He nodded again.

"Why?" I asked.

"She stole from me. Cheated."

"Really? How?"

He stared at me for a few seconds. I couldn't read any emotion there. I didn't know if he thought I was an idiot for asking, or whether he was deciding to share that information with me or what. The guy had a hell of a poker face, for sure. I could sense Kirk getting frustrated. He fidgeted next to me.

Ari placed the chip back in his pocket, and reached around to pick up a deck of cards. He shuffled them easily. "She and a man named Frank Weller were in it together. I didn't know they were dating at first, so it took me a while to catch on."

"Go on."

"Jean was the dealer, and it's a simple trick, really. Has to do with how she collected the cards after each round." He shuffled again. "Do you play Hold 'Em?"

I shook my head and Kirk nodded. "But I've seen it on television," I offered.

He walked to behind the table, discarded the first card, and dealt four hands of two cards each, but they were face up. Average

164

hands, mostly, but one held an ace. Then he dealt the flop and the turn and the river, the cards in the middle of the table that everyone played. An eight, a five, two kings and an ace.

"So they play one hand, like so. Now watch." He gathered the cards. "See how I did that?"

"No," I said. Kirk shook his head.

"Watch." He dealt the same hands again, and the same flop, turn, and river. He collected the cards again. I watched carefully, and this time I could see him covertly slide the ace from the third hand into the deck, about four cards down. The other ace was on top of the deck, the one from the river.

"Oh!" I said. "You're stacking the deck."

Ari nodded. "Now it's just a matter of a false shuffle." He demonstrated. "Now watch. If Frank Weller was sitting in the first position, which he usually was..."

He dealt again. The first position got the two aces.

"Pocket aces," Kirk said.

"Exactly. Like I said, I didn't catch on at first. But Frank was winning. A lot. More than a person normally would, so I started to pay attention. Did a little investigating and found out they were a couple. I confronted Jean and she admitted the whole thing. Gave me some sob story about how his construction company was about to go under. I'll tell you like I told her. That is not my problem. I fired her, put the word out about what she'd done. She wouldn't have worked in Birmingham again. Not doing this."

"I'll bet she pissed you off," I said.

He gave me a condescending grin. "I didn't kill her. I don't know who did. But my first guess would be Frank. He has a temper, you know."

"Did you ever meet Jean's daughter, Samantha?" I asked.

"No. Jean told me about her, but she never brought her here, of course. No place for a child. I wouldn't allow it."

Laughter rang out from the front of the room, and two gentlemen entered. Kirk and I turned around to look. Both wore suits, ties loosened. One carried a paper bag that looked like it might contain a bottle of booze. Ari stood up straight and called, "Guys, I need a moment, please."

They both sobered, quickly, and walked back out the front door in a hurry. Ari returned his attention to me. "Anything else?"

I scanned the place again. I was full of questions, but didn't know how much I should ask. What the hell, I thought. "I just – I mean – all this is illegal, right? I mean, don't the police ever give

165

you any trouble?"

"We're a private club."

"But it's still against the law."

He shrugged. "My members are men who just want to get together and play a little game. The police have better things to do than bother us. Now, if you'll excuse me, I have some things I need to attend to." He walked past us, arm extended toward the door. We were being shown out, like it or not.

Ari locked the door behind us after wishing us good evening. A nervous tightness in my chest disappeared. The two men who interrupted us had vanished, but I suspected they'd be back.

Kirk didn't say word to me as we walked to his car. He opened my door for me and slammed it shut once I was inside. Then he strapped himself into his seat and cranked the engine.

"Look," I said.

"Thanks a whole hell of a lot for that!"

"Well, hell, you weren't getting anywhere turning the whole situation into a cock fight!"

"I was doing just fine, damn it."

"He wasn't even going to let us in the door. Besides, what did we even learn that you could put in an article?"

"That she worked there, for starters. Fuck!" He slapped his hand on the wheel.

I gave up. I wasn't going to argue with him. He took a right onto the highway and made his way to Tyler Road, which led to my neighborhood. He drove much too fast around the curves in the dark. I gripped the door handle. He screeched to a stop in front of my house a few minutes later. I scrambled out of the car.

He got out, too, and walked me to the door. He waited while I searched for my keys and unlocked it.

"I still don't see why you're so mad," I said. "I consider the whole night a bust. Ari didn't exactly confess to Jean's murder, you know. I don't think we learned a damn thing."

"Sure we did."

"What?"

"Did you see the two guys who came in?"

"Yeah. So?"

"One of them was Brad English. He's a big-time public relations guy. The other was Joseph Lawrence. He's a prominent businessman here, in technology services."

"How do you know? And so what?"

"It's my job to know. And what that tells us is that Ari Levi is not running a penny-ante poker stall. At these games, they bet a lot. A whole lot."

"Really?"

"Really. If Jean and Frank did get away with any money, it was probably thousands."

And that was enough to kill for, I thought.

I said goodnight to Kirk and entered the house. I heard his car roar away a minute later. I went into the kitchen. The microwave clock said twenty to ten. I wanted a glass of wine, but morning was just a few short hours away and wine would not do me any good. I reluctantly poured myself a glass of orange juice and wandered back into the living room, where I sank onto the sofa.

My answering machine light was blinking. I reached over to the end table where it sat and hit play.

"Hey," Grant said. "Call me when you get this. I don't care how late it is. I've got something you have to see."

Chapter Twenty Seven

I dialed Grant's number and he picked up after the first ring. "Where are you?" I asked.

"At my apartment," he said. "I'm sorry, but you have to see this, and you're not going to like it."

"What is it?"

"Something from Jean Chambless's computer."

"I'll be there as soon as I can."

I packed something to wear Wednesday, along with my makeup and hair dryer, and got to Grant's at nearly eleven. I was tired and ready to go to sleep. Whatever the hell he'd found had better be good, I thought. I let myself in the door and called out to him.

"Back here," he said. I made my way to his second bedroom, the one he used as his office. Trestle tables like the ones at High Tech lined the walls, and there was always at least one computer humming softly. He was seated at one of the tables, in front of a machine hooked up to one of his large monitors. I kissed him hello.

"Have a seat."

I rolled a small desk chair over and sat down. "What's so important?"

"I was going through the forensic copy of your girl's hard drive. I checked the browser cache to see if anything important had been deleted. Look." He clicked a button.

The monitor filled with a picture of a naked girl. My stomach tensed, then dropped. I felt sick. It was Samantha. Otherwise known as Sandy, or so the picture was labeled.

She was draped across a round, oversized brown leather ottoman. It sat in front of a stately marble fireplace, orange flames clear in the shot.

I looked away and swallowed, hard. Forced myself to look back at the screen.

She was on her back, her head hanging off the end of the ottoman, her lips parted in a sexy way. She wore a ton of makeup and her large brown eyes met the camera directly.

Her hand held one of her small breasts, gently. The other lay delicately, fingers slightly splayed, on her genitals.

I looked away again and said. "God Almighty."

"I know."

"Where'd that come from?"

He minimized the picture and brought up another window from

169

the hard drive. "This is her browser cache. It shows all the websites she visited." He pointed to the second column of information. "And this is where the picture came from. A website called Seerotic.com."

"How did it get there?"

"I would imagine someone sold it to this website., Who knows? Maybe this girl, what's her name again?"

"Samantha."

"Samantha could have uploaded it herself for all we know."

"Really?

"Sure. Some kids send stuff like this over the web all the time. I read one article that said one in ten kids have sexted."

"Sexted?"

"Texting sex-related pictures of themselves to someone. Then, of course, it's out of their control and could wind up anywhere."

"Can I see the picture again?"

He brought it back up and I studied it, trying not to focus on the pornography of it, but to learn more about it. "It's a professional picture, for sure," I mused. "Not something snapped with a cell phone or cheap digital camera. Look at the detail in the flames."

"True. You recognize the location?"

"No. It's not Samantha and Jean's living room or anything."

"Probably a professional studio, then."

"Like Keepers of Time Photography, maybe."

"Maybe."

"I've got to get over there. Tomorrow."

"I'm not so sure that's a good idea. Jean was murdered. Suppose she found out that her daughter was posing for these kinds of pictures and confronted the person who took them. You could get in big trouble."

"I doubt it."

"Why?"

"Do you think someone would be taking these types of pictures at a studio? Of kids and teenagers? Seems kind of a stretch. Too public. Too easy to get caught."

"You never know," he said. "Just be careful."

"Can you print me a copy of that picture?"

"Sure. I even think I've got some photo paper around here somewhere." He rummaged around in the closet and found an open package of it, and printed the picture for me on a four by six piece. It seemed even clearer--and sicker--on the shiny paper. I slipped it into my purse.

"Can we go to that website? Seerotic.com?" I asked.

"Sure. We probably won't be able to see much."

"Why?"

"I'm sure it costs something to download. Maybe not to look." He copied the address to his browser and hit enter.

A soft photo of a long-haired brunette girl filled the screen. She was much older than Samantha and her naked back was to the camera. She gave a sexy look over her shoulder. "Welcome to Seerotic.com" said the title. Under the photo was a place to enter, after you entered your credit card information.

"I'm not joining that." Grant said.

"Me neither." I was frustrated. I wanted to know if there were more pictures of Samantha there.

"I wonder who owns the site." I said.

Grant laughed. "That, we will never know."

"Why? I thought you said all sites had to be registered."

"They do, technically. But that doesn't always happen. And if they are registered, a lot of times with porn sites it's a fake company. Out of Singapore or Thailand or someplace. Believe me, if they don't want to be found, they won't be. I'll see what I can do, but I wouldn't get your hopes up."

The next morning I rushed to work as usual. My calendar was full: two meetings in the morning and I still had to find time to update Mac on all that was happening. I left him a message and was summoned to his office at ten till eleven.

"You said you wanted to see me?" he asked, after I entered his glass-fronted office. He was busy today, his desk piled with files and papers. The papers had overflowed onto one of the two chairs that faced his desk. I sat on the other, and updated him about the events that had happened, about Kyle and finding the computer. We talked about Kyle for some time, and Mac decided we didn't have enough to re-file a petition to have Kyle taken into custody.

"Really?" I asked in disbelief. "But Frank was drinking again. Not to mention the whole tie-in to Jean's murder."

Mac shrugged. "There's no evidence against him yet. And if we took all the kids into custody whose parents had fallen off the wagon—"

"I know, I know."

"But I want you to watch this carefully," he said. "If his father is arrested, or the drinking gets worse, we would probably need to open it again. Stay in touch with Kyle for a while, okay?"

I agreed, and made a mental note to call his mother to do some additional investigating. I rushed to my lunch-hour meeting with a client, and at one-thirty had a free hour. I made my way through Southside toward the Redmont neighborhood, looking for Keepers of Time Photography. I called Grant in the car on my way there, and he warned me again to be careful.

Keepers of Time was located in an old house, imitation Tudor in style, with lots of plaster and big wooden beams. I drove by it twice, thinking it was a just a house, until I noticed the small painted sign by the door. I turned into what must have been the driveway some time ago, now expanded to hold four or five parking spaces. The view from the back of the house would be one of downtown and no doubt spectacular.

I made sure the pictures of Samantha - clothed and otherwise - were in my purse and walked toward the front door. As I walked, out of the corner of my eye I noticed something.

Two spaces down from my Honda sat a dark blue SUV. It was a Honda, a Pilot, and it was new. And it was navy blue. I studied it for a minute from a distance, wondering if this could be the mysterious SUV that had picked up Samantha from the gas station in Midfield. It would make sense, especially if the SUV was Patrick Merrick's.

I entered the photography studio at the main entrance. A young girl of about twenty or so, dark haired and very pretty, sat at a small desk by a large staircase and asked if she could help me. I asked to see the owner, which got me a strange look but no questions. She asked me to have a seat and made a quiet phone call to someone.

Ten minutes later a man emerged from the back of the house. He was a lot younger than I expected, maybe thirty. Maybe. His attractive body was well-dressed in jeans and an untucked oxford shirt. He was also very effeminate. I started to doubt my supposition that this could be someone Samantha was dating, or at least sleeping with, because if I had to guess, this dude was gay.

"Hello, can I help you?" he asked.

"I'm Claire Conover, with the Child Welfare Department."

"Patrick Merrick." He extended a hand and I shook it.

Patrick. Pat. His voice was familiar, too. He was the definitely the man who'd left the message on Samantha's voice mail.

"Is there a place we can talk?" Pretty Receptionist was eagerly listening to every word.

"Can I ask what this is about?"

"Can we talk in private?"

His eyebrows went up in surprise. "Why don't you come back to my office?"

I followed him past the staircase to the back of the house. Dozens of framed photos hung in the passage. Weddings, graduations, birthdays. We reached a large room at the back of the house. It looked like some walls had been removed, leaving a large open space. The space overlooked downtown, with a glass wall at the back. I was right: the view was amazing and would have made a great background for portraits.

I studied the space. Heavy shades that I guessed could be drawn if the photographer wanted the light changed. Several random pieces of furniture scattered the room, a wingback chair, an armchair, and a stool, but no ottoman. Several large lights were in the room, and what might have been a camera case.

Patrick led me through the room to a small messy office that sported a computer that would have made Grant smile. A large monitor towered on the small desk, and little thumbnail pictures were lined up on the screen. An older man was the subject, neat in suit and tie, bland burgundy background behind his stiff smile. Patrick offered me a seat.

"Are you a photographer here, too?" I asked.

He nodded. "The only one," he said.

"And you own the modeling agency, also?"

"That's right. Beautiful Ones. I'm sorry, I just don't understand what this is about. Has there been some kind of complaint against me?"

"No, no." Poor guy, I thought. He did look a little nervous. I should clarify. "I have custody of one of your clients. Samantha Chambless."

"What happened?"

"Her mother was murdered a few days ago, and now Samantha's missing."

His face paled a bit under his fake tan. "Oh, my God. I had no idea."

"I found your website and info on her computer, and saw her picture. I was hoping maybe you'd heard from her."

"I haven't, no."

"But you tried to call her last week. On Tuesday. There was a message from you on her cell phone."

He flinched, just a tiny jerk. I'd surprised him, knowing that detail.

"Well, yes, I merely had a quick question. She never called me back."

"What, exactly, do you do for the girls you represent?"

"Put together a portfolio. Connect them with companies who may want to use them in advertisements."

"And has Samantha been successful?"

"About as much as can be expected. She's been in a television ocommercial for a local hamburger chain."

I opened my purse and found the nude picture of Samantha Grant had printed for me. "Have you ever seen this?" I set the photo on his desk.

He glanced at the picture and looked at me quickly, his skin going even paler. "Good Lord! Where did you get this?"

"Did you take it?"

He shoved the photo towards me. "Of course not!"

"It looks like a professional photograph."

"Most cameras sold today can take very high quality photos. I would never photograph any of my young girls like that. It's wrong. I do boudoir photography, but never, never with minors."

"Boudoir photography?"

"Sexy, intimate photos. Private. For couples. And never that," he pointed to the picture on the desk, "vulgar."

"Oh." I had a fleeting thought of me taking a boudoir photo for Grant, and nearly burst out laughing. Patrick saw it.

"What?"

"Nothing. You also represent a young girl named Marci Silva, correct? She's Samantha's best friend."

"Yes, Sam brought her in a couple of months ago. Beautiful girl, but she hasn't done any work so far. I had one offer, but her mother wasn't pleased with it and wouldn't let her do it."

"When was..." My cell phone rang. I pulled it out of my purse and checked the caller ID. The office. I hit ignore. "Sorry. When was the last time you talked with Samantha?"

"Let see, maybe a couple of weeks ago. She called—"

My cell rang again. I checked the ID again. It was the office again. "I'm sorry, I need to take this."

Patrick nodded and I walked back out to the large studio. "Hey," I said, after hitting "answer".

It was Nancy, at the front desk. "You remember that scary-lookin' guy you met with last week? The Call Tom one?"

"Sure. Kenny Thigpen. Why?"

"He's here, and he's pissed off."

174

Kenny was pissed off, indeed. I could hear him in the background, yelling something unintelligible.

"Who's he screaming at?" I asked.

"Mac," Nancy answered. I could hear Mac's low voice, calmly trying to talk him down. I heard the words "understand" and "talk". Then the shouting started again.

That made me mad. I'd asked the SOB to stay in touch, and he hadn't. Now he had the nerve to march into my office and scream at my boss. And he hadn't mentioned his dark blue SUV, even after I told him his missing daughter had been picked up in one.

"Nancy," I said, "please tell Mac to park him in an empty conference room. I'll be there as soon as I can."

"You got it."

I returned to Patrick's office, where he was studying the thumbnails of the old man in the burgundy tie again. "I'm sorry, I have an emergency at the office I have to go deal with." I handed him one of my cards. "Please call me if you hear from Samantha."

"I will. You know, I hate to say it, but I may have to drop her." He handed me the picture of Samantha that had been sitting on his desk.

"Because of this?" I nodded to the picture.

"I've never had this happen before. What if one of my clients were to see it? Associate it with me? It could be very bad for business. Do you see what I mean?"

"I do. But Samantha has just lost her mother. She may be moving away, to a relative's home, if and when she shows back up. If she enjoys modeling, I hate to take that away from her, too."

He thought about that for a second. "I understand. I'll do nothing for now. I'll talk to her when she returns."

"Thanks. Oh, and one more question. What kind of car do you drive?"

"An SUV. A Honda Pilot. Why?"

"Is that yours, in the lot outside?"

"Yes, why?"

"Samantha was picked up, after she ran away, in a navy SUV."

A worried look crossed his face. Just for a second. "Oh. I see. I'm afraid it wasn't me."

"You didn't pick her up at a gas station in Midfield?"

"No, I'm sorry. I wish I could be more help."

We shook hands and he walked me to the door. I sped back to

the office. I thought about Pat/Patrick on the way there. He didn't seem to have anything to hide. He'd been forthcoming with his answers and appeared to be genuinely shocked when I'd shown him the picture. So why didn't I trust him?

I parked in the back lot as usual and made my way to the front door around the corner. Nancy greeted me when I walked in. "Wow," she said.

"That bad, huh?"

"Mac's got your guy in the second floor conference room, the one closest to your cubicle. He said don't go in there alone."

I made to way to Mac's office. He was on the phone and I waited until he finished. He skipped the greetings as usual and barked, "What the hell did you do to that guy?"

"Nothing. He's Samantha Chambless's bio dad. I found out he relinquished custody. I have absolutely no idea why he's so mad."

"Let's go talk to him. And try not to get him all riled up again. I almost had to call security."

What Ancient Earl would do about Kenny, other than call the police, was beyond me. Mac followed me to the conference room. Earl was outside, keeping an eye on things.

Kenny was seated at the table, rocking back and forth and expending an overflow of angry energy. I swallowed and pushed open the glass door. "Hi, Kenny."

"Where the fuck is my daughter?"

"I don't know." There was a smell in the room. A little bit of earthy body odor from his sweat and booze. He was drunk.

Kenny stood up, a little too quickly, and wavered. His balance was off. I stood planted by the door, next to Mac, who kept the door open.

"I thought you said you were gonna find her!" He pushed the table and its legs screeched on the tile floor.

"We are. Look, I'll be glad to talk to you about the progress we've made, but not if you're going to shout and shove things around. Do you want to sit down and talk?"

He was shaking. Barely controlling himself. But he sat in the chair, hard. He ran a hand over the side of his tattooed neck and cursed again. I wrenched my feet off the floor and sat down across from him. Mac stayed by the door.

"I want to know where she is!"

"I do, too. What's got you so upset?"

"Wouldn't you be, if your daughter was missing? And the cops and the shitheads at DHS weren't doing anything about it?"

"Kenny, I talked to Bobby, Samantha's stepdad. He's her adoptive father."

"So? Sam's mine."

"Legally, she's not."

"Fuck!" He slapped a hand down on the table, then punched it again. I saw Mac nod to Earl in the hallway.

"Kenny, I really want to talk to you but I won't be able to if you don't calm down, okay?"

"She'd still be mine legally if that fuckin' bitch of an ex-wife of mine hadn't took her away. I don't know why I signed away my rights. I never shoulda done that to Sam. I miss her." He took a deep breath.

A lot of sadness underneath the rage, I thought. He was unstable, to say the least. "I know you do. Why didn't you go to the police station, after we met last time? Detective Stringfellow said you never showed up."

"I'm on probation. I got freaked out about talkin' to the cops."

"And you left my office in a dark blue SUV after I told you Samantha had been picked up in one. Why didn't you tell me that's what you were driving?"

"What the hell does that matter?" Tears glistened in his eyes now, though from which emotion I couldn't really tell. "I told you I don't know where she is."

"Were you the one who picked her up in Midfield? Did she call you?"

"No! Goddamn it! I haven't seen her! In years!"

He pushed the table again and it hit me in the stomach, but not hard. He stood up and began pacing the room. "I'm going to find her, and when I do, she's mine. He can't have her."

I stood up, too. "Who?"

"Her stepfather, you stupid bitch! Who the hell do you think?"

He stomped around to my side of the table. "You are not going to take her away from me! Nobody's gonna!"

Mac stepped into the room and nodded to me. I took that to mean the cops were on the way. I gave it one more shot.

"Look, Kenny, calm down. I don't want to take your daughter away from you. But you can't come in here screaming and making demands. And you need to stay sober if you want her back."

He raised his hand so quickly that when the back of it connected with my left cheekbone it was a total shock. I don't remember hitting the wall, or the floor.

When I came to, I was flat on my back. My shoulder was

wedged up against the grimy baseboard and I was staring at the industrial tiled ceiling. Mac was leaning over me and my face hurt. My eyes were watering, and Kenny was still screaming obscenities.

"Claire? Claire? You okay?"

"Yeah." I tried to sit up and Mac helped me. I felt my face. "Am I bleeding?"

"No, but your cheek is starting to swell."

Over Mac's shoulder I could see three male coworkers and Kenny. They had Kenny pinned against the glass wall, and he was fighting back. "Fucking bitch!" he screamed.

Russell appeared in the doorway, wringing his hands. "Oh, my God. Oh, my God."

Mac turned to him. "Go get her an icepack," he barked.

"She's my daughter!" Kenny yelled.

"I'm calling an ambulance," Mac said.

"No. I'm fine." I struggled to my feet.

"You lost consciousness."

"For, like three seconds. I'm fine."

Moments later Russell rushed in the door, eyes wide. "Here."

He handed me a plastic grocery bag with ice in it. I put it on my face. It had carried someone's lunch, and I could smell chicken salad.

A crowd had formed outside the conference room. Among them I could see Nancy and Beth and Michele, and Danessa from the foster care unit, all staring at me. The police arrived and added to the chaos. Four of them, from Birmingham City, all dressed in black uniforms with guns and badges and radios. In moments they had Kenny in handcuffs, and he started to cry. Then they hauled him away.

I sat down in one of the chairs at the table. The ice was making my face numb, which helped, but my nose was running. So were my eyes. One of the police officers interviewed me briefly about what happened. As we were winding things up, Grant walked in.

"What are you doing here?"

"Russell called me. He thought you might need a ride home. You okay?"

"She should go to the hospital and get that x-rayed," Mac said.

"I just want to go home."

Grant waited while I gathered my stuff and walked me out to my car. "I had Vijay drop me off. Where are your keys?" I dug them out of my purse and closed my eyes once I was in the passenger seat and my seatbelt was fastened. The ice in the bag was melted but I kept it on my face anyway.

Grant drove carefully to my house and opened the front door with my key. I threw away the grocery bag and changed into cotton shorts an oversized t-shirt. I checked my face in the bathroom mirror, and sure enough, my cheek was swollen and turning a yucky shade of blackish blue. I met Grant at the couch, where he held a yellow blanket he'd gotten out of my guest room closet. I sank into the sage green cushions and propped my head up with a throw pillow. Grant covered me and tucked me in, then disappeared into the kitchen and returned with a sandwich-sized storage baggie filled with fresh ice.

"I'm going to make you dinner," he said. "What do you want?"

"I don't care." was exhausted and wanted to go to sleep.

"Chicken soup?" he asked with a chuckle.

"Fine." He gave me a very gentle kiss on the non-bruised cheek and went to the front door. He opened it just as there was a knock.

"Oh," Grant said.

It was Kirk.

They shook hands. Grant said he was on his way out and pointed to me on the couch. Kirk walked over and saw me laying there with the icepack on my face and burst out laughing.

"So someone finally decked you. I've wanted to do that since I met you."

"Kirk—"

"Ha!"

"Kirk, what are you doing here?"

He was practically in tears, he was laughing so hard. I was getting tired of it. "Kirk, please."

"I heard there were officers called to the DHS building downtown. I knew somehow you were going to be in the middle of whatever it was. Nancy said you'd been injured and went home. What happened?"

"Jean Chambless's ex-husband hit me. Kenny Thigpen."

"Samantha's biological dad?"

"Yep. He's now in the Birmingham jail, I'm happy to say."

"What'd you do to piss him off?"

I sighed, and shifted the icepack. "I don't know. Nothing, really. He's mad about the fact that we can't find his daughter. He's mad at his dead ex-wife for making him sign away his parental rights. He's just mad, in general. And he was drunk."

"You think he killed Jean?"

179

"Well, he certainly has a violent streak!"

Kirk perched himself next to me on the couch. "Let me see." He removed the icepack. "You should get that x-rayed."

"It looks that bad?"

"It's a nasty shade of black and blue." He traced the bruise with his thumb, softly. Then did the same to my lips.

His light blue eyes were intensely focused on mine. His knuckles gently stroked my cheek, the one without the bruise.

"Kirk--"

"Sorry." He got up and started to pace. "So what's next?"

I thought for a few moments. "You know," I said, "I think it's time to let the proverbial cat out of the bag."

Chapter Twenty Nine

"What do you mean?" Kirk asked.

"I think it's time you wrote a story about Samantha being missing. Don't use my name. Quote other sources. Like the principal from the school, and maybe Detective Stringfellow."

"You sure?"

"Yeah. What could it hurt? It might open up some new leads."

"I'll see if I can get the whole thing together tonight. Maybe if we're lucky we can get it in tomorrow's edition. I'll call you later."

After he left, Grant returned, arms laden with bags of groceries. He went to the kitchen. "What did you get?" I called after him.

"Chicken and dumplings. Homemade. My mother's recipe. She wants to meet you, by the way."

Fantastic. The thought of meeting my boyfriend's parents left me with a feeling that registered just south of panic. Not that they weren't going to be nice, I was sure. But what would they think of me? Especially with a busted-up face. "Can we at least wait until the swelling goes down?"

Grant laughed. "Sure." He came back from the kitchen with a bag in his hand. "Here."

"What's this?"

"Little present for you."

"A bag of peas. You thoughtful thing."

"The least I could do." He removed the baggie with the half-melted ice and replaced it with the peas. "These are softer, see?"

He was right, they felt better. He resumed whatever he was doing in the kitchen. A few minutes later, there was a rapid tapping on the carport door, and then my father barreled in.

"What are you doing here?" I asked.

"Grant called me. Somebody hit you?"

Honest to God, the men in my life were enough to drive me nuts. "Grant called you?"

"And invited me to dinner. Are you okay?"

"I'm fine."

"You should really get that x-rayed."

"I'm fine. It's a bruised cheekbone. I'll be okay. Are you staying for dinner? You don't eat what we're having—"

"I'm making a vegetarian version," Grant called from the kitchen.

"But that's just dumplings."

"Pretty much."

My father was poking at my face and it was getting annoying. "Quit it," I said, brushing his hand away.

"Did they catch the guy who did this?" Dad asked.

"He's in the Birmingham jail."

"Good. Hope he rots there."

"He might."

Grant's chicken and dumplings were delicious. I had second thoughts about meeting his mother if she could cook like this. Dad left shortly after dinner, and Grant offered to stay the night, but I sent him home. I was sore, and very tired, and wanted to be alone. Grant said he'd call me in the morning.

I fetched the bag of peas from the freezer again, changed into my favorite pajamas and crawled into bed. Snuggled under my comforter, I thought about Samantha, as I had every night. Wondered again where she was sleeping. I felt frustrated. I was nowhere with this case. Absolutely lost. I had no idea where she was, and didn't know where to look.

What did I really know, anyway? The hour or so I'd spent with Samantha led me to believe that she knew more about her mother's death than she'd said. Why did she run away? And what was she running from? She'd radically changed her appearance a day or so after her mom was killed. She didn't want to be recognized. Why? Had she pulled the trigger?

But then why come back? Why show up at child welfare's doorstep? She must have known I'd insist she talk to the police. She didn't want to meet with Stringfellow, for sure. Once again, was that because she was guilty? It was where the crime was committed that confused me. How would Samantha lure her mother out to the area by the new golf course? And why there? And where would she have gotten the gun?

The golf resort. That was Frank Weller's baby. Jean and Frank had schemed together to rip off Ari Levi. Frank had been so desperate for money that she helped plan the whole deal. Maybe she needed money, too. But why risk it, if she'd gotten a huge check for her house damage in Mississippi? Then again, she'd bought a house, all new furniture, a computer, and the list went on and on. Maybe she was in debt, and did need the money. But so did Frank. His company was in financial trouble. And Jean had told Ari she cheated for Frank. He was still at the top of the list. His sneakiness didn't help me have faith in him either. And where was all the money now? My guess was Frank had used it to keep his company going. But what did any of that have to do with

Samantha, and her running away?

And that led me to Ari Levi himself. They'd taken him for thousands of dollars, possibly. Was this a revenge killing? The motive was there, for sure. Ari was hard to read. He was running an illegal gaming stall and apparently making a fortune doing it. What would he do to protect his little business?

I had to email Denise Weller tomorrow. Detective Stringfellow was right, she should be on the suspect list. If my husband had been caught with another woman, I'd be tempted to kill her. And him, for that matter.

I pulled the comforter further over my head and adjusted the bag of peas. My cheek hurt. Damn that Kenny Thigpen, anyway. He was a violent drunk. And he was mad about losing custody of Samantha. Had his anger led to Jean's death? Did he come to Birmingham on Friday and confront his ex-wife? And did Samantha know about it? Was she running to escape her father? Or to avoid turning him in? He was a likely suspect, too.

It all came back to Samantha. She was involved somehow, and I had to find her. Where the hell was she?

No answers. No ideas. I threw off the covers and made my way to the kitchen. I put the peas back in the freezer and took two ibuprofen. They didn't help, either. I settled myself on the couch under the yellow blanket again and wished I hadn't sent Grant home. I wanted his company. I flipped on the television and fell asleep halfway through *Meet Me in St. Louis*.

My cell phone woke me up at quarter to one. Kirk.

"Hey," I answered, yawning. It hurt.

"How's your face?"

"Sore. Where are you?"

"At the office. I finished the article. Stringfellow gave me a couple of good quotes, and I've got Samantha's yearbook photo from last year included, too. You want to hear it?"

"I'm not in it, right?"

"Nope, I promise. Not even a mention of your department."

"Then I'll just read it with the rest of the world."

"Sleep well, then."

I called in the next morning, telling Mac I would work from home and come in later if I felt like it. He urged me again to get an x-ray, which I ignored. I checked the mirror in the bathroom. My face looked worse. The bruise was darker, although the swelling had gone down. I showered and put on shorts and a t-shirt and got the paper off of the driveway.

Kirk's article was on the front page, below the fold. The picture of Samantha was in color, a larger version of the same small one I had seen at her home. DAUGHTER OF MURDERED WOMAN MISSING, said the headline. I read on.

Samantha Chambless, thirteen year old daughter of murder victim Jean Chambless, was reported missing last Tuesday, it said. Kirk briefly recounted the story of Jean's body being discovered last weekend, and mentioned her relationship with Frank Weller and his being questioned by the police. Kirk mentioned Jean's two previous marriages and the fact that her first husband had been recently released from prison after serving time on drug-related charges.

Samantha, he wrote, had disappeared from her placement on Tuesday, reappeared briefly on Saturday, and disappeared again. He quoted Stringfellow about how her appearance had been changed, and now she had black hair and wore lots of jewelry. The police, Stringfellow said, were anxious to talk with her. Kirk quoted James Eddy, saying that Samantha was a valuable member of the E.W. Dodge student body and a good student, and everyone missed her. He quoted Bobby Chambless, too, who said he was sorry to hear about her mother and he wanted Samantha to be safe. He concluded the article with a plea for the readers to study her picture and contact the police with any information.

It was a good article. Kirk had a talent for giving all the important facts as well as drawing on the emotions. If Samantha read this, she'd know she was being missed. Whoever was hiding her would know that people were looking for her, especially the police. Maybe that pressure would help get her found.

I went to my home office, strong cup of coffee in hand. I called Kirk's cell and left him a message, thanking him for the great article. Grant called at eight-thirty, on his way to High Tech, to check on me. I told him I was taking the morning off and wished him a good day at work.

I cancelled my appointments for the day, then logged on remotely and checked my work email. I answered a few items and then pulled up Outlook to compose a message.

I thought for a while. I didn't want to frighten Denise, or lead her to believe that Kyle had been injured again. I entered her email address and typed:

Mrs. Weller,

My name is Claire Conover and I'm with the child welfare department in Birmingham. I'm aware of your family's history with us and Kyle is in no danger. However, one of his friend's parents has been murdered and his friend, Samantha, is now missing. I would appreciate the opportunity to talk with you at your convenience about this case. Thank you.

I left my cell phone number after my name and hoped I would hear back soon. I answered numerous other email items, and updated my calendar. Then I checked my voicemail at the office. I had twenty-eight messages. I used my cell phone to answer those calls, none of which, thankfully, were emergencies. Then I checked my cell phone's messages.

The second message was from James Eddy at E.W. Dodge Middle School. "Miss Conover, I hate to bother you, but I was wondering if you had any information for Marci Silva. She's been quite upset today, very unfocused. She's crying a lot, and I'm sure she's worried about Samantha Chambless. If you could give me a call, I'd appreciate it."

Huh. Interesting. I wondered what was going on that would make Marci so upset. Did it have something to do with the article this morning? She hadn't exactly been honest about the computer and the phone that she'd hidden in her locker. What else did she know?

The third message was LaReesa, calling from school: "Hey, I got something I really, really need to talk to you about. It's like, real urgent. Bye." I wondered what was so important that she'd gotten out of class to call me. Something about her grandmother? Her safety? Or was this merely a reason to skip her schoolwork and go to the office to make a phone call?

The phone rang as I disconnected from the voice mail. The caller ID said WELLER, DENISE and had a 256 area code. I answered it.

"Miss Conover, it's Denise Weller. I got your email." She had a trebly voice, and it was breaking a little.

"Thanks for calling me back," I said. "You know what's going on with Samantha Chambless and her mom?"

"The police were here yesterday. They wanted to know where I was Saturday night. They wanted to know my--my alibi, I guess. I was at home, alone. I just can't believe what's going on."

She was becoming more distraught. "I'm so sorry, Mrs. Weller. I know this must be difficult."

"And my son. Poor Kyle." I could hear her crying, softly.

"He's a great kid."

"He is. He doesn't deserve all this."

"Mrs. Weller, would it be possible for us to meet in person? I

185

could really use some insight into Samantha. Anything you know might be helpful."

"I'm supposed to come talk to the police again tomorrow, first thing in the morning. I should be finished about nine." We made an appointment to meet at my office and hung up. I wondered how the meeting would go. Denise sounded so fragile.

It was close to lunchtime. I made myself a sandwich and then changed into pants and a different shirt before heading to E.W. Dodge. I entered the office and the secretary had me wait. Mr. Eddy arrived a few minutes later.

"Oh, Miss Conover, I'm sorry. I didn't mean for you to come all the way down here."

"It's fine. I needed to check on Marci anyway."

He led me into his office. The desk was more cluttered with folders this time. He gestured to a chair and I sat down. "Sorry I kept you waiting. I was monitoring the chaos in the cafeteria."

"I saw your quote in the paper this morning. Thanks for doing that, by the way. You said you had concerns about Marci?"

He nodded. "Something's changed about her this week. She's normally one of our best students, but her teachers are reporting to me that her grades are suffering a little. She's not turning in homework. I mean, I'm sure she's upset about her best friend being missing, and I've reminded the teachers of that fact and asked them to go a little easy on her. I was hoping you could talk to her and maybe ease her mind a little."

"I'd be happy to, but I really don't know what to tell her. I don't have much information."

"Maybe just knowing people are looking for Samantha will help."

"Sure."

He went out to the main office and summoned Marci over the phone. He left us alone.

He was right. There was something different. She'd lost weight. Not that she had much to lose in the first place. And her hair was stringy and looked unwashed. Her face was paler underneath it, and her eyes were red.

"Hi, Marci."

"Hi."

"You okay?"

"Why?"

"Mr. Eddy is worried about you, that's all. I know you're worried about Samantha. We all are."

She nodded.

"You haven't heard from her?"

"No."

"Did you see the article in the paper this morning?"

She nodded.

"What did you think?"

I got a shrug as an answer.

"Is there something else going on? Something else you're worried about?"

She shook her head. "I'll be okay." Her eyes welled, and she wiped away a tear.

"You know, I didn't get a chance to know Samantha all that well, but I'm sure she's going to be fine. She's a tough kid."

"I know."

"Something does concern me, though. We found a picture of Samantha on her computer. A very sexy, naked picture. I'm very disturbed by it. Do you know anything about it?"

She swallowed, hard. Twice. Suddenly, she appeared to be shaking. "You saw that? Sam said she deleted it."

"There's ways to find it."

"Oh, God." She buried her face in her hands.

"It's on the Internet, did you know that? At a site called Seerotic.com."

"Oh, God."

"Was that what Samantha's mom was so mad about?"

She nodded, slowly. "Her mom was furious. Said she wouldn't let Sam ever have a computer again. Or a phone. That's why she gave them to me. She didn't want her mom to take them away. That's all I know, really."

"Why didn't you tell me? At least you could have told me you had the computer and the phone."

"I didn't think it mattered."

"Marci, Samantha's mom was murdered and she is missing. There might have been something really important on that computer, or on the phone."

We sat in silence for several minutes. I was hoping she'd open up, let me know what was bothering her so much. Finally I said, "It might help to talk to someone. I can keep a secret."

She shook her head again. "I just want to go back to class."

"You've got my number if you need me, right?"

"Yes."

She left, and Mr. Eddy rejoined me. "See what I mean?"

"Yeah, she's a wreck. I get the feeling there's more to it than just Samantha being gone."

"Me, too."

"Problems at home?"

He rested his fingers under his chin. "She doesn't have a history of that. Her parents are both professors, and they've always been supportive, and involved. Very involved, in fact."

"Have you talked to her parents?"

"Not yet."

"Maybe I'll stop by her house later, check in with them."

"Good idea. Can I ask you a question?"

"Sure."

"Are you okay? I mean, your face..."

"Oh, yeah. Unhappy client. He's in jail now."

"Oh, well, I just thought I'd ask."

I bid Mr. Eddy goodbye and headed for my next destination. It was close to one-thirty, so I hurried across town to Midfield Middle. School would be getting out soon and I wanted to make sure I had time to talk to LaReesa. Whatever she needed, it'd better be good.

I checked in at the office, like I had at Dodge, and the secretary sent for her. She arrived, neatly dressed in one of the white shirts and navy pants that we'd picked out together.

"Well, don't you look nice," I said. She did, too. Her hair was newly styled, still with a lot of curls. She'd toned down the makeup as well.

"What the hell happened to you? Yo' boyfriend do that? You should break up with him."

My hand went to my face. "No, just an unhappy customer."

"You okay?"

"It's just a bruise. You said you wanted to speak to me." I asked the secretary if there was a place where we could talk. She pointed, while answering the phone, and mouthed the word "library". It wasn't as private as I would've liked, especially if LaReesa was about to disclose something intensely personal like abuse. Still, it would have to do. We walked down the hall together. The library was a little short in the book department, and what they did have looked old and worn. We found a veneered, square table at the back and she sat across from me.

"So, what's so important?"

"I made an appointment."

"Where?"

"Keepers of Time Photography."

188

Chapter Thirty

"What?"

"Keepers of Time Photography. You said yo' missing girl might be there, so I called them. Told the lady I wanted to talk to somebody about modelin'"

"What?"

"Didn't you hear me?"

"I heard you. I just... how do you know about this?"

"I heard you talkin' on the phone about it."

"LaReesa, this is not a good idea."

"Why?"

"First of all, stop listening to my private phone conversations. Second of all, my missing girl's mother was murdered a week and a half ago, and this could be dangerous."

"So?"

"I don't want you involved."

"Why?"

I buried my face in my hands, accidentally hitting my cheek and regretting it. I winced. "LaReesa—"

"What's the big-ass deal? If you think your girl's chillin' at this place, let me go check it out."

"No."

"I have an appointment tomorrow at four. It don't cost nothin' for the first time, the lady said. An initial consultation, she called it."

"This is not a good idea," I said again.

Or maybe it was. What could happen? It was a public place. There'd be people around. I was fairly certain that Patrick was hiding something. I doubted he was convincing his clients to pose for pornography, but maybe I was wrong. Maybe having LaReesa look around wasn't such a bad idea. It would also give me an idea about how Beautiful Ones was run.

"You're changin' your mind. I can tell. I'll need a ride."

"There's a modeling agency being run out of this place. It's called Beautiful Ones."

"I know. The chick on the phone told me that."

"Just go and do the consultation, and tell me what you see."

"Duh. So you'll pick me up at school?"

"Is your grandmother okay with this?"

"She don't care what I do."

Somehow I figured she was right.

189

I sent LaReesa back to class. I couldn't shake the feeling that this was a big mistake. I went to my cubicle and was trying to distract myself by filing stuff in my charts when Russell walked in. His tie was loose around his neck and his highlighted blond hair was mussed. He was in a bad mood, again.

"God!" He threw his satchel on his desk.

"Tough day?"

"Why do I put up with this shit?"

"I take that's a yes."

"She was court ordered to go to the damn counseling, and now she wants to blame me, in front of the judge, for why she didn't go. Ridiculous."

I knew how he felt. We all had clients that we had high expectations for, and it was hard when they fell short. He was angry because he cared. "I'm sorry," I said.

He started unpacking the satchel. "You can only do so much, right?"

"Right. Hey, listen, let me ask you something."

"Shoot."

"There's this guy who owns a modeling agency here. His name's Patrick Merrick. I think he's gay. Do you know him?"

"Oh, I get it. Because there's only four gay men in all of Birmingham, I'm supposed to know him?" He slammed a folder down.

"Well, Christ, don't snap my head off. I just thought I'd ask."

"No, I don't know him."

"Could you ask around for me? See if anyone knows anything about him? One of his clients turned up in a pornographic picture on the web. I'd love to know if he had anything to do with it."

"I doubt I'll find anything out, but I can ask."

Russell and I both worked quietly for a while. I was just about ready to pack it in for the day when my cell phone rang. It was Kirk. "I got your message."

I filled him in on my day, about Marci my meeting with Mr. Eddy. I was frustrated, and he heard it.

"You okay?"

"Yeah, I'm just worried. I've got a friend—a young friend-- who's going to check out Keepers of Time and Beautiful Ones for me."

"I did some asking around here at the paper, by the way, about that place. He's pretty successful, especially with ads for local companies. Both print and television. He's just now breaking in to

190

some web stuff, too. I asked if there'd been any talk about pornography, and my guys seemed pretty shocked."

"He's hiding something. I just know it."

"Well, I'll keep my ears open. I'll call you later."

I went back to my paperwork briefly after we hung up, and then decided it was time to go. If I got out of here early I could beat the traffic home. Russell was on the phone behind me, muttering into his receiver. I stood up and he held up a finger to halt me.

"Okay, yeah, thanks, I appreciate it." He said, and hung up the phone.

"What?"

"I've been playing six degrees of separation. I called a few friends to ask about Patrick Merrick. Turns out one of my friends knows someone who knows a guy who used to date him."

"God, there really are only four gay men in Birmingham."

"Tell me about it. Anyway, my friend called Patrick's ex and got the scoop. Nice guy, he said. Very smart and determined. Started his studio about the time they got first together, and I got the feeling it had a lot to do with why they broke up."

"What do you mean?"

"Oh, who knows? I mean, why does anyone break up, really? It's usually complicated." I could see sadness in his expression. He was reminded of his own ex, I could tell. "Anyway, my friend said Patrick was busy all the time, working a lot, trying to get the agency off the ground and didn't really have time for a relationship. They drifted apart. He hasn't talked to him since. My friend mentioned the porn thing and his ex said no way. Said Patrick was very honest. Almost moralistic. He'd campaign against it, rather than participate in something like that, you know?"

"I know." So Patrick was a good guy, at least according to his ex-boyfriend. What that had to do with anything, I had no idea. It certainly didn't get me any closer to finding Samantha.

Russell looked miserable. I felt bad for him. "Do you want to go grab a drink?"

"I can't, I've got plans, but thanks."

I gathered my stuff and told Russell I'd see him tomorrow. I was ready to head home, but then remembered I'd told Mr. Eddy I'd run by the Silva's to check on Marci.

I peeked in the garage when I arrived. Two cars were there, the Mercedes I'd seen before along with a black Audi. I knocked on the door and Mrs. Dr. Silva opened it.

"Oh, oh hello," she said. She looked flustered. "I'm sorry, I was not expecting you." She was dressed more casually than the first time I'd seen her, in jeans and a feminine, floral top. Her hair was loosely clipped in the back, threads of grey running through the black.

"I'm Claire Conover, from DHS."

"I remember. Won't you come in?"

I followed her into the living room and sat where I had before on the firm couch. "I saw Marci at school today. She looked upset. How's she doing?"

Cecile Silva was trembling. It was subtle, but there, when she raised her hand to brush a piece of hair out of eyes. She looked like she was at the end of her rope. "That girl! Ah, I tell you. She is having a hard time."

"Because of Samantha?"

"Yes, yes. Her principal called. Her grades, they are lower. I am worried. I have told her she needs to concentrate. Pull it together."

"And she hasn't heard from Samantha?"

"No, not that I know of. Her father, he is very frustrated, too. It is bad when he is like that. There's much tension in the house."

"I'm sorry. Dr. Silva, can I ask, do you own any guns?"

"Guns? No, of course not. This neighborhood is very safe. We do not own any guns. Why?"

"It's nothing."

"Why?"

"I just wondered if Samantha had anything to do with her mother's death. And if she did, where she would get the gun, that's all. Odds are she'd steal it from someone she knows."

"Oh. I see. Would you like to see Marci?"

"Is she home?"

"She is watching television in the family room."

Dr. Silva rose and walked to the short hallway that led to the back of the house. I followed her. The hallway was lined with framed family photos, some of them black and white and very old. We emerged into the family room, and suddenly I felt a little dizzy. I'd seen this before.

Light aqua paint on the walls. A beautiful gray marble fireplace graced the end wall, framed by gorgeous built-in bookcases. A large screen television was mounted on the wall, across from an ornate leather sofa. And in front of it was a large, round, leather ottoman.

This was the room where Samantha had taken the nude

photograph.

I hid my surprise, quickly, as Marci stood. She had on a t-shirt tied at the waist and a pair of jeans. "Hey," she said to me. She didn't acknowledge her mother.

"Hi. I wanted to talk to you for a few minutes." I couldn't get Samantha's naked picture out of my head. "Want to go get a Coke somewhere?"

She glanced at her mother, who shrugged. "Sure," she said. "Let me go get my shoes."

Her mother and I waited in silence as she went out of the room. Did Dr. Silva have any idea what had transpired in this room? I wondered, but didn't want to ask. Not yet.

Marci rejoined us, in flip-flops. Her mother didn't walk us out, and I told her we wouldn't be long. Once in the car, I turned to Marci.

"What?" she asked.

I didn't know where to start. I took a deep breath. "Marci."

"What?"

"You know those naked pictures of Samantha I mentioned?"

She looked afraid. She wouldn't look at me. "What about them?"

"They were taken in your family room."

She covered her eyes and burst into tears.

Chapter Thirty One

"Drive!" she cried.

"Marci—"

"Just drive, please!"

I put the car in reverse and pulled out. I drove around the neighborhood for a few minutes while Marci bawled. I found my way out of the neighborhood and down busy Lakeshore Drive, to a McDonald's. I went through the drive-thru and ordered a couple of Diet Cokes. By the time I pulled to the window, Marci was better. She was still crying, but had calmed down some. I handed her the drink and a straw. Then I parked in a parking lot across the street, in front of an abandoned grocery store.

Marci had the hiccups. I told her to sip the drink quietly for a minute, and I did the same. Her hiccups went away and her breathing slowed. Finally I asked, "Were there pictures of you, too?"

She wiped her face with a napkin. "Yes."

"Just like Samantha's?"

She nodded. "Lots of them."

"Does your mother know?"

She nodded again. "We were just foolin' around, me and Sam. You know, Sam's mother got this big wad of money because she lost her house in the hurricane?"

"I know."

"She bought Sam a bunch of really cool stuff with it. The computer, the phone, and this really awesome digital camera."

"Uh huh."

"So we were at my house one day after school, and she had the camera and she said she wanted to take some pictures for her Facebook page. It started out just normal. We were goofing off, making silly faces. Then she said she wanted to do some pictures for Brendan. She said he'd love them. And that I should do some for Kyle. I shouldn't have done it." She started to cry again.

I reached out and rubbed her arm. "And then what happened?"

"She sent the photos to him from my computer. Then, like, a week later, we found out they were on the Internet. Brendan showed us. I don't think Kyle did it. I think it was Brendan. He thought it was funny. For all I know he's showed them to the whole school. I just want to die."

"What did Samantha think?"

"She didn't care. Not really. She's proud of her body, you

195

know? She thinks she's hot. And she is pretty. But still, for everyone to see it..."

"Does your mom know?"

She sobbed again. "She knows. She found the photos on my computer. Sam had saved them. She's so mad. She told my dad, and he's not even speaking to me. God." She wiped her face with the napkin again. "She told me I wasn't allowed to see Sam any more. That we weren't allowed to be friends. Sam's my best friend, for God's sake. I can't not talk to her! And now her mom's dead and I don't even know where she is and she hasn't called me or Brendan—"

"Whoa, whoa. Slow down. Breathe."

She did, taking two long breaths and then sniffled. "Where could she be?"

"I wish I knew. Did your mother do anything else?"

"What do you mean?"

"Did she call Jean? Did Samantha's mom know about the pictures?'

"She said she was going to call her. Said her mother had a right to know that her daughter was acting like a whore. That's what she called us. Whores. I'm so ashamed."

Now for the hard question. "Marci, do you think you mother had anything to do with Jean's death?"

Silence. Then a soft whisper. "I don't know. I mean, I don't think so. She's really mad, but I don't think she'd kill anyone."

My list of suspects was getting ridiculously long. Jean and Samantha had managed to anger just about everyone they knew. Except one person. "Tell me about Beautiful Ones. Samantha got you involved in that, too, right?"

She nodded. "It was really fun. And Patrick, he owns the agency, he said I had real talent. He wanted me to do this ad campaign a few months ago. For the water park. I went out there with him and did all these shots, and it was freezing, but we had a great time, but then Mother said no. She said she wasn't going to have the whole city ogling her daughter. That's the stupid word she used. Ogling. It was, like, just an ad, you know. No biggie. I was so mad. I tried to go ahead with it anyway but Patrick wouldn't let me. He said he had to have my parent's permission. Sam was so lucky. Her mom let her do whatever she wanted."

"She's not so lucky, now, though."

Marci's eyes filled with tears again. "No, I guess not."

We sat for a few minutes longer while Marci collected herself and then I cranked the Civic to drive back to her house. "You won't tell my mom what we talked about?" she asked.

"I don't see any reason to. Your mom loves you, you know. That's why she's so concerned."

"I know."

"And you don't have any idea where Samantha could be?"

"I don't. I wish I did."

I pulled into the Silva's driveway again. "I don't want to go in," Marci said. "I wish I didn't have to live here. I wish we could just go away. We almost did, Labor Day weekend."

"What do you mean?"

"We went to Atlanta. To the airport. Mother was freaking out. Seriously. She was going to take me to Brazil. To her family there. She said living here was a privilege that I didn't appreciate and hadn't earned. Dad found out where we were and talked her into coming home."

I felt bad for Marci. I remembered how difficult eighth grade had been. All the peer pressure and the confidence issues. It was bad enough without a difficult relationship with your parents, and a missing best friend whose mother had been murdered, and the possibility that the entire eighth grade had seen you naked.

I encouraged her to hang in there, for Samantha if nothing else and watched as she entered the house before I pulled away. I replayed our conversation in my head as I drove home.

Marci's mother was furious about Samantha's influence over her daughter. And, I had to admit, if I had found pictures of my buck-naked thirteen-year-old on the internet, I would have probably reacted the same way. I'd have grounded my daughter from everything but eating and breathing. Marci had limits, and Samantha didn't. I could see why Cecile Silva didn't want Marci picking up Samantha's habits. And, with all of Jean's recent issues at work and with her husbands, I wondered how much attention Samantha got, anyway. She was certainly seeking it, one way or another.

But was Jean's lack of parenting motive for murder? I'd seen, over the years, how mad parents got when it came to their children. Like lionesses with their cubs. What would Cecile do to protect her daughter?

Grant's van was in my driveway when I got home. He was typing something on his phone when I walked to the vehicle's window.

"Hey."

"I was just texting you. You okay?"

"Yeah, a little tired."

I heated some soup for us while Grant made a salad out of the half-wilted veggies I had in the fridge. It was past time to do some grocery shopping. We watched TV for a while after supper, but I couldn't keep my mind on what was happening on the show.

I didn't think Samantha was at Brendan's. His parents would have noticed and called me. They didn't want her there, didn't want their son to date her. I couldn't imagine that Brendan would be able to hide her out this long at his house.

And Marci's house was out of the question. The Doctor Silvas kept a tight rein on their only daughter. Marci said she didn't know where Samantha was, and I believed her. Her worry for her best friend was real and genuine.

Kyle's house was out. Samantha was angry with Frank Weller for dating her mother. She didn't like him, and I seriously doubted she would have run to his home. And Frank certainly wasn't the nurturing parental figure who would help her through a crisis.

Her biological father had been driving the type of dark blue SUV that had picked her up when she disappeared. But now he was in jail. I supposed he could have stashed her somewhere before he was arrested, which meant she was now out there with no resources. But he said he didn't know where she was, and hit me when I said I didn't either. And her stepfather lived too far away. She had no money for a bus ticket or any kind of transportation. I doubted she could get to Mississippi, even if she wanted to.

And that just left one place, other than the street. One last adult who may be helping her. Patrick Merrick, at Keepers of Time Photography. As Grant and I went to bed, I hoped LaReesa would find out something tomorrow.

Beth buzzed me at my desk at five till nine. "Mrs. Denise Weller to see you."

No conference rooms were available, but Russell was out, so we met in my cubicle. Denise was a tiny thing, maybe five-two and thin. It horrified me to think of the damage that Frank Weller could have done to someone her size. She had thin brown hair and large brown eyes that reminded me of a rabbit's. And she looked just as scared as a rabbit, too.

She sat small in Russell's chair, clutching her purse. I was desperate for some way to make her more comfortable. "Would you like something to drink?"

"No, thank you."

"How did it go with the police?"

She licked her lips. "Fine. They're testing my gun. They want to do ballistics tests on it."

"Your gun?"

"My revolver."

"I see. You have a thirty-eight?"

"I do. Frank bought it for me when we first got married. He worked late a lot, and I was scared to stay home alone. I've never fired it. But it's the same kind of gun that Jean was killed with, and she was sleeping with my husband, so I guess that makes me a suspect."

"I guess so."

"I didn't kill her, but I'm not sorry she's dead. I guess that's a cruel thing to say, but it's true."

"Because of her affair with Frank?"

"Yes. She was a terrible person. Who does that to someone? She knew he was married. Of course, Frank's at fault, too. He cheated on me before. I tried to forgive him. Tried to make it work. But he never did anything like this before. Never slept with someone I knew."

"You were friends with Jean?"

"A little. I mean, we'd talk occasionally at Kyle's football games or when we were picking the kids up from the mall or someplace. I used to think she was nice. Not the best parent in the world, but nice."

"Why do you say that?"

"Samantha didn't have a lot of limits, if you know what I mean. No curfew, no rules. She could stay out as late as she wanted, go anywhere she wanted. It used to make Marci and Brendan and Kyle upset. They wanted to stay out late, too, but they weren't allowed. Especially not Kyle. Frank is very strict. I got so tired of explaining to Kyle that not everyone has the same rules, and he had to follow ours."

"I see. Do you have any idea where Samantha might have gone?"

"Marci would be the one to ask. Samantha and Marci are very close."

"They modeled together, for a place called Beautiful Ones. For a guy named Patrick Merrick."

"That's right. I'd forgotten. God, Cecile hated that. That's Marci's mother."

"Do you know why?"

"She didn't think it was appropriate. Didn't want her daughter seen in that way. I guess I can understand. She wanted Marci to be focused on school, and not much else."

"Have you filed for divorce, from Frank?"

"Yes. Sorry." The rabbit eyes filled with tears, slowly. She reached into her purse and found a tissue, and wiped them gently.

"That's okay. Divorce is tough."

"I hate to do this to Kyle. He's been through enough."

"Are you filing for custody?"

"As soon as I can get the money."

I was out of questions. I stood up and offered a hand to Denise. "Thank you so much for coming in, Mrs. Weller."

Her handshake was soft. "I didn't kill her. I'm glad she's gone, but I didn't kill her."

I walked her down to the lobby and returned to my cubicle. Denise Weller was a broken woman. Did she even have the ability to pull the trigger and kill Jean? I doubted it. She didn't strike me as the type that would be able to pull it off. Still, she'd been pushed to her limits, it seemed. I wondered what the ballistics tests would show and how long they would take. I'd ask Stringfellow when I got a chance.

I cleared my schedule for the afternoon and met LaReesa when the final bell rang at Midfield Middle School. She looked nice again today, in another of the new shirts and black pants.

She met me at the car. "I'm hungry."

"Hello to you, too."

"We got time to eat?"

"I think so."

"You got any money?"

"I do."

"Will you buy me some French fries?"

"I will. How was school?"

"Fine. Got an A on my English test. Not so good in Earth Science."

"What's not so good mean?"

"I got a B plus."

"That's not bad. You're smart. You'll pull it up to an A if you try."

We made a quick trip through a Wendy's drive-thru for fries, which she ate quickly. As we drove across town to the studio, she fixed her makeup in the mirror in the sun visor.

"Look okay?"

"Real pretty."

"I wonder what he's gonna say." She glanced down at her torso, then her legs. "I mean, I ain't got the body of a model. And my teeth are effed up."

"You'll grow into the teeth. Besides, I think it's more about attitude. Whether or not you can sell something."

"It don't matter, I can't do it no how, not for real." She sounded a little sad. I wondered what other dreams this bright, outgoing girl had that no one encouraged.

I showed her Samantha's picture--not the naked one, but the one of her and her friends on the picnic table--before I dropped her off at Keepers of Time. I told her I'd be back in forty-five minutes. I watched as she went in the front door. I found a coffee shop in nearby Mountain Brook and tried to work on some forms from my briefcase. I had to redo one of them twice. I was nervous. I didn't know why. LaReesa was going to be fine. I needed to relax. She was in no danger. Finally, forty minutes crawled by and I drove back to the studio.

She was waiting for me in the parking lot, a small stack of papers in her hand. She got in the car.

"Yo' girl's there," she said.

"You saw her?"

"No, but how many adults do you know runnin' around with a red bookbag?"

Chapter Thirty Two

"You saw the bookbag?"

"Uh huh. A backpack, like. Dirty. It was in a chair in the room where he takes them pictures. That Patrick dude saw me looking at it and got all weird."

"What do you mean, all weird?"

"Like nervous. Talking real fast. And I heard somebody upstairs, too, walking around."

"Where was the secretary?"

"It wasn't her. She was at her desk. I'm telling you, she's there. So what's next?"

"I'm taking you home." I put the car in gear.

"What? Seriously? We got to do something."

"I am going to do something. I'm going to call the police. The detective who's investigating this case is very good, and he'll come check it out."

"Yeah, like, next year. You can't trust no cops."

"He'll be here." I turned left onto the Expressway.

"Can't I hang out with you? I want to know what happens."

"Listen, LaReesa, you've been a great help. Really. Gave me exactly the information I needed, and I appreciate it. But I have to take you home and get the police out there, okay?"

"Are you going back to Keepers of Time?"

"I'm going home. I'll let the police handle it."

"Oh."

There was a few moments of silence, then, "Where do you live?"

"In Hoover. In Bluff Park."

"In a house?"

"Yes."

"I bet it's a big house."

I laughed. "Oh, I wouldn't say it's huge. It's nice, though. It suits me."

"How many bedrooms?"

"Three."

"You got any kids?"

"Nope."

I get questions like this all the time from the kids I take into care. Some of them are just curious, some of them want to know what it would be like to live with me. To have an adult around who cares for them, who doesn't scream and yell and slap the hell out of them for no reason. Someone who could afford them, who could buy them nice school clothes and three meals a day. The questions always make me sad. "Why do you ask?"

"Just wonderin'. Can't a girl wonder?"

"Sure."

She was quiet the rest of the way into Midfield, and I was curious about what was going through her mind. Was there something going on? Something I'd missed?

I pulled to the side of the street in front of her grandmother's house. LaReesa was looking at it with a disgusted expression on her face. "You okay?" I asked.

"Yeah. I just hate it here."

"What do you mean?"

"My grandma's so mean. And we're always broke. We ain't got shit. Barely enough to eat."

I reached over and massaged her shoulder. "I'm sorry."

"I wish I could live someplace else."

"Like where?"

She shrugged, her gaze focused on her lap. "Ain't no place else. Except maybe with you."

That got to me. "Oh, honey. I can't take you away from your family, as much fun as I think that would be. Your grandma would miss you."

"Ha!"

"Sure she would."

"She just wants less mouths to feed. I heard her say that."

"Reese, listen. You are a very special, very smart girl. And if you were my daughter I'd be so incredibly proud."

She smiled. "Really?"

"Really. I want us to be special friends, okay? You ever need anything, you call me. And I'm going to stay after you to finish school and get good grades, you hear me?"

"I will."

"I mean it." I pulled her to me and hugged her neck. "I'm not going to give up on you, and I don't want you giving up on yourself."

"I won't. Will you call me and let me know what happens with yo' other girl?"

"I will. Go get your homework done."

She giggled. "Yes, ma'am."

I waited until she was safely in the house and Estelle Jones had waved to me from the front door. I felt a weight on my shoulders concerning LaReesa. I wanted to help her, but I didn't know what else to do.

I have to admit, there are certain kids I really get attached to. I like all of my kids, of course, but there are some that manage to burrow their way into my soul and stay there. LaReesa was becoming one of them. Maybe I could help Estelle, at least with the financial burden of raising four kids. Was she getting food stamps? Child support from the fathers? I made a mental note to schedule an appointment with her for next week and ask these questions. If nothing else, I could hook her up with agencies that could help.

My cell phone was ringing. I kept one eye on the highway and felt in my purse to find it. "Silva" was on the caller ID.

"Hello?"

"Hey, it's Marci." She was crying.

"What's the matter?"

"Oh, it's just my stupid mom."

"What happened?"

"It's nothing. She's always mad. Have you heard anything about Sam?"

"I have, actually. I think she may be with Patrick Merrick."

"Really? So she's okay?"

"I don't know, but I think so. I'm going to make sure, and I'll let you know, okay?"

"Okay."

Silence.

"Marci, what is it?" Now she was sobbing softly.

"I'm just relieved, that's all. I miss my best friend."

"I'll keep you posted on what's going on. Was there anything else?"

"No, I'll be all right."

"You sure?"

"I'm fine."

We said goodbye, and I hung up with an uneasy feeling. Marci was on a downhill spiral, fast. I was worried. If she and her parents didn't find some way to learn to live with each other, Marci's depression would only get worse. Maybe it was time for some family counseling. I made another mental note to make a list of some qualified therapists, one that included my father, and deliver it to the Silvas, soon.

I dialed the Homewood Police Department's number and was connected to Detective Stringfellow after holding a few minutes.

"What's up?" he asked.

"Did I catch you at a bad time?"

"I'm interviewing Frank Weller and Ari Levi."

"Together? You didn't leave them alone, for God's sake?"

He chuckled. "Yeah, it's been real interesting. Lot of anger with those two. Don't worry, there's an officer in there. What can I do for you?"

"I think I found Samantha Chambless. I believe she's staying at the studio where she models. Keepers of Time Photography. It's on Pawnee Avenue." I gave him directions. "Someone saw her red bookbag there."

"I need to finish up here, and let these guys go. Then I'll go over there and see what's up."

"Thanks." We disconnected, and I drove toward the interstate to go home. It was raining a little. This month had been particularly wet. It was miserable driving in it, but at least we were out of the drought that had parched us last summer. And I seemed to remember that a lot of rain made for pretty leaves in the fall. Or maybe that was just an old wives' tale.

I wasn't happy leaving things the way they were. Detective Stringfellow was going to go over to Keepers of Time, but then what? Would Patrick even open the door? Stringfellow wasn't going to have a search warrant, so how was he going to be able to look around? Patrick could keep Samantha upstairs and nobody would ever know the difference.

I turned off I-65 onto University Boulevard, drove through the UAB campus to 24th Street and up to Niazuma to Pawnee. I wasn't going to knock on the door. I'd leave the investigation to Stringfellow. But it wouldn't hurt to keep an eye on things until he arrived.

Traffic was heavy. I drove past Keepers of Time twice, looking for a place to park where I would have a good view. I settled for across the street, up a hill, in the parking lot of an apartment complex. I had good view of the premises, looking down on the building and the studio's parking lot. This was a steep part of Red Mountain, and behind the apartments was mostly earthen wall.

I watched the traffic. I counted cars. First the blue cars. Then the red cars, then the white. I listened to the radio, sang along with the classic rock. I called Grant.

"What are you doing?" he asked.

"I think my runaway's at the photography studio, so I'm watching the place until the cops get here."

"And you will not do anything until they get there, right?

Promise me."

"I promise."

"Be careful."

I called Kirk. "I think I found Samantha. I think she's at Keepers of Time, with this Patrick Merrick. I'm sitting in my car watching the place until the police get here to check it out. Stringfellow's on his way. I don't know if he'll get in the door, but we'll see."

"I'm glad you found her."

"We'll see if the police can get her out of here."

"Keep me updated."

"I'll call you when we're done."

I counted more cars. Counted SUV's versus cars, then trucks. I waited. The rain stopped and the clouds thinned a bit, then turned brilliant oranges and pinks as the sun set. I was losing patience and was about to call Stringfellow to find out where he was. As I reached for my phone, I spotted the car.

It turned into the lot of the studio and parked. I could barely see it in the twilight. But I recognized the car, and the two people in it.

Chapter Thirty Three

The car was a black Audi, the same one I'd seen in the Silva's garage. Cecile Silva exited the car, followed by Marci.

Cecile Silva walked with purpose--and anger--toward the front door of the converted house. Marci was right behind her, running to keep up and wiping her eyes like she was crying. She was pleading with her mother about something. Begging. This was not good.

I grabbed my cell phone as Marci and her mother entered the studio. I got out of my car, locked my purse in the trunk, locked the car and headed down the hill, phone in hand.

I was almost to the street when I heard the gunshot. Then the scream.

I dialed 911 on my phone and told the dispatcher a shot had been fired at Keepers of Time Photography. I gave her the address. No, I didn't know if anyone had been hit. I told the dispatcher that Detective Stringfellow was supposedly on his way. She wanted to ask me a bunch of questions I didn't have time for. I hung up.

I ran across the street. A silver Nissan Murano nearly hit me, the driver leaning on his horn in one long, loud blast. My phone rang. I was sure it was the dispatcher. I hit ignore, turned it off, and shoved it into my pocket. I reached the door and quietly opened it.

The entryway was dark and empty except for the secretary's neat desk. A light shone from the room at the back. Voices were coming from down the hall, from the studio. A young girl was crying and saying "Oh, my God," over and over. I thought it was Samantha, but I wasn't sure. I wished at that moment I had a weapon. A gun, a club, anything.

I crept down the hall to the large room. I slowly peeked inside through the doorway, my body as close to the wall as I could get it.

Patrick Merrick lay on the floor, on his back. Blood soaked the front of his purple shirt and the stain was getting bigger. Samantha knelt over him, eyes wide and terrified. He was pale.

"Mother, please. Stop. Please stop," Marci was hanging on to her mother's arm, the one with the gun. It was a pistol. A revolver. I'd bet it was a .38.

Cecile was trying to point the gun at Samantha's head, but Marci was pulling at her arm so she couldn't aim.

I stepped into the room. "Dr. Silva."

She turned to me quickly. I saw the hand that held the gun twitch and dove back into the hallway as she fired. The bullet hit the wall in front of me. I heard the plaster crack. My ears were ringing.

"Stop! Mother!" I peeked in the room again. Marci was now standing between me and her mother. "You've already killed one person! Maybe two!" She pointed to Patrick. "How many people are you gonna kill because you're angry at me?"

Samantha wailed and burst into tears. The stain on Patrick's shirt grew even bigger.

I stepped into the room again, behind Marci. "Samantha," I said, "See those curtains on the table?" I pointed to the stack of white fabric.

"Ye...Yes."

"Get one of those and put pressure on the wound. Got it? Lots of pressure or he's going to bleed to death."

She followed my directions. I could see her hands shaking as she retrieved the folded curtain and pressed it onto Patrick's abdomen. He groaned and moved his arm. She flinched.

"Keep pressing," I said. "Dr. Silva, you need to know that the police are on their way. I called them when I was outside."

As if on cue, I could hear sirens. Lots of them, getting closer.

Dr. Silva was trembling, the gun in her hand moving back and forth in front of her daughter. "Do you have any idea what I've been through?" she asked.

I shook my head. Please don't fire the gun. Please don't fire the gun.

"I grew up in a box. A box, in Brazil. In a shack with my parents and sisters and brothers. I worked. I worked hard all of my life. I got scholarships to private school and to college. Got my Ph.d. Came to America so that my only daughter would have the best education. She is going to go to the university. She is smart."

"I know."

"She could go to Harvard. To Yale. Anywhere she wants to go."

"I know."

"I will, Mother, you know I will."

"I have worked to make that happen. And then this slut, this slut with her wicked mother almost ruined everything!" She pointed the gun at Samantha, who froze. Her gaze was locked on Dr. Silva. The sirens were very close. Three, that I could hear. Please hurry. Please, please hurry.

"No rules. Samantha has had no rules. She gets whatever she wants whenever she wants it. She does whatever she pleases. Including taking nasty pictures of herself like a whore. And nasty pictures of my daughter that are now on the Internet. How is my

210

daughter going to get into college with those pictures out there?"

She steadied the gun on Samantha.

"Dr. Silva!" I cried out.

She turned to me. I thought, quickly, of something to say to get her to put the gun down. "Marci is a wonderful kid. Very smart. Mr. Eddy told me."

"Yes, she makes the best grades in her class."

"I'm sure she's going to do well, even after everything that's happened. But--but don't you think you're hurting her now? I mean, this is traumatizing her."

"I'm protecting her. Protecting her from the scum." The gun was still pointed at Samantha's head.

Marci jumped in. "Claire's right, Mother. I've been a wreck since all this happened. Since you killed Sam's mom."

"I did what I had to do."

"You killed Jean Chambless?" I asked. Please, just keep talking. The sirens had stopped.

"I spoke to her about her whore of a daughter. She didn't care. She said she was going to do better at parenting her, but she wasn't. I went to Frank's workplace on Saturday. She was sleeping with poor Denise's husband. She was there, waiting to talk to him. I asked to speak to her, outside. She didn't have any idea what was going on. About those pictures. Those horrid pictures. One gunshot, that's all it took. And believe me, Samantha is better off without her mother."

The front door burst open and before I could move there were police everywhere. Black uniforms, guns drawn. And Stringfellow, also armed, his weapon pointed at Dr. Silva. "Put the gun down." He said, calmly.

Dr. Silva didn't move. Didn't put the gun down.

"Mother, please."

Cecile took two steps backwards, her gun rising. She aimed the revolver slowly, at her own daughter's head.

Stringfellow fired first, then another officer. I closed my eyes and turned my head away as Marci screamed.

The ambulance was there already. They radioed for another, and the paramedics focused first on Patrick. He'd lost quite a bit of blood. It didn't take them long to get him onto a stretcher and take him away.

Cecile Silva was alive, breathing shallowly, and the bullets had hit her in the torso and the shoulder. She was unconscious and losing blood fast, too, and was soon on her way to the hospital.

Samantha and Marci huddled together, arms around each other, both crying softly. Stringfellow brought them bottled water from somewhere and was talking to them. He had planted me in a chair across the room from them and told me to stay put. Mr. Dr. Silva arrived and spoke to the police, then his daughter. He looked a wreck.

I buried my face in my hands, ignoring the pain from the bruise on my cheek and tried to stop shaking. I felt someone sit down next to me, put a strong arm around my shoulders, and kiss me gently on the temple. "You okay?" Kirk.

"Nope."

His arm went around me again and I buried my face in his neck. Held it together, barely. I was not going to break down in front of him.

Stringfellow came over and I told him the whole story, about Cecile Silva's frustration with Samantha's lack of rules, and apparent lack of morals, and how that led to Jean's death. Kirk scribbled notes in his notebook, then offered to drive me home.

Samantha was mine, legally, and I couldn't leave until I knew she had a place to stay. She and Marci wanted to be together. She went to the hospital with Marci and her father, they would spend the night there, and I'd meet them in the morning. Fernando Silva said he'd look after her. And that it was the least he could do.

Still shaken, I drove my car home, and Kirk followed me in his Infiniti and used my key to open the door. Then he poured me a shot of bourbon.

"I don't want that."

"I don't care. Drink it."

I did. Then laughed. "You trying to get me drunk?"

"Would it work?"

"No."

"Then, no."

I laughed again. I sounded borderline hysterical.

"You going to be okay tonight? You want me to call Grant?"

"I'll be okay."

Kirk took the shot glass back to the kitchen, then fetched the comforter off my bed. He covered me with it, on the couch, and kissed my forehead. "You sure you're okay?"

"I'll be all right."

He shook his head. "No you won't. Because you, darling, are one disaster after another."

Chapter Thirty Four

I took an over-the-counter pill to help me sleep and slept long and hard. Woke up early the next morning and went straight to the University of Alabama-Birmingham hospital. Cecile Silva had been in surgery most of the night. The gunshots injured her lungs. The damage was serious, and from what Fernando Silva told me, it was touch and go. She was being guarded by a police officer. Marci and Samantha were asleep in the waiting room.

Patrick Merrick had surgery, too, but was awake and doing much better. They'd repaired the holes in his small intestine. He'd be in the hospital for a while because of the risk of infection, but he was expected to make a full recovery. He and I talked for a long time about Samantha. He admitted he was the one who picked her up at the gas station in Midfield the day she ran away. She'd been living at the studio the whole time. He'd convinced her to turn herself in to me and drove her to DHS the night she reappeared. She called him again when I revealed I knew who she was. He said Samantha had known from the beginning who had killed her mother, and was terrified that I'd find out. She didn't want me to turn Cecile in. She couldn't take her best friend's mother away. She knew how it felt to lose her mother.

I went to my office after the hospital, on Saturday, and had a long meeting with Mac and Dr. Teresa Pope and updated them on everything that had happened. They were very relieved that I was okay. I called LaReesa and told her everything that happened, and thanked her again for her help.

I called Bobby Chambless in Tunica after I spoke to LaReesa, and told him the whole story. He'd throw a few things in a suitcase and be in Birmingham in five hours, he said. I brought him to the hospital that afternoon, and choked up a little as Samantha threw herself into his waiting arms.

My next call was to our attorney, who scheduled an emergency hearing for Monday morning to get Samantha out of my custody and back with her adoptive father. I checked with Tunica County's child welfare department to make sure Bobby didn't have any complaints against him and he didn't. Judge Myer gave him custody of Samantha on Monday morning, as expected. Bobby rented a truck and went with Samantha to her mother's townhouse to pack up their stuff. They had Jean's body transferred to Tunica and buried her there, close to Bobby's house. He told me later that

Samantha was going to counseling and puts flowers on her mother's grave once a week.

Kenny Thigpen was transferred out of the Birmingham jail and back to Mississippi. He's charged with violating his probation, since he left the state twice without permission. The assault charges against him for punching me were dropped. I was fine with it. I figure he's got enough problems. He sent me a letter of apology from prison. I wrote him back and gave him the numbers of some lawyers in Tunica that I got from one of the child welfare workers over there. When he gets out, if he gets clean, I hope he'll get an attorney to file a motion to get visitation rights.

Kirk's two-page story of the shooting and capture of Cecile Silva after her murder of Jean Chambless ran the day after Cecile was injured. The college where Dr. Silva taught was in shock and disbelief over what she'd done. Several students were quoted, reminiscing about her as a professor. The article was thorough, and well-written, and I wasn't mentioned. At all. Again. I called Kirk to thank him.

The day after the story ran, forty-two hours after she was shot, Cecile Silva peacefully passed away, her husband and her daughter by her side. She never regained consciousness. Dr. Fernando Silva resigned from his job, and was preparing to take his wife's body and his daughter back to Brazil. I checked in with Marci, and she was doing as expected, all things considered. She didn't really want to leave Birmingham, but was looking forward to starting over.

Six days after Cecile's death, I was back at work as usual. I was in my cubicle, working on a court report for one of the numerous new cases I had when Russell arrived. And he wasn't alone.

He had three kids with him, two girls and a toddler. A boy. It took me just a second to place them.

"DeCora! DeCaria! What are you two doing here? And DeCameron, too, I see."

"Hi," DaCaria said. DeCora raised her small hand in greeting.

"Have we got any diapers?" Russell asked.

"In the closet in the hall. What's going on?"

"You know these kids? We don't have an open case on them, do we?"

"I'm friends with their older cousin. What's going on?" I repeated.

"Their grandmother had a stroke. She's in the hospital, and after she gets out they're sending her to Lakeview for rehab. It'll be

214

a while before she gets to go home. If she gets to go home. Both of her daughters are in jail, so they're mine."

"Both of her daughters are locked up?"

"Yep, one of them got arrested ten days ago for prostitution, the other's been in prison a while for possession."

Oh, how could I have been so stupid?

"Where's LaReesa?"

"Who?" Russell asked.

"The older cousin. She's thirteen, and she lived with Estelle, too. Sort of."

Russell gave me a blank look. "These three were all I got. There wasn't a report on any thirteen-year-old."

I looked at DeCaria, then at DeCora. Finally, little DeCora poke up. "Reese's gone."

"Gone where?"

Her big brown eyes stared up at me, and she shrugged her tiny shoulders. "Just gone."

Acknowledgments

So many people have helped make this book possible. Without a doubt, this project never would have happened without input from the members of my writers group throughout the years: Joan, Heidi, Sonny, Coco, Linda, Cindy, Pam, Karen, Jack, and Fred.

To the members of the Birmingham Chapter of Sisters in Crime, thanks for the eight years of mystery-related fun so far.

To the Top of the Hill Social Club, thanks for giving me your invaluable feedback and friendship.

Very special thanks to Brian R. Overstreet, lifelong friend and attorney at law, for answering some vital legal questions, and to Christina L. Brown, CRNA for her help.

Thanks to Jan and Tim of the Children's Services division of JBS Mental Health Authority for a great first career. To child welfare social workers in Jefferson County, Alabama, and elsewhere, thank you for all the very important and difficult work that you do.

As always, thanks and love to my family for their encouragement.

Last but not least, my love and thanks to my wonderful husband, Bill, for supporting my pursuit of this crazy dream.

Other books in the
Social worker Claire Conover Mystery Series

Little Lamb Lost

Social worker Claire Conover honestly believed she could make a difference in the world until she got the phone call she's dreaded her entire career. One of her young clients, Michael, has been found dead, and his mother, Ashley, has been arrested for his murder. And who made the decision to return Michael to Ashley? Claire Conover.

Ashley had seemingly done everything right - gotten clean, found a place to live, worked two jobs, and earned back custody of her son. Devastated but determined to discover where her instincts failed her, Claire vows to find the truth about what really happened to Michael.

What Claire finds is no shortage of suspects. Ashley's boyfriend made no secret that he didn't want children. And Ashley's stepfather, an alcoholic and a chronic gambler, has a shady past. And what about Michael's mysterious father and his family? Or Ashley herself? Was she really using again?

Amidst a heap of unanswered questions, one thing is for certain: Claire Conover is about to uncover secrets that could ruin lives - or end her own.

Little White Lies

Claire Conover is drawn into another mystery when the office of black mayoral candidate Dr. Marcus Freedman is bombed. Marcus is found safe, but his campaign manager Jason O'Dell is found dead in the rubble. Claire's office gets a call about Jason's daughter who was left at her daycare, and she becomes Claire's latest charge. Further investigation reveals that Jason was living under an assumed name, and is really Jason Alsbrook, son of prominent local mine owner James Alsbrook. James holds many records in Alabama, including the most accidents and deaths in his mines. Any number of people would wish harm to he or his family. Claire works to keep little Maddie safe as she faces new challenges in her relationship with computer programmer Grant Summerville. She investigates Jason's death with the help of her friend and reporter Kirk Mahoney, and they become closer, The addition of a foster child further complicates everything as she must make some decisions about her future with Grant.

CPSIA information can be obtained
at www.ICGtesting.com
Printed in the USA
BVHW050218190123
656596BV00022B/155

9 781958 02